Nitro Express

by

Robert Blake Whitehill

TELEMACHUS PRESS

CALAVERAS
MEDIA

This book is a work of fiction. Names, characters, places and incidents are either the product of the author's imagination or are used fictitiously. Any resemblance to actual persons, living or dead, or to actual events or locales is entirely coincidental.

NITRO EXPRESS

Cover Designed by Carol Castelluccio at Studio042
With Photographs by Michael C. Wootton

Cover Art:
Copyright © Calaveras Media
Photography Copyright © Calaveras Media

Published by Telemachus Press, LLC
www.telemachuspress.com
and
Calaveras Media, LLC
www.calaverasmedia.com

Visit the author website:
www.robertblakewhitehill.com

ISBN: 978-1-939927-60-6 (eBook)
ISBN: 978-1-939927-61-3 (Paperback)

Version 2013.09.17

Printed in the United States of America

10 9 8 7 6 5 4 3 2 1

PRAISE FOR NITRO EXPRESS

A nifty thriller. Intricately plotted and excellently paced.
Richard Marek, Author, *Works of Genius*

Ben Blackshaw is back and at the top of his game in NITRO EXPRESS, the latest offering from author Robert Blake Whitehill. The action is fast-paced, the characters engaging and the storyline keeps you turning the pages. If you thought lightning couldn't strike twice for an author, then this book proves you wrong. Whitehill brings his literary best with Nitro Express.
Cyrus Webb, Host of Conversations LIVE, Editor in Chief, Conversations Magazine, www.conversationsmag.blogspot.com

Nitro Express is an exciting, fast-paced thrill-ride even better than the first. I couldn't read fast enough, and was racing through the pages to reach the conclusion, which blew me away. Fans of action, suspense, speed, and big guns will not want to miss this.
Brinda Glatczak, Editor in Chief, WiLove Books,
www.wilovebooks.blogspot.com

Ben Blackshaw, Robert Blake Whitehill's uber-spy, is back in Nitro Express, clear-sighted and strong as ever. In the league with Jason Bourne and James Bond.
Gene Pitts, Editor in Chief, The Audiophile Voice,
www.audiophilevoice.com

Nitro Express draws you in right from the beginning and takes you on an exciting thrill ride whether it be a drone strike, or shots from a far-away sniper. Whitehill sets the stage, then throws the unexpected at you. Like Deadrise before, Nitro Express delivers excitement, great characters and has you guessing right up until the end. Mission accomplished Mr. Whitehill.
Cindy Swabsin

Ben is back! Nitro Express is a ride you don't want to miss! Impossible to predict. Impossible to put down. Whitehill's prose is profound and glitzy all at once. You will want to live in this world a little longer than the pages permit!
Kirsten Lagatree, Author, *Feng Shui: Arranging your Home to Change Your Life*

An absolutely hair-raising, on the edge of your seat, riveting novel. If you thought Deadrise was a home-run, then you will find that Nitro Express is a Grand Slam. Robert has a way of taking you completely by surprise with his endings. Loved it all.
Walt Whitehill, *The Ice Man*

Author Robert Blake Whitehill has hit gold again, in his second installment of the Ben Blackshaw series. In Nitro Express, Blackshaw traverses the world, and explores the good, bad, and apathetic human psyche, in this operative-laden espionage thriller. He opens windows of what could be happening right here and now in a socio-politically charged atmosphere. Make no mistake, this high-action page-turner will keep you riveted to the very end.
Naomi Dschaak

Notch another hit for Whitehill, Nitro Express is an often light-hearted, always gut-splattered dance with death that finds Ben Blackshaw partnered with a new nemesis. Nitro Express's bloody misdirections are built upon eloquent riffs on ballistics, planes, jihadists, genetic hang fires, and political abuse. The bad guys and gals who try to put the "dick" in "Blus ist dicker als Wasser," get theirs in the end.
Diane Wilder

Fast and engrossing, Nitro Express delivers on the legacy of Mr. Whitehill's first novel, Deadrise, and builds on the growing bona fides of reluctant protagonist Ben Blackshaw. Nitro Express draws you in with all the intrigue of classic Cold War spycraft. The world that Mr. Whitehill has created once again teems with complexities of multinational politics, rogue militants, and government agencies fraught with the morally compromised. Whitehill regales his readers with over-the-top characters constructed like a multi-tiered cake, rich with distinctive language and piled high with hidden motives and machinations. The familiar characters of Blackshaw and his compatriots are joined by a chorus of new allies and enemies, and leave the reader to wonder just how much difference exists between them.

Adam Gubar

PRAISE FOR DEADRISE

DEADRISE
has been named in
CONVERSATIONS BOOK CLUB'S TOP
100 BOOKS OF 2012

From the very first chapter it is clear that DEADRISE is a novel that takes you captive and won't let you go until the very end. Whitehill has done lovers of action and suspense a great service with this debut, and we must thank him for it.
Cyrus Webb, Host of Conversations LIVE, Editor in Chief, Conversations Magazine, www.conversationsmag.blogspot.com

Robert Blake Whitehill steams onto the crime fiction scene with his Chesapeake Bay based thriller, DEADRISE. This cracking good tale of mysterious fortune combines irreverent characters, history driven invention, snappy dialogue, artfully managed conflicts, and startling surprises in a sensational count-down-style treasure hunt.
Anita Campos, Editor in Chief, Blue Crabs, Hon, www.bluecrabshon.com

Deadrise is a first rate thriller. The characters are fascinating and so real. The plot was so engaging that I could not put the book down until I finished it. I highly recommend this to all fans of the genre.
Bill Jarblum, Motion Picture Producer, www.jarblumfilms.com

Deadrise takes the thriller/espionage genre to another level by introducing a character whose cultural background is more important than his military experience. It's not a stretch to say that the Chesapeake Bay, and Smith Island in particular, are the true protagonists of this book. Robert Whitehill pits the traditional, solid independence of the Bay's inhabitants and landscape against the modern chaos of terrorism and international intrigue. The conflict between these forces makes a bold statement about the resilience of the Chesapeake's culture and its importance on the international stage.

Marc Dykeman, Chester River Runoff, www.chesterriverrunoff.com

For my precious Mary

Table of Contents

Special Acknowledgments

As with *Deadrise*, the first thriller in the Ben Blackshaw series, the creation of *Nitro Express* was very much a team effort.

Once again, my mother, Cecily Sharp-Whitehill, the relentless stylist, showed me many areas in the story that could benefit from more work.

My beloved bride, Mary Whitehill, came through as ever with her own cogent observations about the manuscript. In particular, our chats about the first draft helped me discover, clarify, and highlight certain themes in subsequent drafts. Beyond fiction, she also helps me understand what actual life is about.

My son, Beau, aged four years now, continues to help me immensely after tough days, often suggesting, "When you stop writing, you can come home and play the Cars game with me. Deal? *Deal!*"

My dear friend, Matthew Bialer, has done my writing yet another yeomanly service by introducing me to the great author and editor, Richard Marek. Richard, in turn, generously lent me his tremendous experience in bashing thrillers into shape. I am forever in his debt for his keen insights and evocative questions as he edited *Nitro Express*. Thanks to him, this is a far better story, a vastly better book, and a genuinely thrilling adventure.

I am fortunate, after some difficult changes in my support network, that Karl Guthrie remains my friend as well as my stalwart ally in the legal field. He continues to protect copyrights, and now trademarks, with an elegant and ferocious brilliance. www.theguthrielawfirm.com

My partners at Telemachus Press, to whom I owe a great debt of thanks, oversee the digital creation of my paperback and ebooks, making sure that they are available in any and all outlets that want to sell my work. www.telemachuspress.com

Shelton Interactive, helmed by Rusty Shelton, has thrown open doors for me that I thought might never be unlocked. In addition to crafting and updating a beautiful and flexible website, they have their collective fingers on the pulse of a wonderful cadre of interviewers and reviewers that it has been my great pleasure to meet since the publication of *Deadrise*. For the inspiring web design and regular care of my website, I must give thanks to Allison Bright, Whitney Burnett, Amber McGinty, Richard Ricondo, Will Ruff, Susan Savkov, and Jeremy Strom. For the dogged, tenacious PR work, I am so grateful to Sara Pence, Andrea Sanchez, Shelby Sledge, and Travis Wilson. www.sheltoninteractive.com

Adam Gubar and I still meet for lunch each week when we're both in town, and inevitably our conversations turn to rare and exotic arms and ordnance. Curious restaurateurs and servers overhearing snippets of our conversation often wonder if they are feeding anarchists instead of the Quakers we actually are. My sincere thanks to Adam for helping me find so many exciting new ways to create mayhem in *Nitro Express*.

I received crucial technical, tactical, and character insights on the manuscript from my dear cousin, Walt Whitehill. He is a decorated Vietnam veteran who served two tours, training in light weapons, in demolition, and as a medic. He was known by his counterparts as *Nguoi dan ong bang*, which translates as *The Ice Man*. Draw your own inferences as to how he got that name. Walt served with the Special Forces until volunteering to join the elite MACV/SOG, where his ability to reach out and touch someone was put to great use. Not only is he a licensed pilot, a PADI Dive Master, and a firearms expert (qualifying as Master with a large variety of weapons), he recently retired after 34 years of police work. Walt knows Ben Blackshaw's world backwards, and is very kind to share this wealth of hard-won experience to improve my humble efforts.

Studio042, and Carol Castelluccio in particular, created the exciting cover for *Nitro Express*. I also go to Carol, and to Pilar Kennedy, Scott

Kennedy, and Colleen Van Dorn, for every single piece of marketing material I need, from banners to cards, and everything in between. I am so grateful for all their terrific ideas. www.studio042.com

The wonderful copy editor, Suzanne Dorf Hall, has proven for a second time that I have no hope of success in a spelling bee. Sometimes it's a typo. Sometimes it's unnecessary haste, or plain ignorance. However my faculties, or my fingers fumble, I am ever grateful that Suzanne sets things true again.

Bryan Clardy at Lightning Source oversees the physical production my print-on-demand paper books. Lucky for you and me, he is satisfied with nothing less than perfection. www.lightningsource.com

I will happily say it again. Michael C. Wootton is a fine photographer with a remarkable eye. I am always grateful for a chance to work with a true professional who is also a great friend. His images appear on my website, as well as on the book covers. Somehow, he manages to make my mug appear less heinous. That's not art. That is magic! www.mcwphoto.com

Andrew Cohen is another gifted photographer with an artist's discernment for the key moments of any event. He has helped me with beautiful pictorial studies from both signings and readings. Though he works with digital cameras, he does not fire them like a machine gun, hoping to find brilliance among the mess of frames. He crafts every shot, makes each one count, and makes me happy. www.AndrewCohenPhotography.com

Bjoern Kils is new to working with me on event videography and photography, but he has long been a fixture on the Hudson River and surrounding waters helping an international list of news and TV production companies get their shots from aboard his doughty rigid hull inflatable boat. Of course he has the chops on dry land, too, particularly in documenting book festival talks I've given. www.BjoernKils.com

Captain Curtis Johns, skipper of the *Karen Ray II*, based in Crisfield, Maryland, was a generous host for an extremely productive Chesapeake Bay photography session. It seems as though he can maneuver his big comfortable deadrise through thought alone. I am remiss for not thanking him at the start of *Deadrise*. If you go down to the sea in ships, like the Psalm says, or at least to the Chesapeake, Curtis is your captain, and the *Karen Ray II* is your ship. www.facebook.com/chesapeakefishing

I used to write my first drafts out by hand on legal tablets. Entering the manuscript into the computer became an easy occasion for the second draft. These days, my early efforts go directly into computers, and without them, I would be sunk. I sincerely thank Troy Craig for keeping the machines humming no matter what disaster befalls them. www.18thConnection.com

I must thank Catcom, including Catalin Ursu and Kyle Wilson, who work hard to impeccably maintain my Internet access. This is nothing to take for granted. Crystal clear, lightning fast connections for both video conferences and research are vital to my work on a moment by moment basis. www.catcomcomputers.com

I have seen the eerie *American Mariner* many times on her shoal in the Chesapeake Bay, but personally, I have never been aboard this old hulk. Ali Whalen, who knows a thing or two about Liberty Ships, was most helpful in rounding out my understanding of the below-decks layout of these noble and storied vessels, and in keeping Ben Blackshaw from getting fatally lost.

James Dissette, Uber-Dean of the Chestertown Book Festival, made me welcome for their very well-attended event in my hometown. I plan to flog my wares there every year. www.chestertownbookfestival.org

It is a sign of the times that I do not place my paper book editions in many brick and mortar stores. I must give special thanks to Margot Sage-El, of Watchung Booksellers, in Montclair, New Jersey, and Tom Martin, of Bookplate, in Chestertown, Maryland, for encouraging me, and for looking after my works with particular care. www.watchungbooksellers.com, www.bookplate.biz

When I get revved up testing character dialogue out loud, particularly the rants of the heavies, I sound like an abject lunatic. My bride gently suggested that our son's naps might be longer, and his eventual time in psychotherapy might be shorter, if I took office space outside the home. Thank goodness Donna Miller, at *C3Workplace* took me in, offered me bright new digs, and a crack team to help get things done. In addition to Donna, I must also thank Peggi Cheevers, Kelly Louro, Janet Neal, Ashley Rojas, Barbara

Ann Ruiz, Delilah Tate, and Karen Weeks for not calling the FBI despite several months of working with me. www.c3workplace.com

Every author should have the pleasure of an evening with the dames of the Gal Pals Book Club. Voracious readers, they show a keen appreciation of their authors' works. During our memorable visit, they kept me on my toes with intriguing, sometimes very personal questions I was only too happy to attempt to answer. Diane Esty hosted the boisterous evening at her home, and most of the roster noted here were in attendance: Tere Bresin, Angela Canfora, Bonnie Jerbasi, Lisa Kelly, Alena Maloney, Ellen Scardena, and Gail Stone. David Oscar's Eastern Shore themed eats were as delicious as the conversation was lively.

And speaking of chow, Chef John Giglio, and his elite staff, created a wonderful event for the launch of *Deadrise* at his Palazzo Restaurant in Montclair. The atmosphere was festive, and the dishes and drink were all wonderful. Never did so many eat so well, thanks to so few. www.palazzonj.com

In addition to the feasts my bride lays on for the family, Sam Codling continues to create delicious savory and sweet pies at *The Pie Store*, in Montclair. Sam saves the Whitehills whenever the rush of life overtakes the dinner hour. I can vouch for the chicken tikka pie as one new item that is particularly special. www.ThePieStoreNJ.com

Natalie Colledge, master baker and owner of *Plum on Park*, also does her bit to keep this author fed, and fed well. She is one restaurateur who has learned to ignore the seditious sounding chat that often crops up when I discuss ordnance for the next book. www.plumonpark.com

There actually is a RailRiders specialty clothing outfitter, as appears in this book. The proprietor, John d'Arbeloff, really does supply both me and Ben Blackshaw with our extreme-ops adventure duds. In the year or so that I've been wearing this durable gear, I have never been so consistently well turned-out, nor so utterly comfortable in every season. www.railriders.com

I am sad to note the closing of *Beans*, which kept me caffeinated in the dark and lonely hours of writing, as well as while I served on the Montclair Ambulance Unit. Though the Writer's Blend, and the Ambulance Blend are no more, I hope you will join me in wishing Corinda DeVingo success and joy in her next venture.

Finally, in 2012, I am proud to report that the selfless men and women of the Montclair Ambulance Unit responded to 120 cardiac calls, 309 traffic accidents, 53 pedestrians struck, 354 falls, and an assortment of other difficult calls totaling over three thousand sorties. Please support this fine group of professionals, or the EMTs in your city, as much as you possibly can. www.mvau.org

RBW
Independence Day 2013
Chestertown, Maryland

Nitro Express

PART 1
QUIETUS

CHAPTER 1

THE MURDER WAS spectacular. Though in the immediate after-math, mainstream news producers and their corporate handlers steered away from calling it an outright assassination, the devoted, some might say rabid fans of Lucilla Calderon reacted as if a Kennedy had been slaughtered in front of them. Compared to Calderon, the death of the short-lived Tejano star Selena was a mere media hiccup.

Tragedy's human hallmarks are simple. At their worst, they include the horror of anticipating doom alone. Tonight, La Luz, as she was called, ago-nized over nothing beyond her makeup, and a *buscanovio* spit curl that threatened to come unstuck from her left temple. She was certainly not alone this evening. Between her lovers and her entourage of handlers, she had not experienced a solitary moment for several years, excluding some, but not all, bathroom breaks. This evening, she fully expected to revel in the company of adoring fans at her movie's Hollywood premiere. She felt the evening would be dazzling.

Lucilla Calderon was huge. Galactic. At twenty-four, she was a break-away crossover success with her roots deep in Latin traditional music, but with updated lyrics and funky, danceable techno arrangements. She wrote mostly about the new struggles of *The People*, that is, anyone who was not a multimillionaire by age twenty. She could krump, or pop-and-lock, or tango depending on the need for her music videos. Her every exhalation for the last six years had charted in the top five on the major popular music rosters, with most going number one. Her fan base spanned the globe. There was an astronaut serving in low earth orbit aboard the International Space Station, a biologist, who was known to play Calderon's tunes while working on his experiments. That story alone fizzed for several news cycles on the major networks.

Yet La Luz, or The Light, as journalists hastened to translate in spavined simile and hackneyed metaphor, was down to earth. So said her ardent fans. She was down with the brown. She represented *La Raza* with a wild kind of dignity that included one of Playboy Magazine's more chaste, yet best-selling pictorials in the last decade of almost anything goes.

And now she was starring in her first movie. It was called *Ganar*—To Win. Calderon played a plucky, big-hearted revolutionary leader struggling in a fictional South American island nation. Her character was a charismatic Valkyrie, like Evita, but she rose to power, not through her President husband's death, but through her own initiative and integrity, uniting disparate political and socioeconomic factions into an unbeatable rebel force. The picture was laced with measured applications of violence, and a love triangle with a male and a female comrade that, while deemed shocking by the more straitlaced, had endeared her to the more open-minded critics who mattered. In an unrealistic plot twist, upon vanquishing her fascist opposition, her character immediately holds multi-party elections deemed honest and fair by European monitors, and assumes leadership of her fledgling democracy. Luz was George Washington with all her own teeth, indeed with no implants of any kind, if her publicist was to be believed.

Advance notices for *Ganar* in the print trades, in the blogosphere, the twitterverse of social media, and in film and television entertainment magazines all led off with breathless predictions of top honors ahead for this picture at the major award ceremonies. Luz was poised to fulfill the glorious pan-media destiny tragically denied to Selena.

After a lackluster year for the film industry, the premiere night's screening at the Dolby Theatre in Los Angeles guaranteed a phenomenal box office for the project in the weekend to come. The smaller Grauman's Theatre located on the same block had been considered only briefly for the occasion, but was dismissed as too small, and too reminiscent of a bygone Hollywood era dominated by the white establishment.

It was a good call. Within a half hour of the premiere's announcement, almost every one of the larger theatre's 3332 seats was booked by Hollywood's most beautiful and most potent, both in front of, and behind the camera. Mere mortals deluged any film industry god or demigod with the most tenuous link to the production and distribution of *Ganar* with fevered demands to find a way to get them in. Even the film's lowly writers, all eight of them, whether credited onscreen or not, were getting offers of lavish gifts, drugs, cash, travel, and even sex if only they would part with, or somehow scrounge up, a single ticket.

A lucky few members of the masses got exactly what they wanted without usury. Luz Calderon had insisted that five hundred seats be reserved for *The People*, and bestowed upon them free of charge by a lottery on specially marked bottles and cans of the soft drink AzteKola, void where prohibited, no purchase necessary, and forget for the moment that the bubbly sweet beverage was originally created in Mexico back in the '30s by a white immigrant from Kansas. This gesture, a slick move some cynics called it, had garnered even more delirious press for a star who already could do no wrong.

Luz Calderon's populist ways played hell with her handlers. She shunned the roided-out security details on which so many industry players insisted. Opening night at the Dolby would be no exception. Her only concession to protection from some lunatic, because only a crazy person would want to hurt La Luz, was a trio of unarmed Cholo friends who had known her since kindergarten back in East Los. At Luz's insistence, these three men had been required to publicly abandon any gang affiliations before she would take them on. The press loved this. Devoured it. So tonight, Luz was on her own, and she liked it that way. There were no artificial barriers, for she had no poseur's need for distance from the very people who adored her, and whom she loved in return, each and every one. It would not matter in the end. Even if La Luz had recruited the fierce yet ragtag rebel army her character led in the movie, it would not have changed how the evening played out.

The presence of Luz's three pals did not stop the Los Angeles Police Department from pulling extra officers onto the *Ganar* detail. Lots of them. There was the usual show of strength at the street level for several blocks around the theatre, with a loose cordon of uniforms starting at West Sunset Boulevard to the south, North La Brea to the west, Franklin Avenue to the north, and North Las Palmas to the east. There were additional uniformed officers in position on the streets closer to the theatre, but they were reinforced by plainclothes detectives pressed from the outlying Valley, Central and South bureaus so as not to irk *The People's* starlet with an apparent police occupation of the area.

Rooftops were another matter. Every structure on the theatre's block and immediately adjacent was secured by teams of spotters and snipers. In an unusual move, Incident Command for the event was positioned on top of the theatre itself to be a less provocative element. This did not make the Incident Commander happy. She was a hands-on officer who had risen through the ranks from her start as a beat cop, but she was used to seeing practicalities bend under the weight of the whims of the famous.

Though six of the twelve Aerospatiale B-2 Astar helicopters from the L.A.P.D.'s Air Support Division were aloft, they were loitering five miles away, so the area around the former Kodak would not look as though an aerial suspect pursuit was in progress during the premiere. All spotlights were on the ground, and they were pointing skyward, not the other way around. There was a ten-mile radius Temporary Flight Restriction centered on the theatre for nearly all General Aviation aircraft. The only exceptions were made for five news choppers. They were more than welcome, provided their networks had filed in advance for their clearances, and they squawked discrete codes issued specifically for the event on their transponders. Luz Calderon demands, and La Luz gets. She got more than she bargained for.

As always, most of the attention around the theatre was focused on Hollywood Boulevard. Camera and color announcer towers were erected overnight by crack crews, many of whom looked like slobs and appeared never to shift out of first gear, but who got the job done right the first time. The towers were tricked out with bunting colored like the flag of the movie's revolutionary army, and populated with camera operators for wide shots of the celebrity get-in. Camera and sound crews for the tighter shots, and network talking heads roved in packs around the cordoned and carpeted gauntlet leading to the theatre's exterior proscenium entrance. A network's rank in the ratings influenced its interviewers' positions. Other crews grabbed and held less desirable spots where the elite had to pass and offer their sound bites. This was a special event for the public, but for the union workers actually making it happen, it was barely more than a drill. They had just done it for the big award ceremony in February a few weeks before. This slightly scaled-back effort coming on its heels was a piece of cake.

One hurdle for the celebrities during the get-in was trying to think up fresh ways to declare that working on *Ganar* had kept them in a constant state of emotional orgasm, that everyone involved, especially Luz, was an absolute dream to work with, and that *Ganar* was the most important project of their lives or anybody else's. Writers had been on call for weeks perfecting seven-second sentences for those movie deities who preferred not to work the gauntlet off the cuff. The lavish writing fees put the scribes in striking distance of buying tiaras, either the bejeweled kind, or the fiberglass speedboat variety with big twin diesels. Big openings made for big business all over town.

It was getting close to curtain time. By now, most of the attending stars, directors, agents, managers and producers had talked into the microphones in the chute outside. They were now gliding past the bars where they scooped up flutes of prepoured Cristal champagne with the zeal of walled-out marathon runners snatching cups of water from hydration volunteers. The five hundred lottery winners were still on Hollywood Boulevard. They would enter after La Luz's arrival. Her car was coming in last. She understood the importance of creating anticipation, of making a grand entrance. It was her exit that everyone would remember.

Tonight La Luz looked like a queen. Eyes heavily accentuated with black mascara, lips a glossy red, the troublesome spitcurls all finally plastered down. She wore a mantilla comb in her hair, a turquoise halter top, and tight black mariachi pants with silver buttons from hip to the snug hem just below her knee. Her only nod to bling was a beautiful turquoise pendant two inches across hanging on a long silver box chain at her sternum between her small gravity-defying breasts. Luz was everyone's *ruca*, their true love.

She was homing in on the theatre in a blazing neon-green lowrider, once a '58 Ford Fairlane Skyliner with the retractable hardtop. She led a procession of other heavily modified cars that hopped and bounced and danced with trunk-loads of batteries boosting 72-volt systems for the hydraulic lifters on each wheel. The car behind Luz's was blasting the movie's theme song, which she had written herself. The windows of nearby buildings pulsed and flexed in time with the bass line, and threatened to send broad glass panes guillotining down into the street.

La Luz's parade of lowriders had already made several laps in the streets outside the police cordon purely for the enjoyment of happy crowds of The People, some of whom had personal reasons for not rubbing up against the L.A.P.D. presence closer to the theatre. Crips and Bloods, as well as the Black P-Stones, Los Zetas, and Mara Salvatruchas, the MS-13, were out in their colors, but the truce that Luz had negotiated among them for the occasion seemed to be holding. She was becoming her movie character; the Great Unifier. Her revolution was well under way.

Finally it was time. The nine parade lowriders behind Luz's peeled off to stage themselves on Sycamore Avenue outside the police cordon where she would rejoin them after the screening. There were several after-parties scheduled, and she planned to arrive at each of them with her full convoy. Luz's Skyliner continued toward the theatre, but of course, it was not alone.

A gaggle of credentialed open paparazzi cars and motorcycles gunned it to fill the paved gap left by the nine lowriders. Flash units strobed the night into ten thousand instants of day. La Luz's car was not bouncing now, so that she could pull up in front of the theatre perched on the trunk, her legs draped over the center of the backseat without risk of getting launched like a rodeo bull rider. She was like a beautiful game animal driven toward the hunters by noisy beaters.

Luz's car slowed to a stop in front of the theatre. Her fans screamed adulation. Gowned and tuxedoed talking heads checked their positions and eyeballed their camera crews. Ready.

The deafening explosion had such brisance that it slugged everyone within two hundred yards in the chest with its pressure wave. Luz's upper body flew into ragged butcher's cuts and landed in pieces across an arc of thirty feet. Her pelvis and legs remained in the back seat of the car. Loving fans, overjoyed at being hand-picked to rush La Luz for autographs, were mowed down on the pavement in bloody shreds of flesh. The Light went out forever, but first there was a wet flash of red.

CHAPTER 2

DEAD MEN ARE supposed to rest in peace. They never tell tales. They are soon forgotten despite the deepest cuts in a headstone. Yet Ben Blackshaw, dead to the world these last four months, was strangely unnerved. This should not be. He should feel nothing like the disquiet now creeping across his skin, hackling the hairs on the nape of his neck. But the writing was on the wall, and he recognized the hand.

Winter in Greenwich Village had been cold and hard. Christmas and New Year's had passed Ben by with little more than an empty longing for people and places too far away in miles, or lost to death and time. His homesickness verged on depression. He would have felt even worse, but his work filled his days, and much of his nights. Sleep eluded him. Fatigue never left him. He was not from New York. The distractions of carving fresh models for the lost-wax molds that his unusual commissions required did nothing to allay the sense that he was a stranger far behind the lines in an alien city. Though Ben was from Smith Island in the Chesapeake Bay, Manhattan was like no island he had ever known. This was nothing like home.

The spring chill clung with icy talons in the shadows between the old factory buildings. Most of the structures in the area were long ago converted to airy or drafty spaces, depending on whether you were realtor or tenant. Now they were high-end homes and trendy minimalist office cube farms with struggling retail joints at the sidewalk level. It was so early in the day that nothing was open.

Ben drudged through twenty-hour days in the raw basement space of a rundown pile that had been shunned by hungry developers because of an encumbering mass of unsettled title disputes, crippling back taxes no one wanted to pay, lawsuits, glaring code violations, and zoning quandaries. An entire five-story building buried beneath paper. If he were alive, Ben would have been called a squatter. Today, he was a ghost.

Or should have been. Now, unlike the many dead he himself had killed, or seen dispatched into oblivion during Gulf War One and other campaigns, unlike the dead man he was supposed to be, he felt fear. That summed it up. Bubble guts. He was afraid.

From fitful dreams of sunrise on the Chesapeake Bay, he had awakened in the chilly dungeon. According to custom, this morning he had emerged from his building's concealed back-alley entrance before sunrise, and walked a cautious seven blocks to an all-night deli. He varied his route every day, sometimes going well out of his way for a cup of bad coffee that cream and sugar could not improve.

If he felt especially homesick, he would impose the meandering pathways and streams of the Smith Island archipelago on the angular urban grid. A stroll to the Drum Point Market back on Smith led him uptown and toward the west side. An imagined visit to the home of his dear friend Knocker Ellis meant heading uptown, but then east. He always broke away from the make-believe path before reaching his fancied destination. It was even too painful for Ben to imagine his bride LuAnna holding his hand on these forays. There would be no miraculous homecoming at the weathered Smith Island saltbox he once called home. No banter with his wife. No jokes or barbs traded with friends. He always wound up at a twenty-four-hour Korean deli where no one had ever heard of putting cheese in the coffee as they sometimes did on Smith Island.

Ben did not need the caffeine. He desperately wanted the fresh air, such as he could find it in New York. Fetching coffee was merely a mission. The deli, an objective. His hunter's mind, honed by years of military service, functioned more easily when there was some kind of plan underpinning his movements. The piecework of his current occupation, however financially rewarding, nearly numbed his soul. Fatigue did the rest, all of it making him vulnerable to a homesickness he never felt when he served in the Gulf; that was an unforgiving sentiment that might cause him to drop his guard and wind up, well, much closer to dead than he was already.

Someone knew he was in town, but Ben's anonymous work clothes had not betrayed him. The threads were dark, dyed by their maker to hide the dirt and grease of hard menial labor over many days between laundering. He zipped his coat up closer to his chin. This jacket was cheap nylon, a subdued navy blue. It was a shapeless, poly-filled item cloned overseas, and sold throughout Manhattan's discount stores to working men who barely got by. He had fixed the few holes, scorched from leaving it too close to his molten work, with black duct tape. He pulled his watch cap lower over his ears. Its wool and synthetic knit was likewise dark. Nothing special. No logos. Head to toe, Ben was a blank. A cipher. He blended in. He was dead to the world, but now someone was trying to bring him back to life.

On the roundabout walk home, he took a sip of coffee every half block or so. Slightly tilting his head back to drink, he let his eyes case the sidewalk ahead and across the street, and the windows above. Without thinking, he filtered out the soft-treaded footfalls of his own rubber soled boots; stayed alert to sounds on the street behind him. Anything sounding remotely like a furtive step on his six o'clock, in military parlance, or directly behind him, earned an easy glance over his shoulder. The first week in town, he had worried this precaution would make him look guilty, thus drawing attention. He quickly learned this was the Big Apple, and everyone had eyes in the back of his head.

Regardless, at this hour, few others were out, and they had bigger problems than some random guy on the move with a lousy cup of joe. Muggers were in bed after preying late into the night on those who had drunk too deeply, or got too high. They fed on the party kids who could not hear a quick and stealthy approach over their blasting earbuds, and on those who had survived to old age, but who were now unable to handle themselves. Ben's stride showed just enough purpose and just enough direction that, when factored with his daunting height and crappy clothes, he was not worth a mugger's trouble. That left police and desperate junkies to hassle him, and had any of those been in sight, they would be watching out for each other, not for a nobody like Ben.

He paused at the mouth of the alley leading to his door, sipped the coffee, glanced around, and peered into still-sunless voids. He let his eyes rest every few seconds as he looked not only at, but through the windows of parked cars for movement, for any sign that somebody was peering back at him from the other side. The street was clear. His heart sank like a convict leaving the prison exercise yard for the next twenty-three hours in solitary.

The electric furnace he had turned on before he left would be plenty hot by now, drawing enough amps to spin the disk in the ancient glass-bubbled Con Edison meter like a Frisbee. Ben could start melting gold for the morning's pour right away. The electricity his work devoured was just another casualty to all the bureaucratic confusion surrounding this troubled old building. When he took up residency, Ben had tapped the trunk line with little risk anyone would report the heavy usage. No one had noticed so far, anyway. If they did, there was no clear owner to serve with a bill. Most phantoms had no money. A more strenuous effort to collect on utilities might have been undertaken if Con Ed knew Ben was a multimillionaire.

Again, Ben scanned the darkened buildings around him from basement windows to rooflines. Satisfied no one was observing him with undue curiosity, he lodged the half-empty blue styrofoam cup into a poorly closed garbage bin from the building next door. Time for work. He turned and entered the alley, passing small patches of grit-blackened snow from the last blizzard that survived in the darkness between a few broken, rotting wood pallets.

He reached the old steel door and stopped, his body tensed, his mind keen for danger. There was no knob on this door, but that was not the problem. Upon arrival months before, Ben had torched a two inch hole in the door's face on the side away from the hinges. After dirtying up a short length of steel chain, a Paclink, and a heavy duty 2170X padlock, he had threaded the chain through the hole in the door and around the steel frame where the masonry had spalled. The inconspicuous security measure, standard in such abandoned buildings, was as sound as he had left it; as sound as he always found it again on coming home. The wall was the problem. Someone had left a message there.

The black spray paint barely showed over the building's sooty grime. The figures, about three inches high, were simple enough, but they shattered his world with more violence than a well-aimed bullet. **BB2AMKIABNRMCG1300ZRIPAU.** He was certain the wall had been bare when he left for coffee. The communiqué was meant for him. Someone was ignoring the fact that a dead man cannot read.

Using a stout key from his pants pocket, Ben unfastened the padlock and went inside. He rethreaded the chain, padlocking himself in the basement. The furnace had made the drafty space warmer. Out of habit, he kicked an old moving quilt against the threshold to block any cold zephyrs until spring got serious. He sat in the dark on the single metal folding chair he had scrounged from a pile of eviction discards on the sidewalk. He had to think.

The first five figures routed the message to him personally. There was no doubt he was the recipient. Though he had not worn his toe tags in many years, he knew what they said by heart. Every soldier did. Reading top to bottom instead of left to right, the first figure in each line of the metal tag was B for Blackshaw, another B for Benjamin, 2, the first digit of his Social Security number, A for his blood type, and M for Methodist. Only a precious few understood this cipher agreed on long ago in more dangerous times. Fewer than the fingers on Ben's powerful hands. Though Ben had been a Navy SEAL, the fact that the dogtag was formatted in the Army, and not the Navy layout was confirmation the message was genuine. The cipher was conceived in the Balkans on a joint Special Operations mission in with soldiers from the 10th Mountain Division.

The rest of the message opened to Ben with a little more study. KIABNR meant killed in action, body not recovered. An expression too well known in the military family. The sender was aware he was hiding, knew where, and knew in particular that his faked death by drowning in the Chesapeake Bay months before had not yielded a corpse for burial. MCG1300Z was the call to action he could not shirk. He was needed by someone to whom he had once pledged life and limb. It was not hard to parse. McGuire Air Force Base. That's where he had to go. 1300Z was one in the afternoon Zulu time, or Coordinated Universal Time. Converting to local time in his head, Ben had to get to McGuire somehow by nine this morning. He still had no idea why, but that would be revealed in due course.

It was the RIPAU that bothered him most, even more than the call to a mysterious mission. Rest In Peace. That was plain enough. But why add that in? A message from anyone who understood this format, and who had taken the trouble to use it instead of meeting him face to face, would have earned his swift response. The sender was telling him two things. The first message was that it was known that Ben's current undertaking had his full attention. His contrived death, and a self-exile to the last place on earth he would ever wish to visit, let alone sojourn, meant big doings. How much did the sender really understand? That was made clear in the second metamessage. *Au* was the kicker. The chemical symbol for gold from the periodic table of the elements.

Somebody knew Ben's business. If the loyalty and the blood obligation demanded by the message were not enough to get Ben moving, curiosity about who was tracking him certainly did. It could be there was a loose end or two to tie off before he and his work were going to be truly secure. The message's mention of gold meant the sender could easily guess there were cubic dollars involved, and perhaps other stakeholders who were relying on him. Somebody was crawling around in his head, in his life. This pissed Ben off. He wanted to scratch the writing off the wall with one of his carving knives. Whoever left this message knew he would do almost anything to avoid having to abandon his current enterprise and break from cover into the unknown.

Ben parsed the whole message. In full, the seemingly random letters and numbers said, I know who you really are. I know where you are. You're not dead. You better be ass-on-curb at McGuire by nine. You can rest easy with your gold, and get on with your life after you help me. Fail me, and it won't be so peaceful.

There was a slim chance he was reading into the last part, the implied threat, but Ben did not take it lightly. With resignation, he turned off the furnace. The dull hum of massive electrical power surging through inadequate wiring went silent. In the new quiet, he glanced around the space. Gray morning light wandered in almost by mistake through filthy gunslit windows. A cache of stolen gold bullion lay under another mover's quilt.

Not a lot. About four million dollars worth in today's market. In five minutes this same boom market would make the gold worth significantly more, give or take a market correction or two. The rest of the gold was stashed on Smith Island. Every bar was stamped with a strangely lopsided smiley face motif. Only small quantities of gold were brought up to Ben in each shipment to minimize risk of losing the entire hoard to theft or a raid to recapture it. Can't be too careful. The former owners of the gold have long memories, and were likely to be irritable for even longer about getting foxed.

A graceful solid gold sculpture of a swan, about ten inches high, lay waiting under another blanket for a final polish. The gold was so pure, so soft, Ben could have carved it with a sharp knife instead of casting it. In fact, many of the finishing details that would make the swan such a precious expression of his vision were added by hand. But that would have to wait. The woman who was expecting this piece at the gallery in Soho would have to wait. The buyer, an arms dealer who lived in London's Connaught Square, would have to be patient, too.

Ben was not laundering money. He was laundering stolen gold. Turning bullion into cash at about 1.38 times the market rate per ounce at the time of final sale, so prized was his artistry. So far the system had worked. Thirty-six million dollars had already been realized from this gambit. The revenue had all been sent to Smith Island. More accurately, the sale price of every piece, less the gallery commission, was wired to a numbered account at Scotiabank in the Caymans. Ben and his people believed in the safety of islands. Manhattan, it was turning out, might not have been foolproof.

While Ben crafted the sculptures, his coconspirators on Smith Island were crafting plans to lease a storefront in the Village to eliminate the present gallery commissions. The Smith Islanders could afford it now. Until recently, lean times meant many at home could barely afford to eat more than once a day. That was changing. The price of gold was rising faster than the cost of New York City real estate. Ben's slow output from his basement studio had its advantages in dollar-cost averaging.

The sender of the strange message was right. Picking up and leaving town was not something Ben wished to do, not if he ever wanted to finish his work here in Manhattan once and for all, and get home to the open skies and waters of Smith Island.

There was no question Ben would accept the summons. On the other hand, he preferred not to walk blindly into this mission. He had to pay a visit.

He left the basement, refastened the chain on the door with the lock on the outside, and glanced at the message again. Ben's anger surged. If there was a real mission behind the cipher, it would delay his work here, and push his return home far into an uncertain future. He had committed to New York for only a vigorous short-term push to convert the gold into currency. He had been willing to sacrifice contact with everything he loved only because there was such hardship and grinding need on Smith Island. He never intended to stay away so long. His father had left home long ago, abandoning everything that mattered. Ben wondered if he had turned out just like his father after all, despite a lifetime of trying to take a different path.

With all of his sniper's stealth, Ben climbed three flights up his building's back alley fire escape. He went slowly because the metal stairs were old, and any regular step might set up a sine wave shudder that would alert the person on whom he was dropping in, or worse, bring the whole structure down on top of him.

On the third-floor landing he peered through a small patch in a grimy pane of glass that had been wiped clear as a peephole by the occupant. She was in there on her mattress, sound asleep. Ω was how she signed her work. Omega. She was black, about twenty or so, too thin, not exactly living *la vida loca* in this squat, but she treasured the freedom to act as she wished. She slept in her baggy pants with a shredded blanket pulled up around her arms. Omega was a one-girl crew, a hardcore tagger getting *up* in the neighborhood. Lately she was expanding into an *all-city piecing* with some brilliant murals dotting the town. Ben had surreptitiously watched her work one night, noted her particular style with admiration, and kept an eye out for new efforts. In her world, she was royalty. He was sure that Omega had written the message by his door downstairs. Having seen and enjoyed her work often enough over the previous few months, he recognized her hand.

Ben worked his fingers in over the sill and slid the window upward. It moved easily enough. It had to. It was the front door into Omega's illegal crib. The interior door to the apartment was barricaded against the addicts lurking in the rest of the building. Like Ben, she shunned attention of any sort, other than through her art.

When he got the window raised about eighteen inches, a chilly draft made Omega frown in her sleep, moan, and pull the blanket more closely around her. Ben noted fifty-plus cans of vibrantly colored spray paint with fat and skinny interchangeable nozzles, all meticulously cleaned and ready for the next night's work. The different hues were arranged in their families on the floor, like an art-school color wheel. One wall of the room was covered by a corner-to-corner mural of an underwater dreamworld infested with demon fish.

This was the first time Ben had seen her up close without the respirator mask over her face and a bandana protecting her hair. She was pretty, with deep golden skin, a narrow face, high freckled cheekbones, a mass of black curling hair, long lashes, full lips, and a little scar on the right side of her jaw. Ben slipped in through the window. He hated creeping up on her like this, dangerous as it was for them both. There was no time now for better manners.

He lowered the window, picked up two spray cans, shook them hard. The mixing marbles inside the cans rattled loud like castanets in a palsied flamenco. He barked, "Omega!"

Her eyes flew open. Ben ignored the knife she flashed out from under the blanket in defense. He was completely taken with her vivid blue eyes.

"What the fuck!" Omega sprang to her feet, stepped bravely toward him into the center of the room, the knife held out in front of her waist high and angled at his throat.

"What the fuck is this!" She was still waking up, but with sleep quickly fading from her eyes, Ben knew she could be deadly. He put the spray cans down, and held out his hands to show they were empty. The universal sign of harmless intent in a touchy situation.

Again she shouted, "What the goddamn hell!" Fear was retreating behind its more common mask of anger.

Ben tried changing the subject. "You been working up some sick bombs lately. You bust a fine spray can. I'm impressed."

"The last thing you can expect to be," she declared.

Ben pressed. "That throw-up you did outside my door. Not your best. Your heart wasn't in it. Who said to do that?"

Omega was not having it. "Get out of here while you can. Don't want your blood messing all over my space."

Ben nodded. "I've worked a fair bit in that color myself. Settle down, tell me who gave you that message, and I'll be on my way. No problems."

Omega said nothing. The knife lowered an inch.

Ben said, "I don't care about racking and mobbing. It's about that *graff* on my wall. Do I look like a cop? Come on, neighbor. You know me from round about. This won't come back to you. It was some tough news you left. I need to know whatever you can tell me."

Omega hesitated. "I thought he was a vig'."

Vigilantes were strangely driven older white men who scoured graffiti off of buildings wherever they found it, or painted over it in the name of order. Police regarded vigilantes who used paint as vandals, just as they did the taggers.

Ben nodded, "But he wasn't a vig'. Could you put the knife down?"

The knife did not move. "No. I don't think I can."

"Alright. Suit yourself. Did he pay you?"

"Girl's gotta eat."

"No doubt. I'm going to reach into my pocket nice and easy. We good?"

She did not answer, rather she watched his hand slip into the right coat pocket. He withdrew it just as slowly, but she coiled tighter for trouble.

Ben opened his hand. In his palm lay a rough sawn rectangle of pure gold the size of a small box of matches.

He said, "Market value, about five thousand dollars. Don't sell it down around here. It might come back on you. Or on me. Go out to Jersey, or even to Philly. I'm not kidding. Any joint with *We Buy Gold* in the window will be glad to try to rip you off, no questions asked. I'm betting whatever you get for it is one hell of a lot more than what that guy gave you to tag my wall. Am I right about that? I mean, you said it. 'Girl's gotta eat.'"

Omega relaxed a little. "Toss that over onto my coat."

Ben hesitated. "We have an agreement?"

"White. Shorter than you by four, maybe five inches, and skinnier. Maybe six feet. But strong. Green eyes. Dark red hair. Little mole on his chin."

Ben took this in. "What did he say?"

"He said toss that gold on my coat before I cut you."

Ben gave the piece of gold an easy lob toward the coat by her bed. It shone in the air like a bright little yellow comet, and made a popping sound as it dented a nest in her leather. Omega was sharp as her blade. She did not take her eyes off Ben.

"He told me what I already knew," she said. "There's a guy squatting in my building. In the basement. He told what you looked like, but he said you had your hair shaved high and tight."

Ben's hair was much longer now, and not exactly neat. So the message came from somebody who knew him in the service, or who had received an old description.

Ben said, "Okay. The message?"

"He handed me a slip of paper with the letters and shit on it. He knew about you. He knew me, too, my work. Said that I had to put the whole thing on the wall by your door where you'd be sure to notice."

Ben said, "You could have put the paper under my door, and I never would have known it was you."

Omega shook her head. "See now, he just let me read it. Made me memorize it, and say it a hundred times, like. Then he took it back. Told me to wait til you went out."

"Did he seem to know what the message meant?"

Omega's eyes narrowed. "No. Matter of fact, seemed like talking to me was a big pain in his skinny white ass. Acted like he was above it, or like he wasn't happy passing along a message he couldn't read."

"Like he was cut out for bigger and better. Ever seen him before?"

"Oh *hell* yes. Seen his kind every day. But not this particular one, no."

"When? When did you meet him?"

The knife shook in her hand. "Four this morning, give or take."

Ben tried to remain patient. "Can you be more specific?"

Omega bridled. "No. I must've forgot to wind my Rolex." She wore no watch.

"Where'd this all happen?"

Omega shuddered with rage, and something else. "About where you're standing. Sick to death of waking up with white men in my damn room!"

"Got it. I'm sorry. Last question, but it's important. What did he pay you to tag the wall?"

Omega said nothing, but Ben thought he saw dew in her eyes. After a moment, she yanked the ratty collar of her t-shirt down hard over her left shoulder. An ugly bruise in the shape of a handprint marred her skin.

CHAPTER 3

THE STRANGER KNEW the mission had been a success. The TV was on in the background in the motel room, and the constant replaying of dramatic video, from news cameras and personal mobile phones, the still photographs, and the eulogies were proving to be a happy distraction from the more mundane business at hand. In the killer's current condition, coming down from a recent self-prescribed application of hallucinogens, packing the small suitcase was slow going, but there was plenty of time before the flight at LAX. The archangel of death chose not to allow time for a nap, for fear that the horrific nightmares would return. So the stranger kept busy, and stayed awake. Wiping the room's surfaces clean of fingerprints would take a little while, but because this methodical assassin practically lived in latex gloves, it would not be burdensome.

News coverage of Luz Calderon's death was important in assessing the work, of course, but it was the telephone call from the stranger's client contact that really counted. The reviews were in. Everyone upstairs was very happy. The next assignment would come shortly.

The contractor was glad to know there would be more work in the future, but this was no time for sloppiness. It was quite possible that in fact there were no further assignments coming, and the promise of another mission was nothing more than a ruse to lull one into a false sense of security while the stranger's own elimination was planned and carried out. The reaper had enjoyed a busy season with this client, but all good things come to an end. Perhaps the client might feel overexposed with the latest effort.

It was certainly the most visible killing undertaken in the series. Making it splashy had been part of the job description, a desired outcome. Make it big. Very public. It was not in the stealthy sharpshooter's nature to work so visibly, especially on American soil, but sometimes the high profile of the target made it unavoidable. Outside a few acquaintances, the killer was indeed a stranger to all. The sheaf of false identities trailing back decades had long assured anonymity.

Unfortunately, the quiet hitter was so good, so perfect an employee, that clients often began to feel fear mixed in with the respect and abject admiration that was due for so many jobs well done. This devolution of sentiment, this waning appreciation had occurred in past business relationships, usually when a client was beginning to think the fee was too steep. No one in this line of work was so good that they would not be viewed, sooner or later, as a liability. Though stiffing a contract killer would seem like a bad idea to a person of even the meanest IQ, some clients tried it. Trying to kill a professional assassin was even more ridiculous, and yet it happened. It was important to stay alert, even in times of great success.

The telephone call from the client had been brief. The real proof of satisfaction had come via the Internet. Through a series of cloaked sub-accounts that routed any online activity through shell servers established in remote countries where bribery was appreciated, the stranger had verified that the final fee for this job, plus the significant expenses incurred, had been wired to the account established in a small financial institution in Bern, Switzerland. Nothing had been held back. Nothing could be taken back. The bank balance was a cool million Euros to the good, not counting the line item expenses. In a few minutes, with more keystrokes on a laptop, the balance would fall back to zero, when the money was divided and routed onward into a cyber-morass of other accounts in other countries, eight in all. If one account were ever traced or hacked, there were many others. This kind of insurance was complicated, but well worth the peace of mind it gave the freelance assassin, who was very skeptical of sure things. A single egg in every basket was the contractor's philosophy.

The plane ticket that the stranger had booked was for First Class. And why not? It was not vanity. Hopscotching flights around the world, covering tracks between the job site and home with a series of false identities backed by expensive forged documents all took their toll on a weary traveler.

CHAPTER 4

BEN BLACKSHAW'S TAXI ride from New York City to McGuire Air Force Base gobbled up almost two hours. The driver, Malik Qadeem, according to his identification, was thankfully not too chatty so early in his shift, other than wanting to be sure Ben had enough money in hand for the unusually large fare. Ben was early as the cab pulled up to the blast-resistant sentry box at McGuire. He held a sheaf of cash at the ready.

The armed sentry was flanked in the booth by a Captain Michaels, white, early thirties, fit, as though his time on a desk had not been the death of his strenuous exercise regimen. Still, Ben quickly figured the rank was too high for sentry duty. Ben rolled down his window, not sure how he was going to explain his arrival at the base. Turns out, he did not have to.

After a quick glance at a photograph in his hand, Captain Michaels said, "Please step out of the vehicle, sir."

Ben complied, taking his GOOD, or Get Out Of Dodge bag with him. It had all his necessaries for a short trip: cash, a change of socks, a change of identity, and a toothbrush. It always lay packed and ready near his door. Captain Michaels' tone led Ben to feel as though he were being busted for speeding, but was under suspicion of something far worse. The officer left the booth and bent down to Qadeem's level. Without glancing at the fare meter, which was in triple digits, he passed over several bills that made Qadeem's eyes open wide.

When he could speak, Qadeem said, "The tolls?"

Captain Michaels did not react. "Back up now, turn around, and go home. Understand me, sir? What I just gave you should cover your whole week."

Qadeem shrugged *Worth a try*, and did as he was told.

Michaels gestured away from the sentry box. "This way, sir." He led Ben past the gate to a Humvee tricked out in the Highet Kracker digital gray-green camouflage that had been popular a few years back. The captain held the door for Ben, but did not meet his eyes.

Though Michaels drove a roundabout route through the base's less active streets, Ben felt exposed. He was risking everything stepping onto this base, and could not help wondering if his identity were common knowledge.

"Were you given my name, Captain?" he asked.

Michaels kept his eyes straight ahead. "No. Strictly need-to-know."

"That's *Mister* Need-To-Know to you."

"Yes, sir. I'll get you where you're supposed to be. That is all."

Ben said nothing more. The base was getting busier with civilian employees by now, and as was usual, no one gave his vehicle a second glance, let alone a first. This was similar to the anonymity he had cultivated in Manhattan, but somewhere up the line Ben would meet a person who knew him very well. Someone in a difficult situation that Ben was supposed to help fix.

The hangars came into view. Michaels pulled up in front of the last, stepped out, walked around the front of the Humvee, and opened Ben's door. Without speaking, he handed Ben the photograph used to verify his identity, and pointed to a modular sally port before driving off into the rest of his day.

Ben walked to the sally port, which from the outside looked like an oversized shipping container, about twelve feet wide by forty long, aligned lengthwise with the wall of the hangar. Probably a blast-resistant number from Lion Industrial Buildings. What the hell was waiting for him inside? The first crash of fear he had felt upon seeing the letters on the wall returned.

Another sentry gave Ben the up-and-down through a small thick window in the end of the building. Ben could see him refer to something, probably another photograph. Without asking for any identification, an anomaly in the post-9/11 world, the sentry activated the heavy door. It opened with a shove from an electric motor geared down low enough to grind a man in half if he did not look sharp. Ben stepped into a ten-by-ten foot space. Still no clue who or what he was dealing with, but the lack of insignias screamed OGA, Other Government Agency, the common euphemism for the Central Intelligence Agency. NSA was another possibility.

When the first door rolled shut behind Ben, the next door cranked open. He walked to the end of the sally port's space, and turned right into a white hallway floored in a broken linoleum pattern that would hide dirt and blood if there were any. There was only one windowless door at the opposite end of this hall, which lay inside the hangar. The second sally port door closed behind him. He waited there for less than a minute.

A functionary in his mid-twenties put his head in the doorway and said, "Uh, hi." Ben was plainly not what he was expecting, a tired man dressed out of a dumpster, looking like he was half a paycheck from racking on steam vents in winter.

Ben said nothing. This kid was dressed in a white shirt, with a WWII style tanker watch poking out from beneath a once-rolled cuff. Khaki slacks bottomed out over comfortable-looking brown brogues with crepe soles. A civilian look, though something about him still whispered *covert*, and well outside any military chain of command. These guys had an impressionistic rulebook, very thin, rarely opened, and constantly being rewritten on the fly. They could do anything they wanted to nearly everyone. Not a good sign. Ben had hoped the Air Force base was just a place to meet an old friend, but this appointment was watermarked by the most ungovernable segments of government.

Ben waited for the spook to gather his thoughts, which took about ten seconds.

The guy said, "Hi," again, then continued, "Come on in. I'm Tom."

Ben followed Tom through the door into another hallway like the one he had left, but much longer. It might run the length of the entire hangar.

Tom stopped walking. "Cell phone?"

Ben shook his head.

"Firearm? Knife?"

Ben shrugged.

Tom digested this for a moment, and said, "Okay, well sir, it seems like you have some things that're pretty heavy in your coat pockets. And something on your right calf."

Ben said, "Loose change. Personal property."

Tom was not sure how to handle this. "I mean, they're pretty dense, you know? No offense, but you mind emptying your pockets please?"

"I mind one hell of a lot. *Tom.*"

Ben realized that somewhere in the sally-port, or in the first hallway, he had received a body scan. It had picked up the four small hand-hewn ingots of gold he had brought along in addition to his cash. Universal currency. Just in case. And the scan had read his knife.

Tom pondered for a few moments. Evidently he decided that engaging with a guy like Ben about the contents of his pockets lay well above his pay grade.

"Right. Would you mind waiting in here?" Tom opened a door to the left in the hallway. The room behind the door was carpeted in an institutional shade of keep-the-crazies-calm green. There were four plush brown chairs against one wall, and a table with plastic-wrapped sandwiches, sodas and bottles of spring water on ice, taking up another wall. And a TV. "Help yourself."

Ben stepped inside. Tom stayed in the hall and closed the door behind Ben. Though there was no visible lock on the door, there was a heavy mechanical clank right away. Ben tried the door. The knob turned, but the door did not budge. Ben was a prisoner. He felt the surge of fear through his chest as adrenalin throttled up the heartbeat. He felt utterly stupid. Lulled into complacent sense of security by the familiar surroundings of the base, Ben had allowed his guard to drop. He was on American soil. Military men would not perpetrate this kind of crap on one another. Then he remembered that Tom was not in any regular branch of the service.

A phone with no keypad chirped on a side table amidst the chairs. Ben picked up, but said nothing. Tom started talking. "Sorry, I don't mean to be a tool. It's not that we don't trust you, but we don't know you. You get it. You're an unknown quantity is all. I mean, I'm sure you're a great guy, but security in here's a bitch for all of us. Can't have people poking around our stuff. Hang in there, and we'll get back to you when everything's ready. Oh, and the sandwiches are made here on base. Even the bread. Really amazing. Try the roast beef. Okay? Okay, great." The line went dead. Ben put the receiver back in its cradle.

Tom's call had given Ben no reason to relax. He explored the room. Tight. No windows. No vent that anything larger than a wet muskrat could pass through. Same in the lavatory that lay behind a small door. Plumbing under the sink's cabinet was cemented into the wall. No access panel for repairs that one might find in a house. No way out through there.

Ben turned on the TV, and got his first glimpse of the world he had not seen in months. He ate a roast beef sandwich. Not bad. Not what he would order for a last meal, but it would keep his body nourished and his mind sharp until Tom and company got their collective shit wrapped.

Suddenly robbed of his freedom, and with it, the busywork of his occupation, Ben found himself dwelling on Smith Island. He should never have left. He could have figured out a way to work the gold closer to home. Fleeing to New York City seemed a drastic step in retrospect, but where else could he have hidden? He had fought well in Gulf War One. He was a local hero, not to mention his reputation as a well-regarded artist. There were evil men angry at the loss of the gold. They wanted it back. They wanted revenge. There was no choice. Ben had to go to ground. The cost was already proving dreadful even before this morning's message.

CHAPTER 5

THE HOLDING ROOM had been well stocked with chow, so Ben was not surprised that hours, not minutes ticked by with no further contact from Tom or anyone else. Ben had lots of time to consider what was happening. The message that morning was a typical military hurry up and wait. Tom had said there were things to get ready for him. Tom was apologetic, almost diffident. Ben had him figured for a terrible liar if called upon. No matter. The food was not drugged. The seals on the water bottles had not been tampered with. And they were a brand he had heard of. All good. He was fairly certain he was not scheduled for torture, or death. For what, then?

The only intel available to him came from the TV, and he would have been thoroughly up to date already if he owned one of his own, or a radio, or bought a newspaper now and then. But work did not allow him the commitment of time required to digest a globe's worth of events on anything like a regular basis.

Media news had never touched Ben's life. Even when he was in the Navy, only his orders mattered. There were no wars. There were only corners of wars for which he was personally accountable to prosecute.

Ben knew many would argue that events great and small anywhere in the world affected them on a personal level, but he felt they were bored or kidding themselves with the misjudged sense of self-importance that everyone was supposed to have these days. Or they were beset with a heavy need for self-validation.

The news never truly touched them either, unless a misadventure of some kind brought the spotlight on them for their personal fifteen minutes of Warhol time. Then they became *content*, in the current jargon. To Ben, the news these days was just another genre of entertainment, storyboarded in gossip, hearsay, and blood, collected by journalists and packaged by editors and producers for sale. Ben thought the only truth of any value was what lay before him; his work, his few dear friends, and his home. Right now he had no contact with those three touchstones of his life. He was alone, far from Smith Island, and not working, though it could be argued that waiting was a kind of work for some. So he ate the sandwich and watched the TV.

Ben got a sense of his mistake over the last few months. He had lived a Spartan life, kept the basement as bare as he could to spur him to work harder. There were no amenities. He had purposefully chosen not to be comfortable. The sooner the gold was converted to money, the sooner he would be paroled to go home. If he had made the basement less dreary, perhaps he might have been less miserable, and less ready to embark on this insane mission. His wife LuAnna could have transformed the cellar into a place of beauty, but she had died with him. She was not in New York. She could not help.

Ben could have bought some kind of CD player, and whiled away the hot dreary hours listening to Chester River Runoff, his favorite newgrass band. He sensed his exile and imprisonment in New York was a not just a tactical necessity. It was a form of self-punishment. What were the charges? Ben did not know upon what evidence he had been convicted. As prosecutor, judge and jury, he should have understood all of this. Yet here he was, hours into a mission he knew nothing about. Had he sentenced himself to death? He had no idea.

Every bite of the sandwich tasted much the same as the last, and every channel was droning out slightly varied coverage of a singer's murder in Los Angeles. Though he had heard of Luz, he did not know her music. The songs sampled in the brief concert retrospectives had been catchy enough. Her moves in the videos were sexy. Her remarks in interviews were gushing paeans to her fans.

Hysterical girl-in-the-street sound bites told of a saint brought down in her prime. It was not as though these tearful people knew the singer personally, but they believed that they did, because their feelings about her were strong, and therefore seemed real. Feelings were not facts, Ben thought, no matter how intense. It was not as though there would be an empty place at their dinner tables tonight now that the singer, Luz, had died. Her recordings were still available, weren't they? And her output of music would probably continue for some time as unreleased cuts were compiled for sale now that her death had raised their value. Ben supposed that concertgoers would be hardest hit, but not really. There would be no more live concerts, true, but try getting a fan to admit that their attention at these events was really focused on the Jumbotron screens most of the time, and not on the gnat-sized figure on the stage hundreds of yards below their nosebleed seats.

The story's coverage was repetitive, hypnotic, with the same concert loops replaying over and over, the same package of shots of the crime scene with Emergency Service Personnel trying to treat or simply calm those who were injured in body and soul. It was clear that the death had been public, and violent, but everyone involved on the scene and in the newsrooms was frustrated that the precise cause of death remained unclear.

The singer seemed to have exploded while sitting on the back of her car just as she was about to go watch a movie in which she had a big important role. Exploded how? No clever phrasing of a reporter's question would induce the L.A.P.D. Public Information Officers and spokespersons to speculate for the record. They were pros, and they could recite the same small set of facts ten different ways without shedding any new light. The talking heads were obviously ambivalent about whether to call out the authorities on their dearth of detail, or jolly them along in order to stretch out the story's value. Reporters did not want to lose eyeballs to boredom, but neither did they want to gin out the full shock value of the story before its natural ebb. Most of the on-camera talent contented themselves with hyping the next press conference, placing the burden of progressing the story, or not, squarely on the shoulders of the authorities.

The phone on the table chirped again. Ben picked up. Tom said, "Hey it's me. We're getting close. So get ready to get ready."

Ben closed his eyes, pinched the bridge of his nose. Tom said, "You have a headache? There's aspirin and ibuprofen in the lavatory."

Of course there was a hidden camera in the room. Ben should have expected it, and he quickly reviewed his last few hours for any strange behavior that might have amused his sitter in Security. Lately, after months of isolation, he had discovered that he talked to himself out loud. Nothing he could do about it now.

Ben said, "No, no headache. About how long are we talking?"

Tom said, "I'm sorry, I can't be more specific. But it's getting dark, so I guess I can suggest, for no particular reason of course, that you lay off the bottled water now, and be sure to use the bathroom." The line went dead.

For no particular reason, Ben followed Tom's instructions. Afterward, he collected the ibuprofen and aspirin, just in case. There were two sealed foil packets of each in the lavatory medicine chest instead of plastic jars, which was good, because they would not rattle like maracas in his pockets. Less bulky, too. He also put a sandwich in each coat pocket, along with two packets of Peanut M&Ms. He was going somewhere soon.

Two hours later, Ben was no smarter about the singer's murder. There might have been developments, but he had turned off the TV, partly in frustration with the lack of movement in the story, but mostly to grab a snooze in one of the chairs. He was awakened from a dream of a crab cake feast by the heavy clunk of the internal door locks rolling back.

Tom put his head in at the door. "Oh, hi," he said, as if genuinely surprised to find Ben still there. "We're ready for you. Did you, you know … one last time?"

Ben said, "No camera in the latrine? Gimme a minute." Shortly, Ben followed Tom out of the waiting room.

After a circuitous walk through a maze of hallways and two additional secured sally ports, Tom stopped in front of a metal door. He turned to Ben and said, "I would give anything to do what you're about to do. But you cannot tell anyone about it. If you do, it's a breach of National Security, and you'll—"

"I'll *nothing*," interrupted Ben. "You have no idea who I am, and you won't ever see me again. And if you ever describe me to anybody, that's a breach of my personal security, and I know where you work, and I know your name, and a hangar is no place to hide. Understand?"

The kid blanched, but rallied like an idiot. "Yeah? Well, Tom's not my real name."

"Say it ain't so."

From inside his collar, the kid produced an ID card which hung from a neck lanyard, and swiped it beside the door. As the card came free of the magnetic card reader, two things happened. The door lock clanked open, and Ben snatched the card out of *Tom's* hands, tugging the card's neck lanyard hard, and his guide's throat in the bargain.

Ben read the card loud and clear. "Howdy Winstedt, Samuel J."

Winstedt *née* Tom choked out a quiet, "Shit."

"So Sam, do we have an understanding, you and I?" Ben asked.

"I guess so."

Ben tried to sound stern, but ended up just sounding irked. "Seriously, kid, do you know my name, or what I look like?"

"I have no idea. I swear."

"Good boy. Let's go." Ben released the card.

Winstedt stood upright, rubbing his neck where the lanyard had impressed a red line. Dejected, he opened the door, and Ben followed him into the enormous hangar bay.

The space was illuminated by overhead lamps to a degree surpassing daylight and well into the lumens of an OR. Maintenance could be performed on high tech military aircraft at any hour with a surgeon's precision. Ben observed the tools were all stowed. There were no Line Replaceable Avionics lying around. All clean, organized, and ready. Nobody in there but Winstedt and himself, and their footsteps echoed under the slight buzz of a few poorly ballasted lights.

There was only one aircraft in the entire space. A Northrop Grumman RQ-4 Global Hawk UAV. An Unmanned Aerial Vehicle. Most people called them drones or, mistakenly, Predators, which were the armed variants.

It was Ben's turn to mutter, "Shit." Sight of the plane left him cold, and flooded with unhappy recollections.

Sam Winstead misunderstood and said, "I know. Amazing, right?"

The Global Hawk was a high-altitude surveillance platform with long, narrow high-aspect-ratio composite wings shaped like an old U-2, spanning one hundred sixteen feet. An Allison Rolls-Royce turbofan, Ben knew, with seven thousand pounds of thrust could push the aircraft along at three hundred fifty knots cruise speed for thirteen thousand miles at a service ceiling of sixty-five thousand feet. Impressive stats, when the bird worked right.

Winstedt was smiling at Ben, "You know what she is? Ever seen one before?"

"I've seen a few like her fall out of the sky for no damn reason. Had to babysit the wrecks behind enemy lines in the desert till the Chinooks and your spook buddies came in to salvage them. That was fun."

Winstedt defended the plane like it was his best girl. "Those were in the first production block! They were practically prototypes for chrissakes. They had no business being deployed in-country before they were fully tested and evaluated, but that's how bad they were needed."

Ben asked, "Winnie, why am I here?"

"I told you, I have no idea why, or even who you are. But we've spent the whole day swapping out most of the Integrated Sensor Suite, the surveillance package, because somebody with a lot of juice said to do that. For you."

Ben hesitated to ask, "What did you swap in?"

"The PTP."

"English, Winnie."

"Personnel Transport Podule."

"Personnel Transport. In that thing? Me?"

Winstedt warmed to his subject, and started walking faster toward the aircraft. "I've sat in it, and it's really comfortable. The chaise is by Oregon Aero. Soft as can be. There's a reading light, and SiriusXM radio, as well as a full mil-spec com package. Air conditioning and heat, the capsule's fully pressurized down to two thousand feet. Steerable Ballistic Recovery System blows out a big parachute in two seconds in the unlikely event something goes wrong, like if you catch a surface-to-air missile. I mean, if you have to get someplace, with nobody the wiser, this is the way to go. Beats a C-130 all to hell. But no lavatory in this generation. Couldn't fit that in. So you get a H.E.R.E. That's a Human Element Range Extender. Otherwise known as a pee bottle. The cover doesn't always fit tight, so don't knock it around once you use it, please."

To Ben, it seemed to take forever to cross the hangar, and the plane kept getting bigger and bigger. Certainly this was the largest UAV he had seen in one piece. The forward payload clamshell was open revealing a high-visibility green pod about the size of a Smart Car. The pod had a hatch in the side like a small car door, and one porthole. He was not getting in that thing.

Ben asked, "Where am I supposed to go exactly?"

Winstedt said, "That's need to know. This flight is autonomous. I personally confirmed that the encoded flight plan was digitally loaded via satellite downlink just before I came to get you, but I don't have clearance to decode it. Our operator will handle take-off via remote control, and the landing will be handled by somebody else, someplace else. Pensacola, maybe, but that's just a guess. You'll be tracked, I imagine, but everything in between is autonomous, the way points, the altitudes, groundspeeds, the works. You'll be up there in the Angel levels, free as a bird. Tell you a secret, and this is huge. Ben, in time of national emergency, this is Air Force Two. This is actually the Vice President's fallback ride."

"And no crapper. Figures. Is your operator any good?"

Winstedt's blush was clear in the harsh light. "She's the best in the business. Actually, we're kind of dating. I mean, when I asked her out a couple months back, she didn't exactly say *no*, did she? Just waiting for our schedules to synch up."

Ben said, "Jesus, Winnie. You're killing me here."

Ben realized someone else had made it halfway across the hangar before he noted the footsteps echoing over the lamp buzz. He turned to see who was coming. It was a man dressed much like Winstedt, but with reddish hair, and a thin wiry build, about six feet tall. As he got close, Ben noticed a little mole on his chin. He carried an aluminum briefcase.

The new guy clearly thought as much of Ben's looks as Winstedt had earlier that morning. He skipped handshakes and introductions. "You're a tough guy to find."

Ben said, "But not impossible."

"No. Not impossible. Not for us, that's for sure. Here." The man with the mole on his chin passed Ben the aluminum case. It was locked shut behind a combination. "You'll get the combo by radio when you're airborne. Think you can handle that, sport?"

"Gosh, I think so. But I did want to ask you something."

The man with the little mole on his chin brightened at the prospect of being either useful, or annoying, or perhaps both. "Sure. What?"

"Early this morning, I think you ran into a friend of mine?"

The operative smiled slyly, man to man. "I suppose. Kinda hot, in a ghetto sort of way."

Ben brought the aluminum case up fast and hard, right into the little chin mole. The impact echoed through the hangar like the report of a pistol. Chin Mole danced backward, arms and legs flailing like a human wind farm. He lost his balance altogether and crashed hard onto the deck.

Winstedt was speechless, eyes wide.

Ben moved in on Chin Mole and stood over him. "Just between us, you don't ever want to see her again. If you do, I'll find you."

Ben snatched the man's ID card so hard that the neck lanyard parted. Ben read the card out loud. "O'Connor, Brian C. You understand me, Bri'? You awake?" Ben slammed a boot into O'Connor's ribs twice. "I don't want there to be any doubt in your mind on that point. Acknowledge!"

O'Connor rolled onto his good side, his tongue probing and pushing loose teeth around behind bloody split lips. He nodded, plenty angry.

Ben dropped the ID card, and wiped a smear of blood off the aluminum case with his coat sleeve. He turned to Winstedt, whose eyes were still big as cue balls. "Okay, Winnie. Tell your gal to make the take-off smooth, because frankly, I'm in a mood. Let's boogie."

CHAPTER 6

THE EXECUTIONER'S SURPRISE was waiting in the blind email drop. Though currently at the airport in Munich, still not halfway through the roundabout flights, trains, and final boat ride to home, there was already a new assignment. Interesting. The pace was definitely ramping up.

The drop account was logged off and would never be used again. There were some travel arrangements to change under another identity, which took only a few minutes. Then the small laptop slid into its travel case, and another passport with a different name was removed. Unfortunately, the checked suitcase would not be rerouted to the new destination if the passenger were not aboard the aircraft with it. The case would eventually be collected by the airline, stored briefly, and then examined and disposed of. Gone was the time when it would be delivered home by the airline, no questions asked. This was a matter of no importance. The luggage was clean. The operative traveled light, but still felt that checked baggage offered the look of normality, of the harmless human need to carry lots of things wherever one went in order to feel at home. The assassin could have carried the case on board. Milling at the baggage carousel with other travelers made this stranger feel almost normal.

A weapon would be procured at the new work site, or smuggled from discreet master gunsmiths in Taiwan if something special were required. The deadly article would be documented and disguised as urgently needed medical supplies. Only donated organs slid through customs faster than the stranger's customized gear. Years of practice, experience, and well-paid connections made repositioning for fresh work easy, even in mid-stride.

There was time at the new gate before the next flight. Time for the killer to consider what the new opportunity signified. On the surface, there would be a large cash infusion, an immediate down payment for the service to be rendered. Half in advance, and that would be verified in the airport after the next flight landed at Tel Aviv.

The stranger was not old, but was old enough to appreciate how wireless internet connections at every gate had made so many aspects of the macabre practice tremendously simple compared to bygone days when a human voice over hardwired telephone lines, followed by actual signatures on paper documents, were required to do practically everything. Independent operators now enjoyed the technological conveniences once reserved for international conglomerates. This was the golden age of contract murder.

The deadly auslander appreciated repeat business with any client, but this new job, coming so closely on the heels of the last, left little time for the usual reflection, the customary contemplation that was important for both quality control and simple human savoring of work well done. A newspaper helped with the latter. As often happened, the higher profile targets were illuminated far more in posthumous media reports than in the brief client *précis* and the stranger's own boots-on-the-ground workups.

The sudden influx of new business cast a shadow, and prompted questions. Was the client losing control of his agenda? Was something wrong with the client's projects such that pre-terminal solutions could not be put into play? The targets for this client were popping up all over the world, so the contract operative was clearly not facilitating a national coup d'état. Those were the purview of petty dictators-in-waiting who commanded sufficient forces to effect a desired regime change in a matter of hours, or days. Any longer, and those affairs became untidy civil wars of attrition. A single bullet through the right brainstem could make all the difference. It was a matter of imagination, and this filler of crypts was nothing if not creative.

Perhaps this additional work was the very engagement that would end everything; the bait, leading into a trap, heading straight to the elimination of a trusted and valued asset that had regrettably outlived its usefulness by becoming overexposed, or as bad, overpaid. The stranger's antennae were up. The next job would require special care. Perhaps, not for the first time, it would be wiser to destroy the client before he got any bright ideas. Perhaps this golden goose should be made into *foie gras*. On that note, the world's most lethal human being rose from the chair at the gate, and wandered away in search of a snack.

CHAPTER 7

THE GLOBAL HAWK'S podule was strangely quiet, despite the Allison Rolls-Royce turbofan howling behind Ben. He munched on a sandwich with no idea what was going on, or what part of the world was passing twelve miles beneath him. He was close to the edge of space up there at Angel 65, the way pilots refer to 65,000 feet, but he felt as though he were in a chair on solid ground.

A voice crackled out of a speaker. "Uh, hi."

"That you, Winnie?"

"No names. We're encrypted, but you know. Can't be too safe."

"If that's the case, I should be on a Greyhound bus, don't you think?"

Winstedt ignored the remark. "That thing you need goes as follows. Ready?"

Feeling a little like Slim Pickens authenticating nuclear targeting orders in *Dr. Strangelove*, Ben pulled the aluminum case from the cabin floor onto his lap.

"Ready to copy."

Winstedt dictated a ten-digit number over the radio. Ben punched the digits into the keypad on the case. An internal lock *kachunked*. Ben opened the case an inch to be sure.

"Did it work?" Winstedt asked.

"Like a charm. Thanks pal." There was a brief pause. "You still there?"

"What's it like?"

Ben thought for a moment. "In-flight entertainment's not so hot. No view. Ride's smooth enough. Flight attendant is homely. It is what it is, Winnie. Where am I?"

"I am not allowed to say. Katie—I mean, your pilot took off great, didn't she?"

"No complaints," Ben said. "Tell her thanks from me."

"Will do." There was pride in Winstedt's voice.

Ben changed the subject. "Say Winnie, I'm looking for a cigarette lighter in this thing. Guess I can use this pee bottle for an ashtray, but—"

Winstedt's voice was panicked when he interrupted. "No! God, please don't smoke! It could mess up the com gear. I mean, you're sitting in one atmosphere pressure, lots of O_2, maybe a fire, and we'll never get the stench out of the upholstery. Like Apollo 1, you know? Well-done meat."

Ben smiled. "Relax. Just having a little fun."

"Really? So not funny." Winstedt regrouped. "Okay. That's it, I guess. Sit back and relax. You're in good hands, I hope. So long, Ben."

The radio speaker went quiet. So, Winstedt knew Ben's name. He was not such a bad liar after all. As if his current position were not precarious enough, Ben felt his control of the situation loosen. He had been lured away from his own clandestine work to a mission that was itself mysterious. Four million dollars in gold lay abandoned and unguarded in a hostile city behind a padlock and chain that could be torched through in minutes. Ben felt like a fool. For the moment, mewed up in the small pod high above the earth, he was left with an overwhelming sense of loneliness.

Ben opened the briefcase wide. His loneliness changed to anger. Photographs quivered in his hand, despite a complete lack of turbulence.

CHAPTER 8

BEN READ AND reread the contents of the briefcase, and studied the photographs. They dealt with the murder of the singer in Los Angeles, a devastating public slaughter. As only another soldier could understand, the senselessness of the killing enraged Ben. In all, the hastily assembled case dossier raised many more questions than it resolved.

An electronic voice, sounding like Perfect Paul, the automated reader of NOAA weather reports, broke in upon his meditations from the com unit. "This is the Captain speaking from the flight deck. If those of you on the left side of the cabin look out the window, you will see there is no window." Some kind of vocal distortion was in use to mask the speaker's identity. This meant Ben might recognize the voice if it were left undistorted.

Ben said, "Been waiting for the beverage service. Time to fasten seatbelts yet?"

The monotonous robotic voice said, "Not yet. Bet you could do with a drink. Know what you're looking at yet in that file?"

Ben almost sneered. "Same as always. Half the story."

"Good. When you get here, maybe I can help with that. For a man like you, that file must be pretty thin. We've pulled a little more intel together since you boarded."

"Such as?" Ben asked.

"You'll see. Sorry for the inconvenience there. You understand, I'm sure."

"I'm sure I don't. What's my ETA?"

The voice said, "Need to know."

"Need to go."

"Improvise, adapt and overcome. See you on the ground."

The com speaker went silent. Ben recognized the last smartass remark as a peculiar form of Marine Corps encouragement. With no tones or nuances of a normal human voice available for clues to the speaker's identity, Ben relied on pace, phrasing, pauses, and the generalities and peculiarities of the speaker's vocabulary. The indicators were for a male speaker, ruling out slightly more than half of the world's population. Assuming an armed forces background of the speaker cut down the potential. The U.S. military currently boasted a little over one million four hundred seventy-three thousand active personnel. Two-hundred thirteen thousand of them were women. That narrowed the pool, yes, but not by much. There was something familiar about the speaker, but nothing specific. Ben had worked with, or at least encountered thousands of male personnel in his career, and every one of them liked a joke as much as the next. The number blossomed again if discharged soldiers like himself were factored in. The voice certainly did not remind him of anyone in the small cadre of friends who knew the code he had found on his wall that morning.

Ben straightened the edges of the papers and photographs, and tucked them away in the aluminum case. Having mined every possible piece of intelligence from them, he resorted to another soldier's credo attributed to Roman legionaries. When you don't have to march, stand. When you don't have to stand, sit your ass down. When you can lie down, do it. When you can grab shut-eye, do that. He had already eaten the sandwiches and the M&Ms.

As he drifted toward sleep, his subconscious kept cranking. In the hazy twilight, freed from the chatter of higher functions of intellect, the animal inside him sensed the full danger, even the stupidity of his position. Perhaps he had been too bored and cooped up grinding out works of art in that dark, damp basement. Perhaps an older need for a mission had drawn him into the open. Whatever the prompting, Ben had broken cover and put his entire venture in New York City at risk. All for a promise made to a comrade long ago. Would he really want to help someone who needed to treat Omega so badly to get his attention?

Other angles jutted into Ben's thoughts. The money. It was every-where. La Luz's career, her chance to become a true legend, that was over. Her label in particular, and the already fractured music industry in general, would take a grievous financial hit with her death. Who would gain? Ben had no answer for now.

The cost of tracking him was prodigious, he reflected. His tradecraft was not sloppy. He knew how to get ghost and stay dead in the eyes of most outfits that might give a damn about him. Rousting him out cost a lot of money. If this errand cost Ben his life, what would it really matter? Most of the world thought he was dead already. This fact provided valuable deni-ability for whoever had called him out; that definitely would be worth the expense to some. And that meant this gig reeked of blackops.

Finally, the fixed and operating costs of putting him aboard a Global Hawk were astronomical. Someone wanted to reposition him a significant distance, but with minimal contact with other civilians. More deniability. That was okay by Ben. The fewer questions he had to field about his incon-venient resurrection, the better. So this mission, this problem he was to solve, it had to be sizable for somebody who had a great deal to lose if he failed. He stirred in his harness. All this time in New York, unbeknownst to Ben, somebody had an up-to-the-minute position on him, keeping him in a back pocket in reserve. Ben mused again that no one was more expendable than a ghost.

Soldier's intuition woke Ben to some undefined danger. As sleep cleared, he noted the flight seemed the same as when he had drifted off. The roar of the jet engine behind him seemed smooth and true. The softly wheezing climate control unit still puffed at him from eyeball vents, even if the air was now slightly stale. The deck angle was level, as best he could judge, indicating neither a climb nor a descent. His lower back was stiffen-ing up. How long had he been asleep? One thing was sure, a growing terror left him feeling trapped like a rat in a box with hungry cats prowling outside.

CHAPTER 9

THE STRANGER WOKE from a disturbing dream. The airliner on which the exhausted operative flew could have been anywhere in the world, between any two points on the long trip to the next assignment; the dream's absorbing disorientation was complete. Lately, the vision, more a nightmare, had ruined more nights' sleep than the killer cared to remember. Always the same. Darkness, at first. Then the sound of marching. An egg sack breaking open to an infinite number of eight-legged hatchlings. Then thousands upon thousands of boots, with a jingle and clank of personal gear. A great massing of infantry forces tromping into a city behind the swath of ruin bashed out of the orderly architecture of civilization by heavy mechanized armor units. The tanks' main guns were always elevated high, like rampant erections bragging to vanquished onlookers that these invaders were perpetually ready for action. As always happened, the dreamer became aware, through no discernible clue or evidence, that these marching soldiers were brash American troops. This was Yankee muscle flexing.

The city into which the troops swarmed began to take shape. The sky-line looked more and more familiar. Old domes. Towers. Spires of churches. The image from millions of postcards sold and mailed, but these were scrawled with, "Wish you had never come along".

The agent of blood, who was used to inspiring fear in others, looked around for the flight attendants to be sure no one could see the sweat-beaded brow and upper lip. The adjoining seat was empty on this flight, but that was little consolation. Often enough, it had been occupied when the stranger woke to find men or women staring, obviously wishing another seat were available to put a safe distance in between.

The dream had to be stopped. Though the operative never balked at the bloodshed of individuals, this spectral invasion somehow abrogated humanity, decency, and felt profoundly unjust. This odd scruple was disturbing to the cold-blooded killer. Why should a dream of war be so paralyzing? The stranger had made a slayer's bones in armed conflict. Remorse had long ago bled away into the churned earth of many battlefields. Now, remorse was skulking back to pollute the stranger's slumber. The anonymous passenger had to take action, and removed a small square of paper from the carry-on briefcase. The little square was brightly decorated with a popular cartoon character. It was also infused with a chemical. Lycergic acid diethylamide. Blotter acid. LSD. Whipped up by a protégé of Owsley Stanley himself. The distempered stranger ate the paper, and waited for the debilitating nightmarish scenes to be displaced by new, more tolerable hallucinations. A handful of Ambien pills followed to encourage sleep through the fresh visions.

CHAPTER 10

PYRAMID LAKE, NEVADA birthed slow, twining phantoms of vapor into the night as cold air from shore drifted over the warmer waters. The four men standing on stepladders out in the shallows cast with their fly rods absently, appreciative that stars winked overhead, but that the waxing moon had not yet risen to light the sky, water, or ground. They were silent. They did not care if a cutthroat trout snagged their lines. In fact it would be damned inconvenient for their plans. They awaited a bigger fish.

An observer from shore might have pointed out that the trout were not running now, and were probably hugging the bottom of the lake anyway. That same observer would note that the anglers' gear was not quite right, did not seem to fit the task, even if their timing for fish had been perfect. The pre-storm nymphs on their lines were wrong, since the good weather was forecast to hold. The landing nets were just out of reach. The wicker creels seemed old school and out of place; both these and the vest pouches the men wore were quite empty of fish. The men's clothing seemed uniformly new and shelf-creased; they had outfitted themselves as much from paintings of Izaak Walton as from Leland.

The first fisherman checked his watch for the fourth time in as many minutes. This time, he slipped his flyrod in one of the holes in the top of his ladder meant for paint roller handles. From his creel, he extracted a computer tablet, and connected it to a small but powerful transmitter with a small USB cable. Another cable connected the transmitter to a port in the flyrod. The rod was actually an antenna. He worked the tablet's touchscreen for a few moments, and smiled broadly through his thick beard, liking what he saw. All systems go.

CHAPTER 11

THIS TIME, BEN'S psychological kit of sniper's tools failed to settle him down. It was black outside the one porthole in the capsule. His breath was coming short and shallow. His pulse had jumped from its usual ambling pace to a brisk trot. Despite no discernible threat in the capsule, his unease only grew more oppressive. Again, he wondered how long he had dozed, as if knowing this would orient him to the direction from which danger might come.

The sudden blare of an alarm kicked his heart into a full gallop. A light on the small annunciator panel flashed DECOY repeatedly. At least eight, maybe ten explosions thumped behind him somewhere in the fuselage. Though no pilot, he knew white-hot magnesium flares had just ejected from the drone to draw a heat-seeking missile off his six. This was shaping up to be a bad night.

CHAPTER 12

THE FISHERMEN GAZED upward, their eyes probing among the stars until they saw their prey. Rather, they saw where their prey must have been, in the black void just ahead of a burst of military-grade fireworks. The drone's burning decoys confirmed to them that their intel was good, and the uplink was working perfectly. Of course there were absolutely no missiles bearing down on the drone miles above their heads, but the flares made a pretty verification that the aircraft's telemetry and command signals were compromised. The angler with the tablet was now in complete control of the Global Hawk overhead.

He played another practiced set of strokes on the touchscreen. His own heartbeat zoomed in anticipation.

CHAPTER 13

ANOTHER ALARM BLARED in the Global Hawk's capsule, louder and more dire than the first, if that were possible. The annunciator panel flashed, just one word in red. EJECT. A silent *oh shit* went through Ben's mind. His harness automatically cinched tight across his upper thighs, hips and chest, almost choking the breath out of him. Though his HALO and HAHO jumps meant he already had many more takeoffs in planes than he had landings, there was no time to get psyched for what was about to happen. He had always parted company from his aircraft as a volunteer.

The comfortable cushion material under Ben's butt suddenly hardened electrochemically to a metallic density. Early in the history of the military ejection seat, softer cushions had compressed upon firing, allowing the chair to accelerate upward beneath aviator's inertia before his body started to move. Even half an inch of upward seat movement delivered a bull kick that had cracked many a pilot's vertebrae. The materials in the podule's seat made for a clever compromise; comfortable most of the time, adamantine when needed. When the ejection motors fired on the Global Hawk, it still felt as though a bomb went off under Ben's seat. Though the force did not break his back, brutal negative Gs wrenched his head forward. His vision greyed and tunneled as the blood was pulled down out of his skull, his brain draining like a sponge in the grip of a god. He tensed every muscle he could get hold of on such short notice, took what breath he could, and said "Hick" to shut his glottis down hard, keeping his chest volume big, forcing as much blood as possible to stay someplace north of his ears. It was his best approximation of the Anti-G Straining Maneuver. He should have started it, and the proper breath pattern, with the first flash of the EJECT warning, but that was the kind of day he was having.

The capsule corkscrewed and pitched as the rocket motors shunted the pod away from the Global Hawk's fuselage. An instant later, another explosion cracked behind him. A ballistic parachute deployment stretched out yards of shroud lines to full length in less than a second. Next, the chute's container was stripped off the canopy itself. In seconds the negative G forces vanished, leaving Ben with a rollercoaster's peak of weightlessness queasing in his gut. Then the parachute bloomed with a milder onset of Gs. He tensed up and *hick*ed again just to be safe.

Winnie had said the Veep rated a GPS/Remotely Steerable Canopy like the big military cargo drops had these days. Ben listened as best he could, and sure enough, he heard the whine of servo motors behind him reeling the steering lines in and out, correcting the course of his descent into the unknown.

It was probably not an older vintage round canopy overhead, though they deployed most reliably. In all likelihood Ben was swaying below a giant rectangular flying ram-air job guided by his flight's watchers, or by some kind of coded program, to a nice soft landing. It would be soft enough, unless the guidance system failed to flare out and brake the canopy's forward speed. That would bring him down hard and ugly.

With horror Ben recalled the day he had seen a big cargo canopy shit the bed in Iraq with spectacular results. The Bradley Linebacker, an air defense version of the armored personnel carrier, had been shoved out of a C141 at six thousand feet. The chute opened and steered the load in true enough, but the system failed to brake and flare. The thirty-ton fighting vehicle bashed into the ground at 60 knots forward speed. Its drop pallet destroyed, the Bradley rolled end over end through a mud brick perimeter wall and into a building where one of the Stinger HE-FRAG warheads blew, detonating the other nine aboard in a fast ragged sequence. That cluster became an *un*-cluster when the impacted building was found to harbor twelve insurgents, all KIA in the holocaust. The happy ending in that case notwithstanding, Ben was not encouraged about his own future.

He sorted through the pod's emergency gear, and found the life vest predictably under the single seat. A few foil-wrapped rations and a small canteen of water were the extent of his supplies outside a rudimentary collection of first aid gear. Gauze bandages, a pair of trauma dressings. Nothing like a proper soldier's blowout kit. It was plain that wherever a Vice President might land, his every need was expected to be met by ground support, and quickly. He checked the knife strapped to his right calf. Somehow, it was still in place after the recent carnival ride. Ben doubted he would have a helpful welcoming committee waiting in place.

CHAPTER 14

THE FISHERMEN WATCHED the ejection rocket motors' fiery tongues lick the night sky, and then wink out. The man with the tablet picked up the capsule's discreet Emergency Locator Transmitter signal on his screen. He whistled loud, just once, like he was hailing a cab.

The four men heard the rumble of a heavy four-stroke outboard motor kick to life. Soon, a skiff bore in gently on the man with the computer tablet, who nodded to his comrade at the helm and stepped aboard from the aluminum ladder. He pushed the ladder over. It sank out of sight. The man's genuine fishing gear quickly followed. He picked up an M70 assault rifle from the boat's deck. The other three anglers were collected, and likewise consigned their rods and nets to the deep in favor of automatic weapons. With another glance at the touchscreen, the bearded man made a chopping motion to the north. The helmsman pushed the big engine around and got the skiff on course.

PART 2
WET WORK

CHAPTER 15

BEN QUICKLY ASSESSED his options and found them wanting. There was infuriatingly little for him to do for the next few moments but wait until the capsule touched earth. From there, depending on how hard he pounded-in, he would collect his rations and find cover until someone exfiltrated him. Ben wondered if his flight plan had kept him over the lower forty-eight or Canada. Somebody was watching his course, regardless. He would meet the person who whistled him up, or his agents, within a few hours. So that was the plan; exit this damn sardine can, stay alert, hydrated, warm and dry, and hang loose.

CHAPTER 16

THREE ANGLERS POINTED into the air at once in case the bearded man with the tablet had possibly missed it. The canopy descended into sight, not so much as a visible thing at first, but as a fast-moving, rectangular shadow in the sky where no stars twinkled. A few moments later, the pod itself, painted high visibility green, was easier to see hanging just where it belonged underneath the parachute.

The helmsman throttled up to intercept the capsule while the man with the tablet played the touchscreen, issuing commands on the compromised frequencies to steer the canopy and shorten the vector line to the landing zone. He overrode the automatic braking and flare-out sequence of the canopy's control unit. With this, he unknowingly also de-sequenced the parachute system's automatic shroud-cutaway mechanism which would usually detach the load from the chute on landing, and prevent it from getting dragged across the ground. The touchdown would be extremely unpleasant for the capsule's occupant. This was going to be fun.

CHAPTER 17

BEN'S PLAN LIVED all of fifty-two seconds past the moment of its inception. The capsule landed hard, and then it rolled. There was no grinding sound of its carbon fiber shell crushing dirt or gravel. Even with the wind knocked out of him, the Smith Island native instantly recognized that the capsule was bobbing in water. Making matters worse, the capsule was not ballasted properly for any kind of sea. This was likely an intentional oversight to meet a weight and balance parameter for the drone in flight. The violent twisting played hell with Ben's inner ear. There was no horizon he could fix on to orient himself. His stomach churned, threatening to shellac the pod walls with the chow he had recently eaten.

Then came the knocking. Hard, loud knocking, a faster tattoo than any human hand could beat, on the external capsule wall. From experience, Ben recognized the unique pace of the blows. It matched the rate of fire of an AK-47. Ragged patches of the headliner, inner trim, and upholstery flew into the small passenger compartment along with 7.62 bullets that were deformed as they transited the feeble armor the Veep's ride seemed to warrant. Before Ben could switch off the light inside the capsule to darken the porthole, and eliminate it as a target, the LED fixture exploded from a bullet impact behind it, sending plastic shrapnel into the confined space. Ben groped, reeling in the dark for his seat harness's central latch. With his other hand, he felt for the capsule's hatch release. He did not care if he opened the hatch when it was pitched high toward fresh air, or rolling down into the water.

CHAPTER 18

THE ANGLERS SHOT at the capsule from the skiff. They knew it was armored to some extent, but did not care. They fired mostly because they wanted the occupant to keep his head down inside the pod.

The bearded man lay down his AK-47, and picked up an RPG-22. The rocket grenade launcher sported the High Explosive Anti-Tank, or HEAT warhead jutting forward from the business end of the weapon like a conical mil-spec lava lamp. Since the RPG-22 was a single-use model, the bearded man waited a few extra seconds until the skiff was close enough for a certain hit, but not so close that shrapnel blowback would injure them. This was a mistake.

Approaching the rolling capsule from downwind, the men all fixed on the target, blind to any danger. The pod was still attached to the canopy, and the giant ram-air's long shroud lines tangled down into the skiff. The chute stalled overhead, and began settling without the weight of its load to maintain the airworthy curved mattress form. This was the only warning the fishermen got before the canopy itself billowed down around them, cutting off sight of everything but nylon fabric. The anglers had enough sense to stop shooting, lest they accidentally kill one another. Over the angry shouts of his squad, the bearded man heard a bang and a loud hiss. The capsule hatch most likely. No problem. Once they cleared this damn parachute, there would still be time for the kill.

CHAPTER 19

A HARD TUG on the hatch release lever detonated exploding bolts on the capsule door; it blew it free into the night. Ben instinctively equalized his ears like a diver because of the sudden change of pressure, unlatched his harness, stooped out of his seat, and leaned across the confined space toward the opening. His shifting weight rotated the capsule. In a moment, the hatch sill dipped well below the surface, and freezing water flooded in over his knees. Ben grabbed the hand-bar over the hatchway, and jackknifed his boots up and through the opening. With a lithe contortion, his body followed his feet into the water. His GOOD bag abandoned, the last thing he heard before the cold water closed over his head was the sound of shouting close by. Angry men. Speaking Arabic perhaps. He shrugged out of his coat, which sank with the weight of the gold chunks sewn in the lining. Ben took a bearing on the tumult and started swimming in the frigid darkness.

CHAPTER 20

THE BEARDED FISHERMAN struggled in the shroud lines, and felt his lion heart grow fearful as wet square yards of the parachute's nylon seemed to mass around his nose and mouth, choking him. He managed to reach his knife, slashed at the fabric, but every layer he cut had another layer behind it. The skiff rocked dangerously. His men, tearing at the lines and lightweight material, cursed and wailed with rage. Just moments before, they had been out in the open enjoying the prospect of holy bloodshed. Now the epithets were underscored by serpentine hisses. The maddening suffocation only worsened when they pulled more wet material aboard. They were waterboarding themselves!

The boat rocked again. The bearded angler shouted for his men to calm down and not capsize the skiff in their tussling. He focused on getting himself free so he could regain control before their panic killed them all. Then the angry shouts changed to screams of terror. This was not the sound of men fighting the inanimate stubborn fabric. This was the gurgling rasp of his men dying, one after another in close proximity. The change in the quality of the sounds came quickly, without warning. Then he heard nothing but one man's ragged breathing.

An instant later, the bearded man felt as though someone had stumbled into his back, and just after this, something burned into his neck, as if hornets had stung him in a line from left to right. Feeling strangely dizzy, he slashed out at the parachute material, extricating himself finally into open air.

He looked toward the skiff's bow. He was on a boat full of dead men. Their throats were cut, their chests daubed in black fluid. Blood in the night. He turned his head, and felt tendons above his collarbone give way loosely over a gush of warmth. His arm felt strangely heavy as he lifted his hand. He touched his neck. His fingertips slipped inside a broad wound. Though dizzier now, he could still register curiosity, and then surprise as his index finger slipped into his own trachea. He coughed weakly, and blood sprayed over his hand. *This was impossible.*

When he looked toward the stern, he saw a demon rise up next to his slaughtered comrade at the helm; the blood-soaked parachute fabric draped the monster like a loose winding cloth. This thing had come from the grave to claim him. The eyes of the ghoul filled the bearded man with dread. Darkness crept quickly into his mind, and he knew nothing more.

CHAPTER 21

THE STRANGER ARRIVED in town, and had plenty of time to assess the state of the investigation in the aftermath of the prior exercise. The devastation was obvious on local television stations, and in newspapers.

A full workup of the new commission was simple. Like a besieging soldier of old, this shooter nonpareil could take a position practically in the suburbs, and ply a brisk trade in death, distraction, and destruction in the city that stretched out below. No exotic weaponry would be required. The necessary hardware was available in a specialty hunter's gun shop. No waiting period. Not for the sum of cash the stranger could offer. Shooting ranges, or just a stroll in the wilderness, would allow the firing of a few discreet rounds for zeroing in the telescopic sight.

The ammunition, on the other hand, would require some effort. The shooter wanted to send a message, and saying it in just the right way would mean painstaking attention to the several bullets that this assignment would likely need. The manner of tailoring the bullets would mean the purchase of reloading equipment, but the gun store where the rifle would be purchased would also likely carry a Lyman Deluxe Crusher Kit which would contain all the basic reloading supplies.

Fatigue was becoming a problem. The nightmare had returned while on the airliner, and once again in the new hotel room. The invasion again. The marching troops. The tanks with the main guns aimed high and hard at the soft targets cowering in the vanquished city of domes. Like the mysterious capital, the stranger's sleep was regularly invaded now as never before. The overwhelming sense of wrongful attack wrecked the possibility of any restorative effect. The overtired assassin put head to pillow with fear, and with little hope of repose. The worst aspect of the dream was the overwhelming sense of regret that the attack was tragic, and unwarranted. While an individual death here and there meant little, this bewildering slaughter in the dream felt as though it would unalterably change the course of human history. The stranger's dream laid out a deep canyon into which mankind was about to plunge without hope of ever crawling out again. *Is this what a moral injury feels like?*

Inside the killer, something was waking. It felt like an ancient conscience. This shootist required dreamless rest to be effective. Just a couple of hours. And yet it would not come. Blotter acid. Another tab. That might help.

CHAPTER 22

BEN BLACKSHAW SWAM quietly for shore. He was freezing, and every instinct urged him to thrash forward with his best Australian crawl as fast as possible to get out of the water. It was slow going with a borrowed AK-47 slung across his back, and his boots tied to the gun, but he had to keep ripples and water sounds to a minimum.

Far behind Ben, the drone capsule sank, pulling the swamped skiff, its heavy motor, and acres of parachute he had belayed to it under water as well. Quick lashings of shroud line around uncut chute panels encased the bodies of his attackers. They disappeared below the chop one by one; large silken links of blood sausage.

Ben's shirt, pants and socks were tied into the bundle. Since leaving the skiff, he wore only his calf sheath and its knife. A breeze disturbed the surface and helped hide his slow progress, even though it also ripped heat out through the top of his head. Cold water would strip warmth from his lean body thirty times faster than cold air. He could expect to last about a half hour before his large muscle groups crapped out.

He side-stroked due east by the stars, toward a glow of blue-white light on the shore. The glow reminded him of xenon headlights. His best estimate of the distance to the shore put him right on the edge of his endurance for cold water swims. This swim was likely not an exfiltration. He figured it would be a position change, an infiltration from one fight to the next. From frying pan, to fire, though not nearly as warm.

After about ten strokes into the journey, Ben second guessed his decision *not* to use the boat to get ashore more quickly, instead of making this grueling cold slog. He could have propped the bodies around the skiff and tried to make them look a little less dead. Anyone waiting on shore would expect to see the silhouettes of his pals. How many would be waiting for him? Unknown. Was there a sign and countersign he would have to exchange with them? Possibly. The men on the boat had died in Arabic, but Ben's facility with the language was rusty, and childish at its best. If he failed to say the right thing, to respond the right way, he risked getting shot up, though a bulwark of bodies in the bow would catch at least a few rounds. It is much harder to take down men on land if they enjoyed the advantage of cover while he was potting away from a moving boat. He had done it before, but his skills as a marksman were as stale as his kindergarten Arabic.

Water carries, almost projects, sound over distances, and gunshots farthest of all. Ben treaded water when he saw the three men on shore. Three men who were probably waiting for their friends in the skiff. Their casual stances said they had heard the gunfire clearly, as well as the shouting, if indistinctly, and believed their job was done. AK-47s were slung casually over shoulders. They even had their Range Rover pointed toward the water with the blue-white headlights on bright as a beacon for the boaters to home in on. Ben cussed quietly. His swim just got even longer. He could not walk out of the water and say howdy. Keeping his profile low in the frigid water, Ben swam farther south, parallel to the shore for another hundred yards.

Ben was getting colder and deadly tired. He sensed the first despondent impulses of hypothermic apathy. *Stop. Rest. Just stop and let the cold disappear into numbness, and then into oblivion.*

At the end of his reserves, he almost swam face-first into a rock. While he recovered from the low-speed impact, he clutched the tufa formation from which Pyramid Lake took its name. This tip-of-the-spear rock was home to one funky smelling colony of American white pelicans. For a second, the ammonia reek of pelican crap reminded Ben of the heron rookery in the Martin Wildlife Refuge back home in the Chesapeake. The recollection was not so different from his current circumstances, fraught as they were with exhaustion, cold, and death. Just like old times. Reminiscences aside, the awful odor acted like smelling salts, a wicked chemical slap jarring him out of his torpor.

The pelicans stirred, flapped, squawked and resettled as he held fast to a jagged piece of their fortress home. He dared not climb out on the rock. The birds would spook, flush, and draw attention. As it was, the apparent leader of the shore party seemed to be getting antsy waiting for his boater comrades to land. They were overdue.

Before the pelicans calmed themselves, Ben eyed the pyramid and realized where he was. The distinctive shape of the rock he was grappling was captured in a photograph that a navy buddy had sent him many years ago. It was summer in the picture, and his friend was holding a respectable trout up for the camera. This formation jutted into the sky in the background of the shot, birds and all. Had to be the same place.

Between the island and the shoreline, Ben could see more, smaller rocks. Realizing that there was a race between fatigue and hypothermia to see which would kill him first, he let go of the island, and lowered his profile as much as he could below the surface. The muscles that did not seize from the cold, slowed in a trend toward drowning. Ben was out of shape. He swam again, slowly, using the next rock as a way point. When he reached it, he took another look at the men on shore. They were in a huddle. Now they obviously sensed something was wrong, but did not know what, exactly.

Through his chilled and blunted mind, Ben tried to break down the shore party's options. They could continue to wait in place. They could leave now without their friends. They could call for help, and wait for backup to arrive. Option three was the worst for them. It meant an admission of concern, if not outright mission failure to whoever answered their mayday. And that meant exposing reinforcements, more men, on a snakebit detail. That assumed this bunch was not an independent team, or a sleeper cell of assholes with nothing but their own training, wits, and resources to rely on both over the long term, and in moments of urgency. This frolic on Pyramid Lake might be their one big gig before heading home to an unspecified 'stan. Screwing it up would be bad for them. Bad for their prospects in Paradise. Worse for any of their family members left on this side of the veil.

Their second choice, bugging out on the water team and letting them work out their own salvation, would be based on assessing and reassessing the gunfire and the screaming. That is what the shore party seemed to be threshing now. Even if it meant writing off everybody in the skiff, did the ruckus they heard also signify the target was terminated? Could they split in good conscience, such as it was? The problem arising later would be any physical evidence left behind. Fishing gear could be accounted for on Pyramid Lake, but automatic weapons, sophisticated radios, and human remains, not to mention wounded men who might survive to be interviewed, these were likely to excite comment. This option presented too many loose, traceable ends.

Another thought raked through Ben's mind. What if these men had intended to abduct and ransom the most likely occupant of the drone capsule, the Vice President of the United States? Holding him hostage would make for some riveting video on Al Jazeera America. A recognizable corpse would be a distant but still impressive second in the ratings war compared to regular installments of a captive Veep weeping and blabbing jihadi cant in exchange for a few more hours of life. Right now, the shore party controlled neither a hostage nor a cadaver. Without one or the other, their claims of responsibility for purple and black swags of mourner's bunting at Number One Observatory Circle could be explained by the Federal spin wonks. Ben could imagine the jihadis in such a case trying to shout "Liars!" while Blitzer or Cooper or Smith read a hastily crafted statement about a cooked-up Vice Presidential aneurysm and the subsequent funeral arrangements for a coffin filled with sand. These guys on the shore already knew that true-blue American news media would win the fight for attention and buy-in, at least at home in the States where it counted. They needed a 9/11 magnitude of irrefutable ocular proof to be believed. They needed a body. Whether it was breathing was becoming less and less important as sunrise approached.

That left option one, staying put. It held no negative consequences for the men on shore until sunup, when they would be more easily noted, exposed, and possibly questioned. Some airdale flying for the Army

National Guard out of Stead, near Reno, might spot these men, and call it in.

Dawn in two hours, by Ben's reckoning. That would be their bingo, the time these guys would retreat regardless of their buddies' status, and the outcome of the mission. It was going to be a cold 120 minutes unless Ben did something. He needed dry clothes. He knew three guys who had some. Their boss, if his stature next to the Range Rover was any indication, would offer the best fit.

Ben released his shirt and pants into the water to float away. With dry clothes in sight, he could do without the drag. If the men on shore decided to hop in the Rover now and drive away, it could be awkward, and possibly fatal, but he had to try. He let go of the smaller rock and made his sluggish way through the water for shore. His brain was slowing down. He fended off an idiotic moment of bewildered self-pity summed up in a childish whine, *but this is America ...*

As he swam, Ben realized that the rocks, beginning with the pyramid in the water, were part of a ridge that continued in a line toward shore in smaller formations at, or just below, the surface. He took advantage of each of them to rest briefly. The rocks did not stop at the beach, but were strewn far enough inland to offer him cover. Finally straggling to the water's edge, he put his face low in the sand and skull-dragged naked onto shore. Then he unslung the rifle, and immediately rolled into a lingering snowdrift. The water clinging to his body clumped into the snow. He hurried to scrape it off, leaving him almost completely dry. The air felt warmer now but not by much.

He inspected the rifle, mostly by touch, in the dim light thrown across the rocks by the Rover. Not an original Kalashnikov. It was likely a Yugoslavian Zastava M70AB2 knock-off of the AK-47, with the folding metal stock. He unfolded the stock from below to full length, reached underneath the gun with his left hand, and pulled the charging handle back. He tipped the barrel down toward the earth and slowly rolled it clockwise. Lake water drained from the muzzle and the breach. Removing the magazine, he drained the water from that as well, then extracted and replaced the four remaining bullets. He was out of practice. Should have checked the magazine before he started swimming. Ben tapped the magazine firmly, but quietly, against the palm of his hand to be sure the cartridges were properly seated, and replaced it on the weapon, hooking the mag in at the front, and then rocking it toward the back until it snapped in. That took care of *rack* and *tap*. All that was left was *bang*. Tying the sodden boots back on his feet, Ben moved east, into the foothills of the Lake Range, damn glad to have a firearm of any kind in hand.

When he reckoned he had gone a safe distance from the men on the shore, he broke into a loping jog as much to warm up as to cover ground. His muscles began to move with more freedom. He turned to the north. After five more minutes of double-timing, he intercepted the Range Rover's tracks and followed them back toward the shore. He slowed his pace and began a hunched-over stalk in toward his quarry. Despite the exercise, he was starting to shake with cold.

Over the brow of the next rise, Ben saw the shore party and the Rover, about thirty yards off. The three men were still watching the water. The Rover's headlights made looking in any other direction tough on their eyes. Now the leader had a cellular phone in his hand. Not good. This guy was on the fence about reporting in, unless he already had. It didn't matter. Ben was freezing.

He heard the long splashing fall of a pee stream just on the other side of the rock that sheltered him. Two more pulses of urine hit the ground, followed by a man's satisfied sigh, and a short zipper's buzz. Ben un-sheathed his knife and held still. He should have anticipated a sentry. Footsteps rounded the rock toward Ben. A moment later, Ben eased the body of a stocky man in his twenties to the ground. Ben wrapped his own legs around those of his target to keep them from thrashing noisily in the scree. Held him still until all the twitching stopped. He wiped the knife, tip to bolster, on the dead man's pants. Another glance over the ridge, and Ben knew the takedown had been quiet enough. The rest of the shore party still fidgeted near the water. Ben plucked a Beretta 9mm from the dead man's belt. Full magazine. No bullet in the chamber.

With no idea how often the sentry was supposed to check in with the other men, Ben leveled the borrowed Zastava at Cell Phone's back for a CBM, or center of body mass shot. This was no time to get cute with a headshot. Ben had no spotter, and no support. He needed to put men down fast. At ninety feet, Ben liked his odds, provided the weapon still worked after its recent dunking. Just before that, when Ben was on the other end of the gun taking fire inside the capsule, it had been working fine.

He pushed the fire selector down all the way to J, for Jedináčna, or semi-automatic. One bullet fired for every squeeze of the trigger. On the range, the 7.62 load would punch a sixteen-inch-deep cavity into a block of ballistic gelatin. But gelatin did not bleed. It never screamed for its mother. Gelatin was easy stuff, unless it was his Aunt Wilma's recipe with those chunks of overcooked carrot stirred in. At this distance, and despite a poorly accommodated weld between his cheek and the stock, Ben could probably shoot the weapon's nominal grouping of six inches across. But he had no spare ammo, and no leisure for test shots. And no need, as it was a type he had fired before. Again, he reached his left hand under the rifle to its right side, and fully drew back the charging handle. Now the gun was ready. It was loaded. There stood his targets. He knew his business. B.R.A.S.S. Breathe, relax, aim, take up the trigger slack, squeeze.

This weapon kicked more than an M-16. Before Cell Phone hit the ground, before the spent shell clinked off the rocks, Ben shifted the gun's iron sights onto the guy standing next farthest away. That one was probably still wondering if the sentry had gone rogue and plugged his boss. He died looking surprised. Ben aimed at the last man, who was taking a first step backward toward the water. Ben took up the trigger slack one final time, but instead of a gunshot followed quickly by ejection of the casing, all he got was a ringing snap and the pop of the bullet's primer. No other report at all. No kick. The target was still on his feet. Water had gotten into that round. So be it.

Rather than waste time clearing the dud and hoping the next cartridge had stayed dry, Ben dropped the rifle, and chambered a round in the Beretta and ran toward the final man. This last guy stared at his dead friends too long, looking up just in time to see the silhouette of a naked man sprint into the headlight beams. Last Guy backpedaled into the water trying to unsling his rifle. Ben fired as he approached, roaring like a lunatic. To Ben's own ears, he sounded more afraid than fierce. Four shots later, the final man's limbs splayed and undulated in the water as if he were relaxing, and not bleeding out.

Ben returned to the shore boss's body and checked the cell phone's history. Seven outgoing calls lasting no more than a few seconds, all to the same number. All placed over the course of the last hour. Ben figured they were unanswered calls to someone on the skiff who was definitely well out of service range.

He helped himself to clothing. Cell Phone was a good enough fit, though his sleeves and pants rode up a few inches short. Ben skipped the dead man's shirt which was soaked with blood, but kept the coat and pants which were spattered to a degree Ben could tolerate for a little while. Cell Phone's fresh blood and his cheap cologne were never going to make a best-selling combination. Not sure what kind of foot fungus the dead man's boots might harbor, Ben put his own wet boots back on after donning the dead man's pants. Then he switched off the Range Rover's headlights, tossed the cell phone onto the front seat, and retreated to the rocks to warm up, wait, and watch.

It was still dark when the chest-thumping roar started reverberating through Ben's body like an extra heartbeat. An aircraft. One big machine. It could be a Chinook helicopter sending supersonic shocks out from its six rotor tips for miles through the air, more felt at first, than they were heard. Ben quickly assessed that the rhythm was too staccato for a Chinook. Ben saw no lights aloft, but the noise came on very fast, loud and strong.

That left an Osprey V-22 tilt-rotor, and so it was. Twin 6,100 horsepower turbine engines swinging 38-foot rotors on either side of a boxy fuselage flew down the shoreline. The aircraft made two recon passes by the Rover. To Ben, despite the engine roar and the rotor downwash, it still felt like he was witnessing an archangel coming down from heaven to rescue him.

The aircraft went into a dragonfly hover. The Osprey's rear ramp door was already lowered. The cargo bay was dark, but Ben knew there was likely a .50 caliber gun manned by a night-vision-goggled crew. In addition to the .50, a BAE Remote Guardian System belly turret with a three barreled minigun traversed through the forward sectors from the Osprey's hell-hole. Now that felt odd to Ben. This thing was armed as if it were deployed to Afghanistan, not flying search and rescue over American soil.

Like a big spider working its spinnerets, two lead ballasted Novabraid
fast-ropes paid out from the aft door to the ground through the hurricane
of proprotor downwash. Ben did not have to wonder what the six-man
team felt descending onto the beach. Likely they were grateful for the grav-
eled terrain. He knew from experience that during a desert insertion, the
rotors kicked up an exfoliating sandstorm that killed visibility. With all the
firepower, Ben had to remind himself he was stateside in a Paiute reservation, and not deployed overseas. This mustering of men and materiel left
him guessing who was really running this operation. Who was paying the
bill for this sortie?

The go-team split, examining the bodies, and the Rover. They set up a
perimeter around the SUV, and must have radioed an all-clear to the
Osprey. It slowly settled to earth, but the pilot kept the rotors turning for a
quick takeoff.

A very thin man, his civilian clothes flapping around him, stepped gin-
gerly out onto the ramp. Ben corrected himself. This guy was not thin, but
frail. Too tall for his feeble musculature to hold himself upright without
swaying. If he had not gripped the ramp doorway, the proprotor turbulence
would have carried him off.

The gaunt man picked up a hardwired mic from the cargo bay wall,
keyed it a few times, and spoke over the Osprey's PA system. "Anybody
from New York City need a lift?"

The loudspeaker could not hide the fact that, unamplified, the voice
would not have been so impressive. There was a puny quality about it. The
cadences of the speech were familiar. Ben sat tight.

The fast-rope team tossed the three bodies into the Rover. Then they
fed a sling underneath the vehicle and cabled it to the Osprey's two cargo
hooks. Ben was witnessing a cleanup operation. Apparently he was one of
the items needing a good tidy.

Again the civilian on the ramp keyed the mic. "It's a long walk to the
highway, sailor, and hitchhiking is against the law."

Whoever this guy was, Ben was now sure he was in bad shape. There
were two clear pauses for breath. The man was ailing, but there was something familiar about him. If Ben was right, there on the Osprey's ramp
stood one of the few men who knew the cipher that called him out. Ben left

the pistol on the ground, put his hands on his head, and stood up from behind his cover. In less than a heartbeat, three fast ropers trained their weapons on him.

The civilian on the Osprey ramp caught sight of Ben, pointed at him
through the proprotors' gale, and keyed the PA mic again. His voice was that
of a man who gargled crusher-run and broken glass. With the amplification of
the PA, he sounded satanic. "That bag of smashed assholes is my man! Let
him come in." With that, the civilian stepped back into the cargo bay.

Three of the fast ropers were covering Ben one moment, and the next,
they were eyes-out to the perimeter again as if Ben did not exist. He felt
invisible as he walked through their line toward the Osprey. Ben said to no
one in particular, "There's one more KIA back by those rocks."

As he stepped up the ramp past the .50's gun crew, Ben saw the civilian slowly lowering himself into a rear-facing seat in the forward section of
the cargo bay. That's when Ben recognized him, and nearly threw a salute.
Commander Jerry Grant, Ben's one-time CO, leered up at him.

Grant had shrunk considerably from his former powerful bulk when
Ben had known him a decade before. He had also lost a lot of hair along
with the muscle mass. The red lensed lighting in the cargo bay could not
hide that Grant's deep desert tan was mottled now, his throat was loose
folds of flesh, ashen and yellow. Grant was bowed forward, tripodding elbows on knees.

Ben shouted over the turbines. "*You*. You bastard. Sir." He put his
hand out.

Grant leaned back and looked up. With a shock Ben realized Grant
was holding a cravat to one side and breathing slow and deep through a
stoma opening in his throat.

The former Navy commander clasped Ben's hand and shook it. The
grip was firm enough, but hardly the crushing vise jaws of former times.
Grant appraised Ben. "Lieutenant, you need a damn haircut."

Ben was saddened by what he saw, and tried to digest the drastic
change in Grant without making him uncomfortable. He quickly gave that
up. "Sir, you look like shit."

Grant smiled again, his voice a rasp. "Stow the *sir*, Ben. No more rank,
either. My mistake. Yeah, it's been touch and go."

Grant looked over his shoulder and nodded at four men and three women who seemed to be waiting for his sign. They surged toward Ben with professional concern and tried to ease him down onto a litter. When Ben saw the stethoscopes and blood pressure cuff, he realized this was a critical care transport team, maybe from the 375th Aeromedical Evacuation Squadron out of Scott Air Force Base.

Ben threw a *What the fuck?* look at Grant, who was chuckling to himself. Grant shouted as best he could at the docs and nurses, but his old bark was more a growling wheeze. "Relax boys and girls! The blood's not his! It's never his."

The medical team had obviously kept tabs on the body count reported by the fast ropers, and expected to have something more to do for Ben. Everyone but a red-headed nurse returned to the team's seating area. The woman wordlessly cleaned cuts and scrapes on Ben's hands and face. She smelled good, soapy fresh. After tossing him a green bag flight suit and a jacket, she too strapped in again.

Ben stripped and zipped while the insertion team reboarded carrying an assortment of rubber and clear plastic bags. Grant got on the intercom to the cockpit. The ramp door rose a few degrees to level as the engines' pitch spooled up. The Osprey climbed, but more slowly than Ben was used to in these beasts. Then he remembered the Range Rover on the hoisting rig below the aircraft. Past the .50 crew Ben could see that the open ramp door pointed toward the early twilight arch where night would soon surrender to morning. The Osprey flew west.

Grant rumbled something indecipherable at Ben, who loosened his harness and leaned close to hear better. Grant repeated, "Anything else I need to know about right now?"

Ben shook his head, shouted, "Deep-sixed."

Grant nodded as if he had figured as much. "Not deep enough."

The Osprey traveled only a few minutes before the crew decelerated the bird into a hover. The load master, strapped into a side-mounted seat, spoke a countdown into the intercom.

Grant looked at Ben, "Ready to go fast?"

Ben cinched down the seat harness again, grabbing the forward-most shoulder strap with both hands.

The load master must have reached his zero count an instant later. He worked a control box, keying a short sequence. The Osprey leaped into an upward right-hand spiral, the roaring Rolls-Royce Allison engines and hammering proprotors augered deep helixes into the sky. The Rover had been cut loose into freefall. The load master leaned toward the down-angled ramp door watching the SUV tumble toward the lake below. He straightened in his seat, gave Grant a thumbs-up.

The Osprey's proprotors tilted farther forward, and the rear ramp door was fully raised. Grant said nothing more for the rest of the flight. He dozed fitfully, never fully awake, never soundly asleep. Ben was hard-pressed not to make any inquiries of his former CO. In the noisy cargo bay of the Osprey, it would have felt like a shouting match. As it was, he had too many questions, but there were too many personnel aboard whose deadpan expressions might hide a curiosity of an innocent or malicious sort. Grant had already called Ben by his first name, and referred to his former rank. His anonymity was at risk. Then Ben realized again that his discreet life in that New York basement might have been illusory for days, weeks, months. This warmed his blood. He had sacrificed so much that he cared about, and worked so hard to hide himself in that city. In the end, he had failed. His whereabouts had been known for some while.

CHAPTER 23

THE STRANGER'S FATIGUE worsened with the long string of flight connections. A more direct itinerary would have taken less than one day. Not for the first time, the killer reflected that most of the last thirty-six hours had been spent above thirty thousand feet. The stale recirculated air, the less-than-healthful food, the near-constant sitting, the temptation to drink alcohol instead of water, and the risk of a loquacious neighbor, all these took their toll.

Fear of sleeping, and the terror of the vivid nightmare that would almost certainly suffuse and corrupt slumber, also kept a constant adrenal seep running through the assassin's bloodstream. Cortisol levels were surging. Stress was degrading the necessary level of sharpness that a minister of death had to maintain to be effective, to survive. This was a less-than-ideal work situation. The commute was deadly.

There was enough money in the various bank accounts if the killer were to bow out of this life and retire immediately. Admittedly, the number, the perfect dollar figure had not yet been achieved, but adjustments could be made. Economies here and there would be relatively painless. The wine cellar was stocked for four lifetimes.

Then there was the question of love. Even a hellhound needed love, and this demon had been very lucky. There was a special person. A wonderful woman, talented, sharp, erotically inventive, with a devastating sense of humor. More time with her, without having to worry that every goodbye could mean the last kiss, the last embrace; this was unbearably attractive.

What would life be like without constantly bustling through airports and train stations, followed by stultifying stretches of inertia in a chair? Until now, the stranger always felt that travel was a matter of going to the job, and coming home again. Upon reflection, perhaps it had more to do with running away from something. From what?

The killer wondered if this trade in death had run its course. Perhaps this assignment would be the last. It might be time to disappear.

CHAPTER 24

AN AUXILIARY FUEL blivet for ferrying missions kept the Osprey aloft and westward bound without a stop for several more hours. With the sun catching up to the aircraft, the pilot tilted the engine nacelles gradually back toward vertical. Ben could not see an altimeter, but at a certain point in the let-down, the regular crew members seemed to tense up. Below sixteen hundred feet above ground level in the descent, a double failure of the engines, or the proprotors sucking up their own downwash in a vortex-ring-state emergency, meant the landing would likely not be survivable.

But the pilot greased the landing, earning Ben's respect, with plenty left over for the Osprey's designers. Grant unbuckled his harness and led Ben slowly down the ramp. No one else aboard even moved before Ben was standing on the tarmac. He was a VIP. Very Important Phantom.

Outside the Osprey, the air was warm, humid, and heavily perfumed with Jet-A fuel. Ben sensed the aircraft had landed at a military airbase shared with a big civilian hub. That was all Ben could take in before they passed through two sally ports and a hallway into a stark borrowed office. Grant gestured to a chair, and sat down heavily. A man who had easily marched twenty miles through the hills of Fort Drum before breakfast with a fully-loaded big green tick ALICE pack was now winded by a six-minute walk on smooth level ground.

Ben sat. Grant caught his breath, and poured them each a glass of water from a plastic pitcher. Grant took one sip. Then another. Ben could sense Grant was not so much thirsty as stalling to marshal his thoughts.

Impatience took Ben over. "Hail fellow. Well met. Who the hell are you working for?"

Grant growled, "And therefore, who are *you* working for?"

Ben nodded. Grant said, "You read the file?"

Grant was clearly struggling with this new strain on his old rapport with Ben. He could not give this or any civilian an order to do anything. After a few moments more, Ben observed Grant coming to the realization that all the face cards were in his old boss's hand no matter how awkward anybody felt.

Grant said, "Okay Ben. I could give you the name of a government group, which is under the aegis of another group. In the end, what does it matter? I reached out, and you came. I appreciate that."

Ben said, "Try me."

"National Defense Watch."

Ben stirred the alphabet soup from his days of active service. "NDW. Sounds like some kind of lubricating oil you can get for $19.99 As Seen On TV."

Grant smiled. "Plus two bits shipping and handling. That's a more apt description than you know."

"Doesn't ring a bell. A post-9-11 thing? Homeland Security?"

Grant said, "Yes and no. Of course, NDW doesn't go back as far as the Knights Templar, but yes, it certainly got a bit more funding from Congress after the towers came down."

Ben thought a moment, "Some adjunct of the National Security Agency?"

Grant shrugged. "Who isn't these days?"

Ben did not smile. "I'm not."

Ben observed that the changes in Grant went beyond the physical degradation wrought by illness. The man was more contemplative now than when he wore a uniform. Or maybe he had sprouted an uneasy sense of finesse for his new job. Maybe it was the illness. Ben preferred the old, decisive, cut-and-dried commander who did not waste anyone's time with sophistries and rationales. Orders were orders. Opinions, feelings, considerations had no place. It was all about the mission. Plan A. Plan B, then C. There would be plenty of time for navel gazing once the shooting, slashing, bleeding and dying was done.

Ben pressed. "What's the deal, sir?"

"*Jerry*, please."

Ben shook his head and said, "That's not exactly going to roll off my tongue. But I take your point. By now, you've got a uniform, or three, for every U.S. branch of the service. Including Coasties. Am I right? Maybe a few for other countries as well."

"You do, too," Grant said. "At least it was true by the time you got out. You covered a lot of ground for a lot of outfits. The liaison work, the loan-outs, and joint task forces must have been a pain, but you had the skill sets that were in high demand. And too damn bad for you, they're in demand again."

"To serve was an honor. And it was a job. And you've heard I had a career change. What about this problem? Why'd you whistle me up? Lay it out."

"So you can tell me to go to hell?" suggested Grant.

"Crossed my mind. I wasn't exactly on the corner hawking pencils when your guy came around."

"*My* guy?"

"That shit-bird, O'Connor, Brian C."

Grant's face darkened. "Thanks to you, he's currently on the disabled list."

"Safest place for him. I don't like how he operates. If he's repping you, or your outfit in any way, then I don't like how *you* operate. And that kid—"

Grant frowned. "Winstedt?"

"The one who still wears Underoos. He knows my name. At least my first name."

Grant waved his hand dismissively. "He's manageable. I can vouch for him. For both of them."

Ben felt his face flush with anger. "No, sir. With all due respect, you can't vouch for them, not for very long. Not from what I see."

Grant was quiet for a moment. "You're right. It's Stage Four. The cancer. All over the place. I mean, if there was a Stage Six, I'd be there, but somehow I'm still on my feet. If this is remission, who needs enemies."

"It's not remission, though, is it?"

Grant shrunk a little more into a suit that already looked too big. "No. A plateau between bad days. I'm a dead man walking."

Ben said softly, "So you don't have a long leash on your own guys. How long have you had this gig?"

"Twenty-five months as mission commander."

"You got the assignment *after* the diagnosis?"

"I was well into a second course of chemo that wasn't working. I thought they were throwing me a bone."

"I don't think so. They don't make kids Pope, do they?"

Grant said, "Don't get you."

Ben hesitated for only a moment. "They give the important but unpopular job to a guy who is going to be around long enough to get it done, but not long enough to turn into a righteous pain in the butt. Nobody to put out to pasture. No time to get bitter. No memoirs. No big interviews in The Situation Room. You just fade to black. End of story."

Grant's laughter turned into a racking coughing fit before he said, "You're a regular Studs Terkel, aren't you?"

"Do you know what it took to put together my cover in New York? You called me out on this BS detail, and blew the whole thing. The word that's coming to mind is sloppy. And I'm going to have to clean up. So spit it, *sir*, and maybe I'll give you two days and a wake-up for old time's sake."

"I get what you're saying. But my health situation works to your advantage, too. You're off the books, off the reservation. Remember where I found you. Dead. And when this is over, you can go back to whatever it was you were doing, just as dead as before."

"I have a feeling you know what I'm working on. How about I go back right now?" Ben already knew the answer.

"There's nothing I can do if you turn me down, but it might work out that other people besides O'Connor and Winstedt get wind of your resurrection. Trust me, those two, they're pipsqueaks in comparison."

"Trust me, I know. You got anything against them?"

"No. Decent guys with promising careers. Wet behind the ears. Heavy-handed with the power of their positions, such as it is. I admit that. Throwing their weight around. Nothing I can't cure."

"If you had the time. Respectfully." Ben had no patience to mollycoddle Grant.

Grant bridled. "My command is under fucking control!"

"Keep them in line," Ben warned. "Remind them that when this is done, whatever it is, they need to forget they ever saw or heard of me." Ben could hear how useless it was to demand this.

"O'Connor got the message already. Jaw's going to be wired shut for at least a couple months. Winstedt is no factor." Grant took a new tack. "What's your opinion of what you read? Of what you saw in the brief. Your assessment."

"Money."

Grant raised his eyebrows in surprise. "Please elaborate."

"It's all over this thing. The woman who was killed. Your calling me. That damn Global Hawk to Shanghai me here. Your ready-ready Osprey with the tactical testicles. A lot of money is flying around this whole business. It's hard to miss. We're at El Segundo, aren't we. Some hangar at LAX. We're close to where the woman died."

Grant seemed uneasy, as if he realized too late that bringing Ben in was a mistake of some kind. "Yes we are. Look Ben, secrecy costs money. I haven't blown your cover, no matter what you think. We got you here as quickly and as anonymously as possible. And yes, that cost beaucoup dollars. Consider that a symbol of your importance to the mission, and to your country. All that bread spent on little old you. I'm trying to make it as easy as I can for you to say yes."

"Or as tough as you can, for me to say *no*."

Grant grinned like a death mask. "Tomato, *tomahto*." Grant coughed again. "You understand what I mean."

Ben probed further. "Want to tell me about the little problem with the CATFUed drone? How about the guys in the water who were waiting for me? Five in a skiff, at least one of them a hacker. Four more on the beach. You don't seem interested. Where'd the drone crash?"

Grant pulled at his shirt collar, which already gapped around his wasting throat. "Need to whine a little before we get to brass tacks? After the capsule ejection, I have it that the drone was successfully retrimmed and landed at an undisclosed field. The reception committee? I have no intel on them at this time."

Ben said, "They spoke Arabic. They carried Zastavas. Had some basic training, but no recency. Degraded skills. More intel's going to be hard to come by, what with all the evidence sitting on the bottom of the lake."

Grant shook his head. "The tactical team recovered a fair amount of material. Cell phones. License and VIN number off the Rover. We got a couple of wallets, if you can believe that. Photos of the four dead guys' faces. Thanks for not popping them in the head, by the way. And fingerprints."

Ben was surprised. "Your operators had time to take fingerprints off four bodies? Forty useable prints?"

"Hell no, Ben. But they did have time to recover eight hands. A couple passes from Cyndi and—"

"Cyndi?"

"Our nickname for the Stryker saw. For field amputations. Battery powered. Affectionately known as Cyndi Lopper. So, yes, we have good prints."

Ben was used to gallows humor, but not so comfortable with acts that would not pass the Geneva Convention, let alone the Rule of Law on American soil. But he believed that now was not the time to climb onto a soap box. "How did they hack the drone?"

Now Grant shook his head with genuine disgust. "Hell, some college kids from UT-Austin already did it once with parts from Radio Shack. Cost them about a grand. Spoofed the GPS system."

Ben could not let it go. "Okay, but I wasn't farting around in some A-block drone, or a kit from Hobby Lobby. The added layers of protection, the signal encryptions—that was the Vice President's ride. That's who they thought they were bringing down."

"And there *you* were." Grant managed a smile. "Must have been quite a surprise for those poor bastards. Relax, Ben. We'll know the color of their grandmother's shit in a day or two. And I'll be sure to share your feelings with the squints. They sure screwed up, I agree."

Ben waited. All this expenditure, and only half the story. He was tired, and might have spoken out of turn, revealing too much of his own opinion. "Okay," he said. "You've looked up my dress plenty here. Now *you* elaborate."

Grant opened a desk drawer and removed a file that appeared to be a duplicate of the materials provided to Ben on the drone flight. "She was huge," he said. "Luz Calderon. You figured that out, right?"

"Doesn't the L.A.P.D. handle things like this?" Ben asked. "What's it called? *Homicide*. They have homicide detectives who find people who kill other people. Given what I've seen so far, you could steer them from off-stage as needed."

Grant shook his head. "That woman was killed by someone with military training. I figured it takes one to find one."

Ben clarified, "I'm a sniper. He's a murderer."

"Potato, *potahto*. On this one we don't want to steer from the rear. We need to lead."

"How did your outfit draw this detail? What's the military connection? What's the government connection here that's got you so worked up you had to call me?"

"Finding me the answer to the politico-military side," Grant said. "That's where you come in."

Ben rolled his eyes with frustration. "She was a kid. A civilian. A high-profile one, sure, but a civilian all the same."

Grant hedged. "Yes she was, to some extent. We think there might be more to her story. And we aren't sure about the person, or persons, who killed her."

Grant's discomfort was more understandable. This might be Uncle Sam's dirty laundry flapping in the breeze, Ben thought, and it embarrassed the hell out of his former CO. Grant was struggling. He could not give a simple order to get things done anymore, and it was clear that even this conversation with an old buddy was taxing his physical resources. All this reasoning and cajoling would have given Grant fits in a former life.

Grant stood, and gestured to Ben to follow him. They walked up to a secure parking deck, pausing several times for Grant to catch his breath. From the lot, Grant drove Ben personally in his navy blue Ford Taurus.

The car was clean inside and out, without looking recently detailed. Ben caught a strong sour tang of cigarette smoke and rolled down his window. Some habits were hard to break, he guessed, even in the face of catastrophic consequences.

They spent time on two freeways before diving to surface roads in Hollywood itself. They did not talk. Grant slowed, and Ben noticed quiet crowds packing the sidewalks. Luz's mourners holding a vigil. Shrines with flowers, photographs of Luz, and handwritten posters popped up amidst fans who were having trouble making their way closer to the murder scene.

At a barricade, a uniformed police officer checked Grant's ID quickly, and waved the car onto Hollywood Boulevard where they parked.

Strained members of law enforcement eyed Ben and Grant with disapproval. No one came over to them. They approached no one. Grant led Ben to a place on the street in front of the Dolby Theatre's entry proscenium. The vinyl marquee banner for the canceled movie premiere still fluttered over the Dolby's arch.

On the pavement were no fewer than four dozen small yellow plastic triangles marked with the capital letter A in black. They were propped up off the pavement by little wire tripods. Many more triangles each had a hand lettered A written on paper and taped to the tripod crime scene markers. The police had run out of A flags, and made a few more in a hurry. The flags covered an area of roughly ten parking spaces.

"Evidence markers," Ben said. "Okay, I'll bite. Which one is where she died?"

"All of them."

Ben looked at all the markers again. "Seriously."

"She was blown to pieces. A little here, a little there. Her three bodyguards and a bunch of fans went to the hospital with Chiclets in them, among other things."

Ben looked at Grant for an explanation, but felt he knew the answer already. Grant confirmed, "Luz's teeth. And bone fragments. And jewelry fragments. Buttons. It was a mess, unless you're into creepy souvenirs. I'm telling you, they're still putting the girl back together at the morgue like she's a crashed airliner. The M.E. doesn't believe she's all there. I'm thinking closed casket."

"Not a bomb?" Ben wondered.

"You saw the file pics."

"I saw sheets on the car. Sheets spread on the ground. And now this."

"Right. The only thing that came apart was the girl, and a few people in the crowd right behind her. The car has some dents, a couple holes, but other than that, it's drivable."

Ben raised his gaze toward the buildings around the theatre. "The area was covered?"

"Keep your voice down. L.A.P.D. isn't happy. I reviewed their procedures, the security, their sniper positions. They did their job."

Ben took in the field of yellow flags popping up from the pavement like dandelions. "If this is doing their job, I'd hate to see a screw-up."

"So you know they're all in a pucker about it. No need to rub it in." He waited a few moments, watching Ben.

Finally Ben said, "Can we get in there?" He was looking up at the El Capitan Theatre across from the Dolby.

"We can go anywhere you like. Want to take in a flick? The Mouse owns that building." Grant caught Ben's look of confusion. "The Disney Company."

Grant started trudging toward Paramount's old movie palace.

"Let's look at the offices above the theatre," Ben said. "I'm thinking third floor, west end of the building."

"It's a tough angle for a shot of any kind, but okay. I'm telling you, this building is well inside the L.A.P.D. security perimeter."

During this short walk to the building, Grant was winded again. Ben said, "Those yellow flags mark a kind of human debris field. If the car she was riding in wasn't moved before your scene pics were taken, it looks like she started out in the car, then got blown north, piecemeal."

Grant hacked up a grim laugh. "She was aerosolized. For Christ's sake, she was a pink mist."

Ben observed a man standing by the glass double doors leading into an elevator lobby for the offices above the El Capitan. Ben made him for a plainclothes detective. The sentry looked at Grant and Ben with dead, unreadable eyes, and let them pass without speaking.

In the elevator, Ben said, "You've got some juice. How come there's a guy on the door?"

Grant stared at the elevator's annunciator marking the quick passage of the floors. He said nothing. The elevator chimed. The doors split open, and the two men stepped into the hall; empty except for another plain-clothes cop, a woman positioned at the far end. They took the corridor west toward her. The offices on this floor were unoccupied, and under renovation.

The officer, a brunette, was carrying a few extra pounds under her windbreaker, and much of that was probably a ballistic vest and a service weapon. She was in her late thirties, olive skin and jet black hair. Maybe Hispanic. With some make-up, and a little rest, she would have turned heads. As it was, a sadness in her eyes told Ben that her daughter, or her niece, or perhaps even she, was a fan of Luz Calderon. She stepped aside, giving Ben and Grant a clear path to the office behind her.

The small space was empty except for two items that caught Ben's eye. The first was a bolt-action rifle leaning upright on its wood stock next to a corner window. The second was a book on the windowsill. Black finger-print powder covered everything, including the window frame.

Ben looked at Grant, who was already holding out a pair of Nytrile gloves. In the empty space, Grant's voice grated, "Help yourself. Go ahead. They've been dusted. They're clean, but the powder's easy to get on your clothes." Grant glanced at Ben's flight suit. "Not that it matters."

Ben donned the gloves and picked up the rifle. "You had them pro-cessed here?" Ben asked.

Grant was abashed, "Not standard procedure, but I needed you to see this with your own eyes. The layout."

Ben sniffed the rifle's receiver and muzzle. Then he jacked open the breach, and put an eye close to the barrel. Another quick sniff. "Oil. Old gun oil. I'm betting Remington Powder Solvent, World War II vintage. She hasn't been fired in a long while. A little rust in her." Taking a slow, deep breath through his nostrils, Ben said, "In fact, nothing was ever fired in this room."

"I don't know. Maybe a secretary who wouldn't put out," Grant said.

Ben replaced the rifle the way he found it, and picked up the powder-stained book. "You're kidding me, right?"

Grant shook his head. Ben put the book down. "An unfired Carcano-type Model 91/38. Chambered for a 6.5x52 millimeter cartridge. And an unread copy of Calvert's, *The History of Texas*. We're supposed to see the Kennedy assassination. The gun. A book depository."

Ben looked out the window to the street below. "But she wasn't shot from here. She wasn't shot with this gun. This room, it's a like a Cub Scout's diorama project. The window wasn't even open. Luz wasn't John Kennedy. It's bogus. All this has more to do with the shooter's opinion of himself than anything to do with the murder."

Grant pointed out the window to the vinyl marquee banner for *Ganar* hanging across the street. "In the movie, she was something like a Kennedy. Political. A controversial leader. Cross-hairs on her twenty-four/seven, so to speak."

Ben went on. "I mean all this is bogus. You knew there was a room of interest in this building, but you waited until I nosed it out. You could have said, 'Hey Ben, let's take a look in here.'"

Ben sighed beneath the weight of a fresh realization. "This was a drill. Did your people dress this set? There isn't even a scope on the rifle."

"We had nothing to do with it," Grant answered quickly. "The gun and the book were both here. L.A.P.D. found the room as is within eight minutes when they cased the building for the shooter. Somebody put it here beforehand. And yes, I could have mentioned it, but I had to get a read on your instincts." Grant waited a moment. "So, what do you think?"

"I've been up since balls, yesterday. I need chow, a shower, and some shut-eye."

Grant shook the cardboard box of gravel in his throat, and his voice came out rough. "I'm dying. I don't have that kind of time."

"That girl has all the time in the world."

Ben preceded Grant out of the office. He stopped at the door, and looked squarely at the female agent, or cop, or operative, or whatever she was, and said, "I'm sorry."

She glanced at Ben, checking his face for any hint of mockery. Apparently convinced he was sincere, she nodded once in acknowledgment.

On the sidewalk, Grant handed Ben a twenty-dollar bill and a folded yellow piece of paper. "Got you a rack at the Renaissance around the corner. Give 'em the name on the paper. No one will ask for ID. Likewise if you get room service or whatever. All taken care of. Meet you in five hours in Twist. That's the bar off the lobby."

Grant walked toward the Taurus; his gait looked like a soldier's last shuffling steps of a thousand-mile march back home from a lost battle.

Ben broke the twenty at a Gap clothing store, buying nothing but a pair of socks. Twenty bucks went nowhere even in a plebian clothier like that. Not in Hollywood. Instead, he walked a few blocks until he found an actual payphone. Then he walked several blocks more until he found a payphone that worked.

He cranked in a fistful of coins from the money Grant had spotted him, and dialed long distance.

The call was answered on the third ring, "RailRiders. Can I help—"

Ben interrupted from three thousand miles away. "John, you know who this is?"

John d'Arbeloff, a salt-and-pepper adventurer, ran a specialty clothing concern for persons who had serious problems staying indoors with unelevated heart rates. "I know who this is. Crazy Pam's been saying she misses you. You coming to town?"

Through the fatigue, Ben managed a smile. "Not even close. I need a package."

"No sweat. Where? When?"

"Are you seeing this phone number?"

"I see all—know all."

"The Renaissance near there." Ben broke the connection and by some miracle, within just twenty minutes he hunted up another working payphone. He fed in more coins, and dialed a different number than he had before. D'arbeloff took the call on this line without salutations this time. He had been waiting, Ben knew, noted the area code, and understood Ben was breaking up his data feed between two payphones, and two separate phone calls. It was a crude way to ensure privacy, but would only work if the RailRiders line was not tapped.

Now Ben unfolded Grant's yellow scrap of paper and read the name written there. *Ribauldequin.* Ben slowly let out a measured shooter's breath, mustering patience. Like its namesake, this was a ridiculous nom de guerre to lug around on the mission. A ribauldequin was a cumbersome multi-barreled, small-caliber volley gun, such as those once used on Smith Island for hunting waterfowl. This was Grant's way of reinforcing the fact that he had Ben's number. Ben gave John the name once. "How soon can you help me out?"

"Sizes the same?"

"Yes. Can you do it? And I'm a little light."

d'Arbeloff said, "No worries. We opened a hub for all our clients out there jumping off to play on the Rim. A half hour work for you?"

"That it does." Ben heard the line click dead, and walked back to the hotel past the barrage of trendy hard-sell signage of the Hollywood and Highland Center.

Inside, Ben approached the model-pretty Asian woman at the registration desk, Song, according to her nametag, and muttered his new handle. Without asking him to repeat it, Song glanced at her computer, made a few keystrokes, and fed a blank keycard into its programmer. When the keycard popped back out, she tucked it into a colorful cardstock bifold brochure on which she had written his room number, and handed it to him. Song did not ask about luggage or his needs for a bellhop. The transaction complete, Song warmed the lobby with her gleaming array of dental veneers, and allowed as how she hoped he would enjoy his stay.

Ben headed for a waiting granite-lined elevator. He hated the little space. It was like stepping into a vertical crypt with control buttons. Since no floor number for Hell was listed, he pressed 20. Top floor. The Penthouse. The elevator panel flashed, and bonged once, and a light went on around a keycard slot he had not noticed. Ben fed the card that Song had just handed him into the slot. The elevator doors slid closed, and Ben felt the slight G-force of an express ascent, which was negligible compared to his ejection earlier that day. Ben swallowed like a diver several times to equalize his ears during the ride.

Moments later, he barely detected the deceleration. The doors split with a whoosh between the different pressures of a lobby elevator meeting an atmosphere two hundred feet above the ground. The hallway on the twentieth floor was lushly carpeted, but it was small, more an antechamber, or a foyer. It was not merely quiet. The walls, floor and ceiling seemed to have sucked away the normal noises of human occupation, like a vacuum of sound in which only stationary air, albeit lightly scented with frangipani, remained. It was the kind of hush that only large amounts of money could buy, or rent by the night.

There were only three doors giving off this hallway. One was marked *Exit* leading to the emergency stairwell. Ben stepped the few feet to the door with his room number and used the card again. The latch gave a Diebold vault's *thunk*, and he went in.

This was not a room. It was a banquet hall with beds. Thick area carpet with swaths of red and blue stretched across a marble floor toward a curved two-story picture window offering a two hundred seventy-degree view of Los Angeles. Near the window, a grand piano gave Ben a sense of the room's enormous scale. The walls were paneled in a light walnut, and hung with pieces by artists who owed debts, if not their souls, to Klimt, Pollock and De Kooning. The mobile hanging like a spray of red melting chevrons from the ceiling in the center of the room had to be a Calder.

Ben made a quick survey. Radiating from the central great space with the window lay three separate bedrooms with king-size racks. A wet bar and separate kitchenette boasted clean, spare chrome and gold fixtures and rough-textured tile in hues of black and green.

The bathroom was the size of his living room in the saltbox on Smith Island. The shower was walled floor to ceiling in thick glass panels tinted pink. He walked completely around the shower, which he realized was free-standing like an aquarium with several nozzles and valves. Big fish swam here. The towels were thick, and cut more like the pelts of weird animals with fur bred to absorb water rather than repel it.

Ben tossed his new socks on the piano. As he contemplated the last twenty hours, their idiocy, lethality, and possible meaning, Ben grabbed hotel stationery and a pen and stood at the big window. He quickly sketched the view in front of him, creating a sniper's range card, but more artfully rendered, and punctuated with details he intuitively sensed were pertinent to Grant's problem.

The suite's doorbell chimed a brief but lovely classical riff. Ben stepped to the side of the door. "Who is it?"

No one replied. Ben faintly heard the elevator door close. In the small antechamber outside the room, he found no one. On the table by the door lay a parcel of taped brown paper. Ben took it inside the room and left it on top of the piano by the socks.

He pulled off his boots which were slowly drying, stripped off the jacket and flight suit, unstrapped the calf-sheath and knife, and rinsed off in the aquarium for two minutes.

Back at the piano and the parcel, he changed into the heavyweight black Versatac trousers and the khaki shirt his friend had sent him. In these threads, if he ever got soaked again, he would dry in minutes. For a few moments, the dry socks made a pleasant buffer between his feet and the clammy boots.

He wolfed three of the parcel's Journey Bars as he studied the last two items d'Arbeloff sent: a prepaid cell phone, and a matte-finished Bersa .380 Thunder Plus pistol. Fifteen rounds in the magazine, and one in the chamber. He threaded a Last Chance web belt through the loops on the pants, fixing the pistol's flat holster at the small of his back. Then he put on the jacket.

In the right-front cargo pocket of the pants, Ben found two thousand dollars in hundred-dollar bills. The phone, gun and cash were definitely not RailRiders catalogue items. Again, Ben had proof that if one is unable to prepare adequately for the sudden onset of hardship, it was good to have friends who could lend a hand. d'Arbeloff was one of those friends, but the thought reminded Ben that at the moment, he was otherwise quite alone.

He returned to the window and looked over the city. He let his eyes stray south, east and west. Something in the panorama nagged at his limbic senses, but the essential idea refused to bloom forth out of the shadows into the conscious gallery of his imagination. He mulled for a few more moments, then realized he was burning daylight.

He also realized he did not trust Grant. If he let the strained camaraderie of their reunion blind him, or allowed pity at his friend's illness to misdirect his attention, he would have missed that one important fact. Grant had secrets that could kill Ben if he were not careful. He was torn between the desire to help, the need to finish the work, and a sickening sense that someone he had once trusted with his life might be rotten. Grant controlled this space. Grant knew where Ben was going to lay his head. This made Ben antsy. There was only one thing to do.

With Ben's greater question about Grant and his mission still unformed, and the answer still a mystery, Ben closed the door of the suite behind him. Though he was unsure of what he was supposed to glean from that instant of half-satori, it was the plush quiet hallway, more than the grand penthouse suite itself, that left him keenly aware once again that money was playing a much larger role in this mission than he expected. The antechamber was a strange no man's land between the street and the money.

Ben appreciated the comfort of being in Los Angeles, and not grubbing face down in a mudhole of a shooter's blind for days on end scoping and doping out a target. Luxury notwithstanding, Ben wondered if deep down he missed the truth of physical hardships that his work usually afforded him. His near-fatal flight, and the swim in the lake hours before, with all its *sturm* and blood, these were more understandable: more acceptable and familiar realities than the mirage of affluence shimmering around him now.

He had nothing against the rich. He had grown up comfortably poor, but had always worked hard, with excellence and with honor, and so bore no resentment toward those whose labor was better compensated than his own. He had always eaten plenty from the Chesapeake's offerings of shellfish and fowl, to his satisfaction, but not to excesses associated with idle wealth, or stagnant poverty. His big frame was a natural Bessemer converter, food into muscle. Like a few of the well-heeled who harbored regrets, his sleep was sometimes disturbed by nightmares. These were flashbacks to his work in the military, and they were common to warriors of conscience in any walk of life. Lately he had made peace with a large phalanx of personal demons conscripted from the men he had snuffed in the line of duty.

Today, Ben was extremely wealthy, now that processing the gold had been under way for a few months in New York. Yet there was something about the sumptuous spending here in Los Angeles that seemed to be an overcompensation, a make-good for some other quality that was missing, either in the planning, the execution, or the resolution of the sorry business that lay before him. He felt it actually helped that he was parted from his affluence, save for the scratch his friend might lend him. He was accustomed to the hardship of forward operations.

Ben threshed the problem as he descended the emergency stairs from the twentieth floor to street level. When he ducked out the door onto the busy sidewalk, he was no wiser. He walked for an hour to make sure he was not tailed.

He felt no irony that it took judicious applications of cash to aid him in getting a room key without any ID at the Orchid Suites Hotel on Orchid Avenue around the corner from the Renaissance. Richard, the desk clerk, was an actor on the cusp of realizing this town was never going to grant him the glitz and bling of a ride to the A-List. Ben guessed he was from a good family back home in a flyover state, but times were hard, acting gigs were thin as ever, and so Richard was not fastidious about registration details. The hotel's business had slowed now that fancier joints had opened close to the Dolby.

Ben had no false identification with which to open the transaction, but cash provided the highest degree of anonymity and safety. No desk clerk would be looking for a driver's license if Ben had to stay past Richard's shift change. On the other hand, an initial infusion of folding money might make a welcome encore appearance down the road if need be. Ben knew that, to Richard's way of thinking, he bore a satisfactory resemblance to Benjamin Franklin's portrait on the hundred-dollar bills he slid across the desk. That was as close to a guarantee of goodwill as Ben could wish in case he required other services. Richard handed over an actual metal key, with teeth and a worn, illegible plastic fob. Ben liked this better than tattling magnetic key-cards, where the opening and closing of every door was recorded by Big Brother.

There was nothing special about Ben's room. This was the likely situation for the entire hotel. A special room, or at least signs of recent remodeling, made a visitor feel unique in a world where nobody really gave a damn. An ordinary room, while perfect for Ben's needs, conferred no

cachet of status on a traveler who, in addition to the desire for clean lodg-
ings, wanted his ego fluffed when he burst onto the L.A. scene. Ben wondered if such a place might be more conspicuous for him just because it was
so anonymous in this bright city. Had he skylined himself here, risking ex-
posure? Would he have blended in better had he played the role of a big
shot?

Ben undressed, and lay down on sheets that were clean without reek-
ing as if they had been marinated in a goulash of perfumed detergents.
Orchid Suites was not the Ritz, but it was no flophouse either. Ben slept,
and dreamed of the Chesapeake Bay, the autumn marshes and the shooting
grounds near his home on Smith Island.

CHAPTER 25

THE HIRED REAPER shifted from one foot to the other, annoyed, and perplexed. The new destination originally posted by the client
turned out to be no more than a way point. This was *not* the work site.
There was no target whatsoever here in Ho Chi Minh City. There was no
time to revisit old haunts, or look up old friends from simpler days. Waiting
in another blind email account lay new instructions with the suggestion of a
flight that would, in less than a day, put the killer right back where this
journey had begun. In Los Angeles.

The stranger was never one to lurk around a former work site. That
was the behavior of an amateur, of a weak-minded murderer trying to learn
how far the police had come in their investigation, or the irresistible impulse of a thrill-killer looking for another adrenal jolt of excitement at the
scene of an earlier conquest. It was not professional behavior. By requiring
a professional hitter to go back to L.A., it was clear the client was coming
unglued. Only a very unstable customer would insist on such slovenly
tradecraft. This killer made a rule of not returning to the scene of a job for
at least seven years to be sure any incriminating closed-circuit surveillance
video recorded in the town was long since destroyed.

The additional money offered for the job, on the other hand, was
staggering. At least the client understood that this hitch, this awkward revi-
sion, with its complications and particular risks, warranted much more
money than usual.

The shooter logged off the blind email address, and booked a flight to San Diego. If the client were attempting to bait a trap, at least he would not be sure of his employee's line of approach.

The hallucinations from the most recent tab of blotter acid seemed to be fading too quickly. It was as if the invasion nightmares metabolized the drug with unheard-of, inhuman ferocity. The stranger had to go back to work in less than half a day. No more LSD for now.

CHAPTER 26

BEN WAS AWAKE, dressed, and seated at Twist in the Renaissance Hotel an hour earlier than Grant expected him. He waited for Grant at a table, and nursed a fifteen-dollar ammonia Coke with lime, to help clear his head. He kept his eyes open. They nearly popped when he saw the woman.

She was tall, with honey-blonde hair. Her green eyes gleamed with a mischief that spoke of purity, but not innocence. Her face was that of a Roman goddess, with a jaw set by strength, and a hunter's gaze in her eye; she was smiling directly at Ben. She did not walk to him, or even stroll, but glided over to his table with a clean, easy motion of her trim hips. Her black sleeveless dress flowed like it was alive and in love with her. She placed her small black clutch on the table. Ben stood and held her chair while she sat down as if she was assuming a familiar throne.

The woman placed her tan forearms on the table, and leaned forward revealing loaves of deep-dish cleavage. "Hello sailor. New in town?"

Ben groaned inside. The approach was so promising. The line was so corny. He signaled to the waitress, and noticed that everyone in Twist, customers, bartenders, and servers alike, had an eye bent on his table. Ben sensed that this woman made people wonder what any companion of hers had done to deserve her least attention.

Ben said, "I'm drinking Coke. With lime. And aromatic spirits of ammonia. That there's the lime in question."

"I'll have the same," the woman told the waitress, without taking her eyes off Ben.

Ben extended his hand. "Ben. Ben Ribauldequin."

She wrinkled her nose. "Is that French for *republican?*"

"I'm not sure. I didn't get a choice in the matter, and I suppose I never thought it through. What's your name?"

The woman smiled coyly. "What would you like it to be?"

"I think, *Loki.*"

"Why that name? It wasn't your mother's name, was it?"

Anger flickered in Ben's chest, but he quelled it. "In Norse mythology, Loki was a shape shifter, sometimes an animal, sometimes male, sometimes female. Definitely a mixed bag when it came to being helpful to the other gods."

The woman sighed, "And if I recall the story, he, or she as the case may be, was bound up helpless at one point, and had serpent venom dripped onto him. Pretty painful. The experience probably changed him a great deal. Or her. But I can live with it. Loki it is."

"You're not from around here, are you," said Ben.

Loki smiled. "This is Los Angeles. There aren't too many people here who're what you'd call local. Definitely not in a place like this, unless they're providing a service." She made *service* sound dirty and appealing.

The waitress swung by with Loki's drink. "Would you like to see a menu?"

"When I've got the house special right in front of me? No, thank you."

The waitress smiled thinly and retreated to a cooler, less humid part of the lounge.

"It's very nice of you to say hello, Loki," Ben said, "but I'm expecting someone."

Loki's face clouded. "Are you married, Ben?"

"To the most beautiful woman in the world."

Loki caressed Ben's left hand. "But you don't wear a ring. Or you haven't in some while. Not by the looks of your fingers, which are quite the mess, if I might be so bold." She drew her finger gently along the scrapes and cuts on Ben's right hand. Her concern seemed heartfelt.

Now the conversation took on a surreal quality. Ben knew the woman was not a call girl, because even in his fresh clothes, he was the least likely male prospect in the lounge compared to other men there whose suits cost the same as imported cars.

Ben drank in her undeniable beauty. "You're sharp."

"So I've been told."

Ben looked at Loki's hands. "My wife doesn't wear a ring either."

She was back in comfortable territory. "Ah. Pictures are forming. You have an understanding. Or she doesn't understand *you*. Or is it an open kind of marriage? Which is it? You can tell me."

Ben was getting impatient. "Nothing like that. She's the only woman I ever loved, or ever will. But the fact is, I haven't seen her in a while."

Loki's face was drawn with worry. "Are you separated? She's not ill is she? I think I've put my foot in it. Did she die or something?"

Ben looked her straight in the eye. "Yes. Several months ago. In an accident. It's kind of you to ask."

Loki covered Ben's hands with hers. He did not shift them away. "That's awful. You must miss her still."

"I've been counting the days until I see her again."

"In a perfect world, you will." She hesitated, then asked, "How did it happen?"

"She drowned. It was shortly after our wedding. So you see, not enough time for ring marks on fingers."

"You poor man."

"I don't need sympathy. I feel very close to her still. Especially at moments like this."

Loki withdrew her hands from Ben's. "I see. Wound's still raw. You're honoring her memory. I respect that. Even admire it. You're a rare bird, Ben, in a world full of snakes. Would you like to have sex with me?"

"I'm expecting someone just now. In plain English, I don't think you should be here when he shows up."

Loki frowned. "You cooking a movie deal? Pitching a script?"

"There's a story involved, but I haven't worked out the details."

Loki smiled her brightest. "You're a mogul. A big-picture, broad-strokes kind of fellow. The little guys sweat the little stuff. Interesting. I could help. I could gaze at you with adoring eyes, and giggle at your jokes. Giggle at his jokes. Or hers, as the case may be. I know the drill. I can help you close the deal, right here and now."

Ben was firm. "No, thank you. I'm on my own with this."

Loki looked disappointed. "Okay. Now, about the sex. You're not on your own for that, I hope. We could call it lovemaking, if it makes you feel better. You seem like the *lovemaking* type, standing as you do when a woman says hello. Holding her chair. Very old school. Very gentlemanly. Was that a yes, or a no?"

"It's a definite yes. But, listen to me Loki. Listen as if your life depends on it. The man I'm meeting here shouldn't see you together with me. It would complicate things. For me, and for you. Do you understand what I'm trying to say?"

Loki opened her small clutch. "Of course I do. You're not really a mogul. You're some kind of dangerous criminal. I'm drawn to the bad boys." She smiled, and tucked a business card under Ben's hand. "I absolutely cannot wait to hear from you, Ben Republican."

CHAPTER 27

JERRY GRANT STOPPED to watch Loki flow out of the bar, glanced at Ben, and put his gaze back on Loki's receding form. He followed her with his eyes until she disappeared amidst the clusters of tourists in the lobby. While Grant ogled the woman, Ben tucked her card into a breast pocket of his shirt, and zippered it closed for safekeeping. The encounter with Loki had been unexpected, weird, and somehow restorative. The lonely ache of the last few months seemed to fall away while he talked with her.

Ben's fantasy ended when Grant sat down at the table. The game was on again. Grant waived off the waitress before she got in range.

"That was something special. Who was she?" Grant assessed Ben, clearly wondering what about him had attracted Loki.

"No idea."

"I mean it, Ben, is she a pro? Local talent?"

"I already answered you."

Grant took a moment to shift gears. "Did you like the room?"

"It was big."

"Did you get some sleep? Are you ready for your close-up?"

"The window was big, too."

Grant smiled as if an idiot student had just moved to the head of the class. "I'm glad you liked the view. I was hoping you would."

Ben asked, "What's going on, Jerry? We could have taken an elevator to the roof if you wanted me to look around. Cheaper by ten grand, I'm guessing."

Grant smiled patiently. "It's not the same, and you know it. To really get what happened here, it's the place where you stand, and what that place means, *those* are just as important as what you're looking at."

"You're joking, right? This joint used to be a Holiday Inn. Now it's a spa. That big fancy penthouse used to be a restaurant. Maybe it even revolved to give everybody a view while they ate a club sandwich and drank a beer on expense. Don't get caught up in the froufrou."

Grant said, "You're used to looking through the scope from the shooter's end. That's why I need you. What did you see?"

"I was in the street. I saw where she ate it."

"We all did, and we're none the fucking wiser."

Ben humored Grant. "Tell me, what's in that room that I don't understand already? What's in the air up there that you think *I'm* missing?"

Ben watched Grant's mind crank through telling him off, to bypassing need-to-know information, to arrive at crafting a reply that would gather more intel than it revealed. "You said it before. The money. But it's not just about bucks. It's about what people *do* with them in a town like this. Like that honey. She stepped out of a stack of bills. Have you seen her before?"

Ben ignored the question. "Things are simpler where I'm from."

"Okay. Tug your forelock and scuff your feet all you like, country boy, but I'm not buying it. What I'm talking about here is power, and how it's— I don't know, *expressed.* Money is a medium here, like oil paints, or watercolors. Having it is great. It's how you create with it that really counts."

"Or how you destroy with it," Ben said. "Give it a rest, sir. This town is Detroit for our country's biggest export. They tell stories here, and sell them like hotcakes. They're good at it. They get paid for it. Good for them. So what if it's a business of fantasy? Maybe the fantasy bleeds into their personal lives, but that's how they think. It's how they conjure the magic. It's in the DNA of anybody who makes it here. You want to dump on an industry boomtown because of what you did or didn't have growing up, go ahead. But if you think your singer was killed by atmosphere, or a mood, I don't agree. This is a kid's sandbox, and a cat climbed in and left everybody a present. End of story."

Grant pushed his chair back. "More like its beginning. I'm sick of this place. Let's go." He got up.

Ben rose. "Where to?"

"Up to you, boyo. I'm still not digging your Chamber of Commerce spiel. I didn't put you in that room for nothing. Show me what you really saw from up there."

"I want to see her first."

Grant raised his eyebrows. "A little late for an autograph. Why are you sandbagging?"

"I need to check a couple things. You need to be there when I do."

Grant's car was parked at a yellow curb, but police and parking enforcement had not touched it. Grant fired it up and headed to the L.A. County Coroner on North Mission.

On the way, he pulled a pack of Larks from the breast pocket of his jacket, and shook out a cigarette. He yanked his cravat to one side, and pressed the charcoal filter into to the stoma in his throat, his fingers molding a tight seal. Ben saw how thin Grant's neck looked after surgery, seemingly too frail to support the cranium and the elongated jaw.

Taking his other hand off the wheel, steering with his thigh, Grant flipped a stainless steel Zippo open, snapped it to life, lit the cigarette and took a deep drag. Ben watched in amazement.

Grant caught Ben's stare. "Fuck you." He jetted smoke at the windshield from between the open wings of his collar.

After the first puff, and a second, Grant flicked the cigarette out the window. He said, "You thought I was a brave man."

"I was there when they pinned on your Silver Star."

"You were there when I fucking earned it. In the end, I wasn't brave enough to quit. And now that it's really the end, I don't have to. No point. Guess I didn't have that kind of intestinal fortitude, right? Stick an AK in my face and I'll kill you with my bare hands, but momma, please oh please don't take away my Larks. And now I breathe through an asshole in my neck."

Ben said, "You eat a lot of sushi lately?"

Grant slewed a suspicious look. "A whole lot, for a few years. How'd you know?"

"Lucky guess. Hard to find Larks in the states. But they're pretty big in Japan."

"You're telling me. I bought them by the case. Enough to see me through."

Ben filed Japan in the mission jacket. If Grant was stationed in the Land of the Rising Sun recently, this business might loop back there, too. A long shot, but those were always Ben's specialty, and he would spare a few synapses to let the possible connection percolate as he learned more.

Grant shifted in his seat as if he was uncomfortable with the lengthening silence. "Got a read on this killing yet? A feel? A goddamn hunch?"

"Who wants her dead? If she were a soldier, and this were war, there would be a clear enemy I could understand. She was a civilian. Makes it tougher to know. Some assassins act to take greatness down a peg. To shift power. Some act to remove an irritant."

"What was she to her killer?"

"Let's take a look at her. Maybe that will help me understand."

They pulled past another throng of Luz's mourners and turned into the parking lot of the old brick Austrian-German Secessionist pile that housed the Los Angeles County Coroner facility. The architecture was from another time. Ben thought a gargoyle, a raven, or perhaps a vulture would suit nicely perched over the high façade, a stark foil to the heaps of flowers that were piling up on the sidewalk.

Inside, Ben saw a gift shop selling beach towels, baseball caps, and bumper stickers, all tricked out with the trademarked motif of a chalked body outline from a crime scene. The loose hand of the design reminded Ben of Keith Haring's work. Tourists picked among racks of toe tag refrigerator magnets and other macabre souvenirs.

Grant spoke so the browsers would hear him. "Nothing's sacred." A little girl clutching a plastic skull that served as a business card holder took a step back.

Ben said, "Everything's sacred, including death."

"Spare me the Goth crap. Let's see how Zen you are when you're hard on the brink and can't gun your way back."

Ben might have mentioned that is exactly where he had been that morning on the lake, but he let it go. Grant flashed his ID as they rolled past the guard at the security desk. They bypassed an elevator, plunged into a dank stairwell with wire-caged emergency lights, and made their way down two flights.

When they pushed through a green steel door on the lower level, all Ben's senses were assaulted at once. Fluorescent overhead lights flickered such that they might inspire a *petit mal* seizure, and examination floods blazed painfully off of steel autopsy tables. The chilly chemical tang of sanitizers, human blood and perforated bowel was so heavy that Ben could taste the odors as well as smell them. The room was chilled by its grim purpose as much as by its thermostat setting.

A black medical examiner in his 50s, with close-cropped gray hair, meticulously wielded an autopsy saw around the skull of what might have been a young woman. The scalp had been incised at the back of the head and peeled forward. Luxurious black hair cascaded over the chin. The cranium was braced in a rubber block with extra steadying clamps since the neck evidenced a full tearing trauma from front to back. The torso, what remained of it, lay on a different table across the room. The crescent saw blade oscillated in a blur inside a half-shrouding cover with an attached vacuum hose that caught bone dust. Ben thought the rig's din echoing off the walls and floor warranted ear protection, but no one else seemed to notice the noise, or the aromas for that matter.

The M.E. put the saw down when he saw Grant and Ben, took off his curved plastic face shield, and peeled off his thin purple gloves. Three other scrub-clad men in their thirties and a young woman looked up from a rolling table covered with small clear plastic bags filled with tissue and blood. Nearby counters held small table scales. Several bucket scales hung from hooks on tracks in the ceiling. Another counter lay paved in shining steel kidney dishes stained with blood.

After a moment, the four other forensic pathologists went back to work. Ben heard the woman examining a baggie say, "I bet this is another fragment of her left iliac crest. Any takers?"

The M.E. washed his hands. "Jerry, we didn't expect you back."

Grant looked at the four other examiners. "This business look done to you, Ham?"

Hamish Aran smiled and said, "I meant, I thought you were going to die fairly soon after I saw you last."

Grant laughed and tapped his head. "I can save you some time with that saw. Nothing up here worth looking at."

Hamish shook Grant's hand. "Nothing but the scorpions? No rush. But I'm waiting."

Grant jerked a thumb at Ben. "This is Ben. He thinks he has a couple questions. Spare a minute?"

Hamish said, "Hello Ben, No-Last-Name," and shook his hand. "What's your pleasure?"

"Your guest of honor was wearing a pendant."

"I reviewed the photographs from before her—makeover," Hamish said. "I know the one you mean. Turquoise. It looked good on her." He glanced at the other pathologists. "We're still sorting her out. Was the piece insured? You don't look like an adjuster. Stars often wear loaner jewelry from the hot designers at these events, but I doubt this pendant was anything from Winston or Tiffany. She had simpler, semi-precious tastes."

"All the same," said Ben, "I'd like to know about it."

Hamish obliged, showing Ben to another area of the room. Bloody fragments of clothing were laid out on a table. The pants were saturated with body fluids that still looked gummy, but the garment was mostly intact. The waistband had been stretched in front to the point that a ragged tear ran down on the right side of the zipper past the crotch and halfway down the right thigh.

The blouse was an unrecognizable rough assemblage of small tatters stained the rusty brown of dried blood.

There was another set of kidney dishes with Luz Calderon's personal accessories. Hamish picked one up and said, "That's it."

Ben saw one small fragment of turquoise in the bottom of the dish. The knapped bit of stone was still fixed to a piece of silver backing by two prongs.

Hamish explained. "The rest of the fragments haven't been collected, and possibly never will. It might interest you to know that this particular piece was fused with her xiphoid process, that's the very bottom of her sternum. That, in turn, was removed in surgery from the left trapezius muscle of a man riding in the front seat of her car. The force of this round was appalling."

"Did it explode before impact?"

Hamish glanced at Grant. They were both getting interested in Ben's question. "Possible. But not that we've been able to determine conclusively so far. There was some scorching or tattooing of the skin fragments of the torso that've been recovered, which supports your point. And the ballistic impact effects here do bring an artillery shell to mind. It was big. It hit her hard. Internal hydrostatic pressure did the rest. Explosive gasses, or vaporized fluids inflated her abdomen so much for a single instant that she would have blown her slacks completely off if her top half hadn't separated from the bottom. She popped, as much as she was broken in two. Here."

Hamish picked up another kidney dish and shook it gently from side to side. Ben heard small metal fragments scraping in the bottom. Hamish said, "We're getting these out of her, as well as from bystanders who were treated at hospitals. We even found one that blew downward all the way through her right leg, lodging at her medial malleolus. Sorry. Her ankle. The authorities are digging more out of the victim's car. See how small they are? Yet how regular? That's how we knew to collect them together, they were all so alike. Weight so far, just proud of fifty-five grams."

Ben was surprised. "So far? That's already close on fifteen hundred grains. That's half again as big as the largest nitro express hunting round. For Elephants. Rhinos. You're saying it's bigger than that?"

Ben reached for the tray, but Hamish pulled it back slightly, and looked at Grant. Grant nodded.

Hamish said, "Scrub in for me Ben? And then glove up."

Ben did as he was told, then held the kidney dish close to his face.

Hamish said, "There'll be a metallurgy report soon, but I think they'll find an alloy of copper, nickel—"

"What's that?" Ben interrupted.

Hamish handed a magnifying glass to Ben. "This piece."

Hamish passed Ben a long, fine pair of tweezers. Ben picked up the small shard of metal, and held the glass over it. He peered at the fragment silently for several minutes.

Finally he said, "Can I suggest you keep this one separate? Got a clean dish?" Hamish's team had stopped their work, not because Ben was fascinating, but because their boss had been effortlessly demoted to their scut-work caste inside of eight minutes.

Ben put the fragment in the new kidney dish Hamish gave him. "Can I see that piece of the pendant?"

Hamish passed Ben the dish and a fresh pair of tweezers. Once again, Ben used the magnifying glass for several minutes. Then he said to Grant, "Okay. Let's hit the road."

Grant and Hamish exchanged a look. They were busy men, and this quiet lunatic had just wasted precious time.

CHAPTER 28

BACK IN GRANT'S car, Ben watched the tall palm trees slip past. Grant held a lit cigarette, but rarely took a neck drag. "Started in my throat. They wanted to cut out my whole voice box and give me a cancer kazoo, or teach me to burp out a few words at a time. Make me a 'lary'. *No fucking way* I said. I'm going down screaming. But the C is shutting down my windpipe. This knothole keeps me going."

After another mile, Grant said, "They don't belong here."

"What doesn't?"

"Mexicans."

Ben looked out the window at a Hispanic world. "This'll be interesting."

"Hundreds of Mexican palms were planted in South L.A. for the 1932 Olympics. Then they caught on with the landscapers. Now they're dying out from fungus, old age, like me. Replacing them with sycamores and oaks. Someday, palms in L.A. will only be in the lyrics of that Neil Diamond song."

"What song is that?" asked Ben, half afraid Grant would hum a few bars.

"*I am I said.* About a guy singing to a chair because he misses New York. Like you, I guess."

"I try never to sing, and New York's not my town."

"Anyway, they'll be replaced, those trees. Like everything, eventually." Grant changed the subject. "You got a family by now?"

"Drop it, sir."

"I've got nobody. I'm the last of the line. Nobody with my blood will be there to say a few words for me. Don't be like that, Ben. I can see you're on your way. Don't screw around."

Ben stewed as they drove three more blocks in silence. Grant twitched with irritation in his seat. He finally asked, "What the hell was that back there?"

"Damn interesting."

Grant gargled gravel in his neck. "I need you to develop your thesis. Out loud. *Show your work.* Didn't you ever get that on a math test?"

Ben paused a moment, searching for a word. "Organized."

Grant put the Lark to his throat stoma, and took a drag. He exhaled hard, vexed, puffing his cravat out to flutter like a smoldering party favor. Ben watched him mentally pare back on some of the verbiage he would have liked to use. Neither of them had adjusted to the shift in their roles from the service to the civilian world. Grant was tiring again. "Organized crime?"

"Maybe. I meant your shooter. Your *unsub*. He's organized. You like it when I use that profiler lingo?"

"We figured our unknown subject wasn't a random kook. In a high-security event, he got the kill. He got away. Bobby Bedpisser Skitzo-Crackhead can't usually swing both on his best day. But, what did *you* see?"

"You're going to get tired of me saying it."

Grant tossed his cigarette out the window. "For the record, I'm tired of everything about you. Say it anyway."

"Rather show you. Let's go to Hollywood and Highland."

"Back by the Dolby." Grant settled down a little. He had a mission. He had a place to go that was not his empty home.

CHAPTER 29

THE ITINERANT SHOOTER tried to think of home, of the woman, of a life after the killing was done. There was no joy in taking life, but there was no guilt. Everyone dies at some point. For an unlucky few, the assassin was merely a cog in the clock that determined when the free rides around the sun ran out.

The invasion nightmares changed all that. Slaughter on the grand scale, warfare, was beyond the killer's comprehension. The idea of winning and losing never entered the equation. Smaller jobs satisfied, where brigade actions simply seemed an abomination. The killer enjoyed a niche. War was a crater.

CHAPTER 30

REACHING THE DOLBY took two hours, with traffic jams from sheer congestion. At one point, rubberneckers slowed to watch a tall muscular black man wearing a red bandana, a red tank tee, and driving in a yellow Corvette convertible get a speeding ticket from a white police officer. Perhaps passing drivers were hoping the situation would deteriorate into a beating, a shooting, or maybe even a riot. Somehow, windshields had become TV screens, with gas pedals and steering wheels changing the channel every second. Tap the brake if you see a show that you like.

Grant drew closer to Hollywood and Highland, and within a few minutes pulled into one of the parking spaces that the L.A.P.D. was holding for investigators. They got out, and Ben noticed the flowers were mounded higher than before. Their scent carried in the breeze, but could not cut through the morgue odors embedded in his sinuses.

Though the police had kept their barricades up on the streets and sidewalks in front of the crime scene, it did not stop fans from paying their respects. The barricades at every approach to the street in front of the Dolby were already obscured by more bouquets of flowers, and more poster-sized messages of desolated adoration. Some mourners held candles in quiet tribute.

Ben observed, "Looks like Diana's shrines."

"Diana Ross? She dead, too?" Grant pulled in, braked. "We're here. What's on your mind?"

Ben pointed to the old Hollywood First National building on the corner. The white Meyer & Holler structure rose thirteen stories into the sky, topped with an octagonal tower turret. "You've been through that building."

Grant nodded.

"Find anything? Do you have another scene laid out up there somewhere? Maybe Lincoln's assassination at Ford's Theatre?"

"Negative. L.A.P.D. had spotters and snipers throughout up there. It's been completely combed. It's clean."

"Okay." But Ben didn't move. He let his gaze range over the crowds of mourners behind the barricades. Within moments, he picked out two undercover detectives, a man and a woman, both Hispanic, positioned among the weeping fans at the closest intersection. "L.A.P.D. has people working the crowds?"

"They'd do a lot better if you didn't stare them down. Why don't you point at them and shout 'Pig' or something discreet like that?"

"They're wasting overtime. The shooter isn't coming back here." Ben moved toward Grant's car. "One more stop."

Grant asked, "Where?" Ben could tell he was gauging his reserves of energy.

"A few blocks. Just down the street. Another building. I saw it from the window of that spendy hotel room."

"You serious?" Grant asked. "That far from the scene I'm going to need a badge along for the ride." He glanced over toward the Paramount Theatre. The dead-eyed cop was still at the door, but he had been joined by the detective who had stood sentry outside the faked shooter's tableau in the third-floor office. Grant nodded at them. The cops swapped glances, and they both sauntered toward the Taurus. The dead-eyed male cop talked into a wrist mic, and within a moment a replacement officer was moving into their old position on the Paramount door.

Grant gestured toward the woman. "Detective Dario. And that's Detective Strahan. This is Ben. He wants to take a little drive and see what he can see."

The detectives said nothing, just looked at Ben, and climbed in the back seat of the car. Ben wasn't sure whether they were still on duty from the day before, or if they had taken a few hours' break. Either way, he could see they were operating on fumes. Nobody was willing to stand down without some kind of progress. Cops.

Ben told Grant when to pull over. Detective Strahan, who had not said a word, looked out the car window at the building that loomed across the sidewalk. "Fireproof Storage. Records vaults. Healthcare. Municipal stuff. Movie master prints and negatives. Lots of clients all over. And they do a big business in shredding as everything goes digital."

Ben stepped out of the Taurus and scanned the building from sidewalk to roof. The nearly windowless white edifice looked like a wall of niches in a giant's mausoleum. He pointed to the roof. "Can you get us up there?"

Detective Dario rousted a tired security guard, and badged him. The guard retreated into his office long enough to alert his boss by phone. When a buttoned-down head of security, ripped and coifed like a Blackwater retiree, appeared, there were two minutes of heated conversation bordering on confrontation, in which words like warrant, court order, and injunction were used.

Grant stepped in close to the security maven, one Lieutenant Borskein, and told him, "Not sure where you served or how bad you had to screw the pooch to end up here, probably with a Big Chicken Dinner, but you're about to do it all over again if you don't get us to the roof now. Right now. No more stonewalling." Mentioning the BCD, or Bad Conduct Discharge, hit home. Several times in Grant's tirade, gobbets of sticky yellow lung fluid sprayed past his fingers sealing the stoma, and backed Lieutenant Borskein up. Grant followed him in uncomfortably close. "Are you with me brother, or agin' me?"

After three minutes, an elevator ride, and a final flight of stairs, everyone was standing on the building's roof.

Ben approached the security head, who was daubing at his shirtfront with a handkerchief, "Take a look around, and tell us what you see."

Borskein tucked the handkerchief away, and scanned the rooftop. "What I see looks good. We done here?"

Ben eyed the two stone structures that rose from the east and west ends of the roof. One held a water cistern. The other housed the massive air handlers for the building's critical climate control system. And there was a small metal shed.

CHAPTER 31

A COUNTER-SNIPER'S STOCK in trade lies in recognition of anything out of place, and recognizing it from far enough away, preferably from one's own well-concealed blind, in time to eliminate the threat before it takes you down. Note the false element, and the shooter, who is being hunted by the counter-sniper, is likely in the neighborhood. Every sense comes into play. Might be a whiff of human sweat, gun oil, chow, or the sewage reek of a hastily buried cat hole. Might be the vegetation on the prey's ghillie suit that would look right if it were a foot higher in the leaves, but stands out as all wrong among the ground cover. Perhaps the sniper stalked in through one kind of cover, but failed to adapt his camouflage to the growth at the final position quickly enough.

Closer in, the *tell* might be the sound of a suppressed sneeze. A movement. A shadow passing behind a backlit crack in a derelict building's roof. One open window in a structure where all the others are closed, or curtained. That is where he, or she, might be lurking, waiting for a shot. Worse, any of these indicators might be the decoy clue that distracts the counter-sniper's survey just long enough for a bullet to fly in from another sector altogether. In the sniper's kit, misdirection was just as important as concealment.

The hide on this rooftop, here in the middle of downtown Los Angeles, was so conspicuous that Ben overlooked it in his first scan. Everything appeared exactly as he expected. There was a window washer's movable scaffold with portable davits to lower workers to the few panes of glass this building had. Insulated piping and conduits to and from the air handlers. A few snack wrappers from workers who put in a full day without returning to the street level for lunch. Instinct drew his eye back to one anomaly, and he instantly held stock-still, a pointer dog with a line on a cowering rabbit.

Grant looked at Ben, who was powering down all his movement to disappear into the background. "What? What do you see?"

The Hollywood Hills, and many distant buildings had the height advantage over even this elevated position. If Ben's working theory proved true, his stealth would be pointless. Ben calmed his concern with the knowledge that the shooting was more than thirty hours old. Luz's killer was not still in town; was unlikely to be watching. But wily snipers often left booby traps behind when they abandoned their FFPs, or Final Firing Positions. Ben stepped forward, slowly, cautiously.

It looked like a sheet metal utility cover, almost a shed, the kind that protected whatever lay inside from the elements, plus a couple of feet of walking around space inside next to the equipment for a technician to service the protected mechanism and its parts.

The problem lay in the ventilation louvers on the side of the structure facing the distant crime scene. There were two openings in the wall, both about ten inches square. The layout reminded Ben of the back of a movie theatre, with the window for the projector, and another window for the projectionist to judge and adjust the quality of the picture on the screen. Ben drew a line from the apertures to the sheet aluminum parapet that walled the entire roof fifty feet away. There was another aperture there, neatly opened in the parapet, and professionally flashed with a made-to-fit rectangular frame; a shooter's loophole.

Grant saw the loophole. "Too high for a drainage duct. I mean, it's too far from that shed for a shot, and the opening's too small. No way to see her roll up, even if the trajectory was clear all the way in, which it isn't. There are buildings between here and the scene. Tall ones."

Detectives Dario and Strahan watched Ben circle the metal shed as if he were insane. They too seemed to be drawing imaginary lines from the shed to the parapet and beyond toward the Dolby Theatre. They too saw all the intervening buildings. Lieutenant Borskein was probably impatient to get back to his office, perhaps to change his shirt, or at least his necktie. Daubing at his clothes with his handkerchief had rubbed Grant's lung butter in deeper.

Ben said nothing. He went to the large aperture and glanced in. He sniffed. Then he turned to Lieutenant Borskein's belt. "Sir, I need your flashlight."

Borskein was petulantly annoyed. He pulled a small Maglite from a soft polyweb sheath hanging from his belt, strolled over to Ben at pace calculated to annoy, and passed him the light.

Ben gave the light a twist, and shined it into the aperture. "I'll be damned."

The others caught the amazement in his voice and unconsciously drifted toward him. Ben checked them with an upraised hand. "Hang back a piece. Let me look this thing over." He played the light around inside the small shed, paying particular attention to the inside of the sheet metal access door, its hinges, and its handle.

Grant said, "Got something?"

"Could say that." Ben moved from the aperture end of the shed to its door on the side. He turned the handle slowly, and pulled the door open half an inch, running the light, his eyes, and then his fingers around the inside of the metal panel. There was an echo inside the shed; metal flexing, the wobbling Foley artist's rumble of distant b-movie thunder. "Want to get a bomb crew up here? Maybe a K-9 unit at least?"

Borskein and the detectives took a few steps back.

Grant said, "A dog? Screw that. Too many eyes on this mess already. What the hell do you see?"

"No explosive triggers in plain sight, but judging by what I *do* see, you might—"

Grant mumbled, "Got no time for this", crossed the roof to Ben, and yanked the door wide open. The three onlookers flinched, and turned away defensively.

Grant looked inside the shed. "Shit."

Ben was never sure if the expletive spewed out because of what Grant saw inside the shed, or because he got no booby trap's flash-and-bang shortcut past a hard death from cancer to oblivion.

"Okay Ben. What the hell is that?" Grant asked.

"That's a dam big gun. Take a gander in that opening around front."

Grant walked to the shed's aperture. "Two inches? That's a fifty mil' bore. Not a rifle—"

"It's artillery. Never seen the like."

Grant looked at Borskein and the two detectives. "I want this roof secured! Start with yourselves. Get your backsides one floor down double-time. One floor only. Do not move from there, and wait for me. Leave your fucking radios and cell phones right there on the deck. National security, boys and girls."

There was a fire in Grant's eye that brooked no pushback. After placing their communications equipment on the roof, the trio entered the stairwell. The sound of their footsteps on the metal treads receded down to the top floor. Grant lit a cigarette. "Okay, Ben. Talk to me."

Ben let his eyes roam along the weapon, observing its matte-black anodized finish. He guessed it stretched eight feet in length, from the butt to the end of the muzzle brake. It was mounted on a quad-pod, and the spirit levels he could see on the legs still had the bubbles centered in their tubes. Likely a recoilless rifle with a mount that was so perfect at absorbing energy, it would not foul its zero between shots if more than one round had been needed. This was not a soldier's gun. It was an artifact of fantasy made real, perhaps by a shooting artist who carved invisible arcing lines through air, and always finished his portraits in the hues of human mortality, of pink viscera and gray matter.

Ben started a running commentary, much like a medical examiner recording findings as an autopsy moved along. Objective as he tried to sound, there was no covering the anger in his voice. "Very high-caliber recoilless rifle. Four-round box magazine. Semi-auto. Huge ammo. There is an external module here. Reckon it's a ballistic computer for complete dope. The shooting solution, with full weather, wind speed and direction, looks like humidity and temperature, too. If I could get all that in a box, I'd also want the corrections for spin drift, or Magnus Effect, bullet drop, maybe even transonic destab' and restab' algorithm, maybe even the Earth's rotation."

"But this gun can't be traversed to correct for any of that dope."

Ben said, "I know."

Grant pointed with his cigarette to four black stubby horns projecting at odd angles from the box that Ben said was the ballistic computer. "What're they, do you think?"

"Maybe ultra-high frequency antennae in here, possibly for feeds from cameras on the target, but there is no scope, and no monitor to see the target from this position."

Grant nodded. "We combed the Dolby crime scene looking for a shooter, for weapons, shells, all that. We weren't looking for security and surveillance cameras that didn't belong."

"Might not be *extra* cameras. Might could be the shooter, or his team, tapped the feeds of existing cameras to predict or fix Luz's position. Can't say from here." Ben went on, "Looks like servos on that quad-pod, to make small adjustments based on the fresh dope."

"Fancy-pants gun. Okay. But how could somebody set it up, set this whole thing up fifty feet from that hole in the parapet over there, and then make such little adjustments to hit that girl. You ever see a firing solution that didn't change up? Sometimes a hell of a lot. Her car was moving until a second before she ate it. Change the shooting solution too much, the round hits that wall, and it's Maggie's drawers." A missed shot on the shooting range.

Ben pointed to the breech. "From what I saw at the morgue," Ben said, "I think your answer's in here."

Before Grant could stop Ben from tampering with the gun, Ben opened the heavy breech. A big bullet sprung out into Ben's hand. Nearly a foot long, the cartridge appeared to be made of a black polymer, not typical brass. And the projectile itself had a strangely light shade of copper.

"What the hell is that horse dick?" Grant asked. "Spent uranium?"

Ben shook his head. "Your life would be a lot simpler if that's all it is. Forget about guns and bullets, sir. I believe the weapon is more a launcher. You were right. All that data from this computer isn't to adjust the gun. It was fed into a guidance system in this round."

"So that's a fucking rocket? Explains why there's no brass from the shot lying around in there."

Ben considered his reply before speaking. "There's no brass because I think this casing is part of the propellant material. It *all* burns away in the breech. No space wasted by inert metal that's nothing more than an arma-ture, or a container holding primer, powder, and the projectile together. When I say this thing is a launcher, I mean all it had to do was get the bullet on its way at the right *time*. Get it out the barrel, out that opening in the louvers, and get it through the loophole over in the wall at the edge of the roof, and just at the right instant."

"Nobody can make a shot like that," Grant chafed. "Look at the flat angle of the barrel. The bullet wasn't lobbed over the obstacles between here and the scene. There're no fins on that damn thing to change its course and help it fly around that first building over there, and then around the El Capitan."

"Not with an ordinary round. And fins can guide a projectile, but the barrel is rifled. Fins would kill the rotation. They are drag. Parasitic drag, I think it's called by the propeller heads. But look close here at the bullet's tail."

Grant took out a pair of drugstore reading glasses from his jacket pocket and put them on. "Little holes. You think they're chemical jet ducts to push the ass-end around and change its heading?"

"No. I saw the ducts on the pieces in the morgue. Not for jets. I'm thinking they're ports for *sound*. I think you'll find this bullet can make major course adjustments, maybe close to ninety degrees, by vectored sound pulses that distort or mold the shape of the bullet's wake and bend the trajectory."

"But that bullet's *faster* than sound."

"For most of its flight, yes. I have no idea for sure, but maybe there's some kind of laminar-flow relationship between the bullet and its shock wave, where the projectile leverages its own wake turbulence like an old-fashioned kite gets stabilized, or steered by its tail. Wave drag. The one ele-ment of aerodynamic drag the bullet can't avoid, it actually exploits. But like you said, the bullet gradually slows, and gets unstable as it transitions from supersonic to subsonic."

"Bullshit," said Grant. "A Cheytac .408 boat-tail will do that predict-ably without all the fancy insides. And it stabilizes again when it becomes subsonic after the transition."

"Yep. Predictably enough for an ordinary shot, but not *perfectly* for this kind of work. We're two miles away from the Dolby."

"So it's the Magic Bullet."

"Exactly. The Warren Commission was looking for one in the Kennedy assassination five decades ago. And here it is. That tableau in the El Capitan is starting to make sense."

"It goes around fucking corners." Grant was taking it all in, but Ben was still way out left of him.

Ben said, "I don't know. It's all too many for me. Maybe there's a final impulse stage, a chemical propellant charge, or more sound, that helps it make a hard turn around the building."

Grant said nothing.

"It's why I was looking at her pendant. Might be it's a transmitter that put out a signal, or passively aggregated or resonated and reflected some ambient signal for the bullet to surf in on, and get the hit just right. Some kind of *Here I am, so come on in and blow up now* kind of thing. Maybe it was planted on her. Given to her as a gift for her big night. Maybe it's just a nice pendant and nothing more. But I'm also betting she wasn't hit by a ballistic impact. The burns on her torso, tattooing, plus all those little fragments Hamish showed us, made me think she was killed by a shaped charge that went off a few feet from her. Pointed right at her. A lot of the other folks who got hit were hit by pieces of *her*. As if she stood right in front of this barrel when the gun fired, but she was two miles away."

Grant looked closely at Ben. "There's a lot you're not saying."

"Because there's a lot I don't know. But nothing I've seen here changes what I told you back in the hangar. Look, this piece is for accuracy. Nothing is wasted. But nothing's spared. This isn't just custom work from a genius gunsmith. It looks like years of research behind it. Lots of input, not from individuals, but from departments, teams. A hybrid weapon. This thing was babied into existence over time, and with an open checkbook. It's perfect for taking down a dictator. Imagine one of these set up next to one of Saddam Hussein's goat paths around Bagdad? He wasn't underground the whole time. Hell, set up five of these, and one of them would've caught sight of him and taken him out when he was above ground and feeling safe. Would've saved a lot of lives."

"In Baghdad? We'd have lost the technological edge right away once the weapon or shooter was found."

Ben played out the scenario. "Not if the kill was confirmed. Self-destruct charges would wreck the evidence, like sinking a submarine's torpedo if it doesn't hit its mark. Which is why I figured a bomb crew would be a help. Look at this setup. It took a while to put in place. There's video of your killer or his crew on Borskein's surveillance footage. He probably signed the shooter in to the building himself. This shed, the hole in the parapet, the Kennedy tableau, all that took time. Invest the time in preparation, and you don't have to get that close anymore. And the bad news? I don't think the shooter was on this roof when the trigger was pulled. Could've been watching those feeds on a monitor from anywhere. I told you, no optical sight, and no monitors in here. Those antennae are inside this blind to hide them along with the gun. That part was like a television signal repeater."

"Always comes back to the money," mused Grant.

"Right. And who's got that kind of money?"

"DARPA." Grant pronounced the word softly, the way others speak of the devil. The Defense Advanced Research Projects Agency was lavishly funded by uncounted billions of dollars to develop new concepts in tactical and strategic warfare, from conventional to all-out nuclear conflict. Their brief included surveillance from the ground to satellites in orbit. Data mining and its interpretation was also part of the DARPA mission.

Grant strategized out loud. "So we don't acknowledge we know about this thing. Act as if the L.A.P.D. is still treating it like a big public assassination. This is a huge break you've given us. Why are you so pissed?"

"You asked who would want to kill Luz. Now you know. She wasn't a giant brought down by a David. She was a guppy eaten by Leviathan. The reason for her death is as large as the entity that killed her. As big as our own government. That scares the shit out of me."

"Only you and I know we found this weapon."

"If Borskein is in on it, your edge won't last very long," Ben said.

"So we scoop him up. Him and the cops. Put all three of them on ice in Gitmo until we figure out who our shooter is." Grant smiled. "Damn, I bet somebody is supremely pissed this gun was swiped."

Something about Grant's bravado rang false to Ben. It seemed as if this weapon was something Grant had heard of before, but was now seeing for the first time. Perhaps he knew the shed was not booby-trapped, and that is why he had thrown the access door open so boldly.

Ben took a risk. "I don't think this weapon is missing. In fact, I think somebody at DARPA is tickled pink their field test went off without a hitch. You're still talking about a shooter. He's the least of your problems. I'd want to know who's pulling the strings. You want a killer, or do you want the truth?"

"You're right. Must be these painkillers slowing me down. Jesus Christ."

Ben saw Grant's cigarette falling to the roof. There was a clang of something striking the sheet metal gun hide. Grant collapsed as if all his muscles had simply switched off. A silver dollar of blood spread on the right side of his chest. With his soldier's instincts punched-up to full alert, Ben put his hand over the chest wound and pressed, glancing at the stairwell entrance. Nobody there. Then he drew a line from where Grant had been standing to an elongated groove dented into the metal wall of the shed. Something small lying on the roof below the groove glinted in the sunlight. Ben grabbed it, and jammed it in his left pants cargo pocket.

With a rough idea of the sector from which the bullet had been fired, he dragged Grant to the other side of the shed, shouting, "Dario! Shooter! Get a medic up here! Strahan!"

Grant had ordered the trio to leave all radios and cellphones on the roof. No help could be summoned with those, and Grant needed care right now.

Pulling Grant to cover had left broad smearing trail of blood from the exit wound by Grant's right shoulder blade.

Detective Strahan ran onto the rooftop with his gun drawn. He saw the blood, and bent to pick up his radio. Then he grunted, and kept bending toward the roof slowly, like a methadone patient, and never straightened up. Though shot in the gut, he reached for the radio again. Strahan's head broke into pieces from another shot. Brain matter hit the roof and stairwell door. His chest rose and fell twice. He went still.

Detective Dario looked out onto the roof from the stairwell door. Ben yelled, "Active shooter! Rifle! Stay back! Grant's down."

Dario shouted, "Strahan!"

"He's down! Stay back!"

Dario wept tears of rage. "The guard's heading down for backup! Strahan!" Cement shards exploded from a bullet's impact on the lintel over the doorway, dusting Dario's black hair to gray as she jumped back to safety.

Grant's jaw worked, but no sound came out. His hand flopped over the stoma in his throat and pressed as blood flowed around his fingers. "Lake. Bravo-Zulu."

Grant grinned. Maybe it was a leer from pain. Maybe it was some other reason. He stopped moving. He stopped breathing. Ben felt for a carotid pulse, held his fingers to Grant's throat long after he knew there was nothing there.

"Dario, stay back!" he yelled. "Keep everybody back! Grant and Strahan are both down. KIA. Stay put. Shooter is north and west."

Ben sat for three more minutes during which no more incoming fire pocked the roof. He held onto Grant's body, and kept his head low. For the shooter to change positions and get a clear shot at him from a fresh angle would have required a car or a helicopter, and significant time. He wanted to pick up Grant and dash to the open stairwell door, but the pathway there lay in the kill zone, so he didn't dare.

Dario called to Strahan three more times, but got no answer. Ben heard her sob quietly once, then pull it together. "You hit?"

Ben yelled, "Negative. Didn't hear any shots. You?"

"No! Nothing." Moments later, she yelled, "Somebody's coming up!"

Ben heard Detective Dario telling someone to keep back and stay low. In reply, a male voice said, "Get the fuck out of my way!"

Ben expected the point man of a SWAT team, or a tactical medic to poke a mirror on a probe from the stairwell's safety to take a peek, or perhaps to creep from the door sporting the latest in ballistic fashion.

Instead, a blond man in his forties, portly, in an overly tight navy blue suit with a white shirt, and a loosely knotted red, white, and blue striped repp tie, stepped onto the roof. He wingtipped fearlessly into the middle of the kill zone, and strode toward Strahan's body. Ben waited for a bullet to cut the newcomer down, not sure if he would feel loss or a sense of justice when it happened.

The bullet never came. Instead, the man scanned the roof, caught sight of the bloodstains near the metal shed and started toward them. He took one look inside the shed, and then moved briskly to where Ben still knelt next to Grant.

"MacCready. You Ben?"

"Yeah."

"You hit? You're a bloody mess."

An L.A.P.D. helicopter buzzed overhead and established a hover fifty yards from the rooftop.

"Blood's not mine. Grant is—"

"Not going anywhere. Anybody can see that. Let's go."

Ben pointed toward the hills. "Shots came in from that way."

MacCready yelled into a handheld radio. "Northwest of my position. Go!"

The helicopter banked and churned away.

"Come on. Let's move." MacCready turned and walked toward the stairwell.

Ben stood up slowly, but stayed where he was. Grant's blood stained his shirt and pants.

MacCready said, "Grant was my direct report. Now you form on me, Ben. I'm not asking."

Ben felt anger surge in his chest. He was charged with adrenalin. "Commander Grant is dead."

MacCready turned. "And that is tons of suck for him. Now, I heard you're good, Ben, but unless you're going to lay on hands and bring him back—just so he can die a slow grisly agonizing death from the Big C, I might add, we need to be on our way before the locals fuck this cluster six ways to Sunday."

Ben did not move.

"Oh, you're a goddamn peach aren't you." MacCready swore under his breath, and walked back toward Ben, unbuttoning and pulling off his suit jacket. He stopped, bowing his head, giving a two-second impression of a man at prayer. Then he slowly draped his jacket over Grant's withered frame, covering his face.

MacCready held his hands away from his sides, palms up, giving Ben the international sign for *Satisfied now?* and made off for the stairwell again. "Seen dogs leave their dead masters quicker than you."

Ben followed MacCready more from a sense of wanting vengeance than out of obedience or curiosity. They passed Detective Dario on the stairwell. She appeared to be in full-blown shock. He made her a silent promise to find who had killed her friend, and fucked up her city. At the moment he had no idea how.

PART 3
BLOODSTRIPES

CHAPTER 32

MACCREADY FLOPPED ACROSS the back seat of a black Crown Victoria, leaving barely enough room for Ben to wedge in after him. A white female driver with a neat Naval Academy ploob's bob under a blue pisscutter cap sat patiently, eyes forward.

When Ben's door closed, the driver put the car in gear and angled out into traffic. Marked and unmarked police cars, as well as two ambulances, were converging Code 3 on the building Ben had just left. MacCready just looked out his window as the flashing lights and screaming sirens receded.

Three blocks later, MacCready cleared his throat. "What do you want to know, my friend?"

Ben tested the waters. "The bus station. Or the train station. You can drop me at whichever's closest."

MacCready chuckled. "You surprise me. Your old CO popped like that, and you want a ticket to ride? So fucking be it. Janie, please take the man where he wants to go."

"Aye-aye," Janie said, and U-turned the Crown Victoria amidst a din of braying car horns, nearly trading paint with a red Ferrari. Throughout the next few minutes, it seemed to Ben that Janie was studying him in the rear-view mirror as much as driving would allow. It was as if she were searching his face for something she half-recognized.

MacCready said, "Of course, you might want take a minute to clean up before the traveling public gets a load of those bloodstains, but that's just me. You set for cash, Ben?"

It seemed to Ben that either MacCready was soft-selling a mission, or he was genuinely pleased Ben was off this detail. "I take it you just got a promotion," he said.

MacCready smiled. "Somebody did. No concern of yours now, is it?"

Ben let the silence hang.

"I'll get him. I really could have used your help, Ben. Grant must have thought you had the patriotic jism, but that's okay."

"You want the shooter for killing the singer, or for killing Grant?"

"Does it matter? Tell me, Ben, where do your loyalties lie these days? Where's your professional curiosity? That weapon up there, didn't it spark your interest?"

"You expected to see it. Didn't bat an eye."

"And we owe you a debt of thanks. You helped us close one important barn door at least. Got us a line on the shooter's tactics. Recovered some pretty cool ordnance in the bargain. Glad to have that weapon under our control again."

"The police will be all over it."

"No, Ben. No they won't. That rooftop is a Federal crime scene. We have people swaggering around up there already using magic words like *National Security* and *Eyes Only* and *Need to Know*. Make no mistake, we have jurisdiction. Tell me, did you ever work with that kind of reachback support, or were you always operating forward, your butt in a sling, waiting for a pansy-ass committee of career brass and bureaucrats to sanction your kills before you could even touch the trigger? Let's face it Ben, you may have shot a bunch of bad men in your day, but we both know every damn one of your targets really died from paper cuts."

Ben could say nothing in reply. Last autumn, he had allowed himself a free hand repelling a savage invasion of Smith Island, but he did not find it any kind of a thrill the way MacCready supposed.

MacCready propped himself up a few degrees in the seat. "Oh wait. You had that little kerfuffle in Nevada just yesterday. Grant filled me in. 'Bravo Zulu,' he told me. Job well done. So, I don't want you to give that mess a second thought, because as you may have guessed, it's also become our jurisdiction. Bygones. You are free and clear. Self-defense. You had absolutely no legal obligation whatsoever to retreat from mortal danger.

Anyway Ben, we sure could've used a man of your talents, but if you're dead set on being a total pussy, there's not a thing I can do about it, right?"

Ben said nothing. Cheap shots at his manhood, his patriotism, or his former scope of practice did not move him one iota, but they said loads about the scum of thought in which MacCready's mind was stewed.

Janie pulled up in front of the Greyhound station on East 7th.

Ben opened the car door. "What's your first name, MacCready?"

"Just MacCready."

"Like Cher?"

"And just as terrifying. Write when you get work, kiddo."

CHAPTER 33

BEN STRIPPED, SHOWERED, and after emptying the pockets
and downrigging the pistol from the web belt, he cold-water rinsed the shirt
and pants of Grant's blood in one of the bus station's truckstop-style
shower stalls in the men's room. The blood had not completely dried, and
the cold water prevented the stain from setting badly. It took some effort,
soaping, scrubbing, and rinsing again and again until the water swirling the
drain stopped running with rust. Though a large area of the khaki shirt was
slightly darker than the rest, the black pants looked clean. Ben believed the
remaining discoloration on the shirt would not draw attention. He dressed.
In a few minutes, the clothes dried completely.

He purchased his ticket for New York City's Wall Street station departing at 11:35 that night, some eight hours off. Then he bought snacks
and waited in the main terminal area, making it very easy for anyone tailing
him to stay close.

At the appointed hour, he boarded the bus. His travel companions appeared to come from the same Skid Row area where the terminal was located. They all seemed poor, dignified, with few options, and quietly bereft
of hope. A few elderly men and women boarded with plastic bags of snack
food. Their main luggage, if they had any, was stowed in the big bays below
the seating cabin. A Hispanic couple with three children sat across the aisle
just ahead of Ben's seat. The children, a girl and two boys, ranged in ages
from about six to eleven. They were quiet, and while they snuck looks at
Ben from time to time, none of them sought to engage him in play or

banter or peekaboo in the relentless way young airline travelers seemed to enjoy.

The bus barreled north for hours through open fields along Interstate 5, pulling over only for a quick halt at a Chevron Station on Route 119. Ben climbed down from the bus, walked aimlessly in the harsh lighting, and stayed in plain sight. He reboarded the bus last, allowing the occupants of the dark sedan he noted idling across the highway just out of the light to see him easily.

There was another stop at a more built-out area three hours to the north in Stockton. Another Chevron station, a motel, an open cafeteria, and a Starbucks, which was closed. The driver let his passengers know this stop was only ten minutes longer than the first pull-off had been. Stray far from the cafeteria at your own risk. The father of the Hispanic family went inside for takeout, leaving his wife and children asleep aboard the bus.

Once again, Ben boarded last, even though there was no sign of the sedan from the prior stop. Maybe the watchers were convinced he was on his way. Maybe the sedan he had seen before was innocently parked.

When the bus left its next stop, the sun was rising. Ben was not aboard. The ticket office opened at nine, and Ben paid the fare for his trip back to Los Angeles. The new bus rolled south along the same freeway he had just traveled. He stepped down in Los Angeles at four in the afternoon. Since taxis rarely waited for a fare because of the high-crime neighborhood, he used the cell phone to call a cab. When the call was done, he field stripped the phone of battery and simcard, offered a silent apology to the janitorial staff, and drowned the works in a toilet.

CHAPTER 34

AN HOUR LATER, Ben was back in his room at the Orchid Suites, courtesy of Richard, the obliging desk clerk, who still thought Ben Blackshaw looked like Ben Franklin as depicted on four 100 dollar bills.

Since Ben had rested on the bus, he spread several newspapers and a Los Angeles map on the table in the room's small sitting area, and perused the classified ads for messages that might jump out at him. There were so many mourning shout-outs in praise of Luz Calderon that *La Opinion*, the *Los Angeles Times*, and *El Segundo Herald* had each added special sections to contain them.

Ben turned the television to a national news broadcast. Luz's very public death was still the big story. The police spokeswoman took several minutes to announce that no progress had as yet been made in the case, and that authorities were marshaling all available resources to apprehend a suspect. A series of politely phrased wave-offs, including *no comment at this time*, as well as *ongoing investigation*, and the like, frustrated reporters who needed progress to refocus desensitized viewers' eyes away from the stale clip packages and to fixate them on something fresh.

There was no mention of Grant's and Strahan's deaths. MacCready was as good as his word. The rooftop scene was locked down tight as a frog's rump. Ben wondered if Detective Dario was stashed in a safe house, a quiet cell, or on the bottom of the harbor. Whatever the case, she certainly was not talking to the press.

Ben passed his hand over the cargo pocket on his left thigh. The object was still there. He removed a small lump of metal. It was a bullet deformed roughly into a shape of a mushroom with a short stem. This round had passed through Grant's thorax, tumbling in its transit without fragmenting, exiting his back, and expending its last joules of ballistic energy to dent the wall of the metal shed on the roof.

This was not the first time Ben had looked at the fatal round. During his ride on the bus, he had already determined it was a full metal jacket .338 Lapua Magnum. At one time, it might have been mated to a rimless .416 Rigby hunting case. Once again, he studied the boat-tail, the tapered area at the rear of the bullet.

Ben was bewildered, yet filled with a grudging admiration. This bullet had been modified. From what he could see, the bullet had been removed from the case, and etched, or perhaps even engraved. Now Ben could read small letters and a number placed around the taper where the lands and grooves of the barrel's rifling would not mar them. A filigree of Grant's blood still lay in the bottom of the figures, highlighting them in gore. **BB2AM**: once again, the first five figures of the message that had flushed Ben from hiding in New York three nights ago.

Whoever had customized this round had taken a risk. Removing material from the bullet's shape at any point would change its weight, its balance, and its aerodynamics and flight geometry. This work had been done with care, probably with various micrometers and scales to check the modifications, so the shooter could allow for them when he aimed. That left a question in Ben's mind. Had the bullet been meant for him? Was Grant killed because the figures on the bullet's taper, shallow as they were, had altered the bullet's flight so that it put down the wrong man?

One thing Ben understood for certain. The shot had been taken from a great distance. A round like this could pass through five layers of military grade body armor at about a thousand yards. But with a stock casing and charge, the end of its effective range was about two thousand yards against a soft target. Ben put the map on top of the newspapers and began to explore his estimated range ring from which the shooter might have fired, which lay from about sixteen hundred to nineteen hundred yards from the fatal rooftop. Fired from that limited arc of a circle to the northwest, he reckoned the round would have enough force to transit Grant from his right chest to his left shoulder blade and all viscera in between, then dent the sheet metal wall without penetrating it, to drop finally on the roof, deformed.

The required elevation to see the rooftop and fire down on it eliminated any hide in the ring below the height of the roof. That left a limited number of likely positions, archipelagos of possible shooting islands surrounded by areas from which the shot could not be taken. The bullet was fired from an area of ground that had to be both high enough and far enough away from the rooftop and Grant to allow the shooter invisibility.

This bullet had not been fired from anything like the shooting machine in the rooftop hide, with its video feeds and computer. This shot had been taken with a handheld rifle, probably a SAKO, for which the bullet was originally designed. Who else knew Ben was in town? Who was tracking him? Who was aware of that ciphered summons? With Ben's growing respect for this killer came a growing fear.

The most likely firing position lay near the famous Hollywood sign. Go higher up that hill, and the shooter was walking away from his target area, increasing the range and reducing the force with which the bullet would arrive. Go lower down the hill, and the range was decreased, in turn increasing the bullet's arrival energy and likelihood of greater deformation, or even fragmentation.

Ben heard a light tapping on the door. He put the bullet back in his pocket. The tapping was repeated. Maybe Richard was suddenly in a jam with his manager, who was insisting upon seeing identification, either of the official or the fungible kind.

Then Ben heard a woman's voice. "Mr. Republican? Are you there? It's your friend, Loki."

Ben thrilled to hear her voice. Here was a beautiful woman who oddly enough seemed to find him fascinating, and who was relentless in letting him know it. Any intelligent man would have suspected that she had ulterior motives. Ben was not feeling intelligent. He felt alone, and the answer to his solitude stood outside the door. He tried to quell any sign of interest. "Are you by yourself?"

"Do you think I need assistance in your particular case?"

"Depends on what you have in mind." Taking no chances, Ben removed the Bersa 380 from the holster at the small of his back and, as quietly as he could, drew back the hammer until it caught and held. "Do you think you were followed here?"

Ben heard the beguiling smile in Loki's voice. "I've been followed before. I tend to attract that kind of attention sometimes, sad to say, but what's a girl to do? I took a very indirect route walking here. I was very careful."

However alone Ben felt, dragging innocents inside his current circle of confusion was wrong. "Maybe you should keep walking. I hear it's very good for the health. Much better for you than hanging around the likes of me these days."

Loki sounded slightly exasperated. "Much as I'd like to keep chatting through this door, I'd much rather see you face to face. I'm coming in, Mr. Republican."

Ben stood back from the door and raised the pistol, his index finger resting loosely next to the gun's trigger guard. The metal to metal scrape at the lock meant Richard, the desk clerk, had betrayed Ben, and surrendered a key to this irresistible woman.

He inhaled, then exhaled in readiness. And there she was. Loki strode confidently into the room, dropped her handbag on the bed, pushed the gun lightly to one side, folded him in her arms and kissed him hard on the mouth.

CHAPTER 35

NAKED, LOKI'S BEAUTY was a revelation to Ben. He expected as much when he first saw her in the black dress. The only flaw in this ravishing vision dozing lightly beside him on the bed was a purple scar on her hip, as if a large graft had been savagely cut from her there, but not affixed to any new place he could see. And this evening, he had seen her body's every curve, every ripe mounding, and every cleft and declivity, exploring her as he had with a wolfen hunger from the part in her hair to the tips of her toes. It had taken them hours to sate one another.

Loki roused from a reverie with half-lidded eyes. "Heaven is a nice place, I'm sure, but I wonder if that angel bride of yours has any idea what she's missing, flapping and harping around up there in her robes and halo." She held out her wrists.

"I believe she knows. We were very close before she left. Remember? Still newlyweds." Ben unknotted Loki's brassiere from her wrists. The lacy ligature was ruined from all the wrenching and tugging it had suffered.

"It's so tragic. And doncha know that makes it awfully romantic."

"You remind me of her." Next, Ben removed his belt from around her ankles.

Loki blushed, and nuzzled her face into his chest. "All except for the dead part, I hope. I pride myself on doubling like a mink."

"That you do," agreed Ben. A shadow crossed his face.

Loki pretended to pout. "What's wrong, Mr. Republican? Afterglow fading already? Cares of the world rushing in at you? You can tell me. I'd like to think that you and I are already intimates, despite our brief acquaintance."

Ben opened up to her, as perhaps he should have done with his wife in times before. "The simple truth is, since I've been on this trip, I've seen ten men die. Two of them didn't deserve it, and one was them was a friend."

Loki's eyes narrowed. "I *knew* you weren't in the movie business. What about the other eight?"

"They all managed to get on and off my shit-list pretty quick."

"Oh. Are you a serial killer?"

"No more than you are." Ben caressed her waist.

Loki shivered. "Then I'm sure you're doing the Lord's work."

"I'm doing *somebody's* work, that's certain."

Loki sat up, her breasts flouting gravity with a natural, unenhanced sway. "Hand me my bag?"

Ben reached across to the other bed, then placed the leather satchel next to her.

"Got this bag in New York not too long back," she said. "And wouldn't you know, as big as it is, I seem to have filled it up already. But a person hard at work needs the right tools."

She handed a plain plastic shopping bag to Ben. He looked inside, and saw three small prepaid cellular phones.

"You are full of surprises."

"Not the first time I've heard that said. I figure you'd know what to do with those."

"Reckon I do. While we're at it," he said, "how did you find me again?"

Loki brushed a tousle of hair from of his eyes. "Ben, I never lost you. Even when you thought we were apart."

"The four-door sedan on the ramp this morning. By that bus stop. That was you."

Loki's light mood darkened for a moment. "No. That car was a hundred fifty yards ahead of mine. Two men. A white man. A black man. Thirties. Short hair. Neat, but not military. They headed back south after you climbed on the bus to keep on going north. They had trailed you all the way from the station on East 7th."

"I didn't see you."

Loki grinned. "Nobody ever does, sweet man. Not if I don't want them to. It's one of my charms."

CHAPTER 36

BEN REVEALED MORE than he intended to Loki, all the while sensing that this was often the case among those she knew. She invited his confidences with the same animal force with which she evoked his desire. After the wringing trauma of his recent struggles, Ben talked to her with euphoric relief; the way a man shares gut-wrenching intimacies with his dearest friend, or his bride. He told her about the strange plea to travel that he had received in New York, the violent end of the flight, and of meeting Grant again after so many years. He confessed his persisting bafflement at Grant's request for help solve Luz Calderon's murder. He admitted his shame at living on when Grant was dead. He let her hold the bullet that killed his friend. He told her about MacCready's cavalier fearlessness on the rooftop.

Concern lined Loki's face, but she did not interrupt. When he stopped speaking, she remained quiet for a few moments. Then she said, "This MacCready's a closed book. You'd get more information from the guy shooting up the town."

"Whoever that is. He seems the shy, retiring sort. Unless you're in his sights, and then the acquaintance is brief and ends badly."

"But he knows the way to call to you. He knows the **BB2MA** thing. How many people know that?"

"One less than used to. Five still standing."

"Right. So you know him, Ben. My money says he shot Grant with an idea you'd see the bullet. He might know you'd look closely at things like that, with your unusual background. Bet he knows you've been to the morgue, and knows what you might have seen there. In a homicidal way, he wants to connect, either to brag and preen, or for something else."

"Grant knew that call sign, and he was up to his eyebrows in government spooks. We'd all discussed using the call sign, but it was strictly for cases of personal need. It wasn't the Bat Signal. It was never meant to be a call to duty. It was conceived as a sworn good-will obligation among friends."

"Then maybe it *is* personal," Loki said. "Not in the movie cliché way, you know, where just before somebody kills somebody else, they say it to mean the murder is just part of doing business, and no hard feelings. This feels like he has a bond with you."

Ben turned Loki's face to his. "Whatever the case, you need to leave, and I do mean it in the most personal way."

Loki gave him a wicked grin. "And no hard feelings?"

"Some, but not the dramatic kind. Of course I'd much rather you took off without a chip on your shoulder."

She raked her nails down his chest and stomach leaving red marks behind. "Okay, but my terms are severe."

"I'm up to it."

She rolled her hips toward his. "Oh my blessing—so I see."

An hour later, Loki was gone.

CHAPTER 37

ALONE AGAIN, BEN undertook any busywork he could think of to help put Loki out of his mind. Being with her had felt too good. He had no idea if he would ever see her again, and the thought hollowed him. At the moment, Ben hated love, and all its shattered promises. *This sailor will not weep*, he repeated to himself. Had he known her long enough to feel this way about her? Clearly, he had.

Desperate for distraction from this mounting pain, he dug into Luz's special newspaper classifieds again. In the extra section in El Segundo Herald, he struck paydirt. The last page, right at the fold. All the little notice said was, **BB 2324 ¡Lo siento, Luz! Nitro Express**. Ben's high school Spanish was up to the task of translating. Was it a self-pitying expression of sadness at Luz's death, or was it a killer's remorse at being the cause of her demise? He felt almost positive the **BB** referred to the first part of his cadre's call sign. The **2324** meant nothing to him. Then he realized that the double B could refer to anything and anyone. His imagination was running away with him.

Whoever signed the ad as Nitro Express added a new twist. Ben had mentioned the large, uncommon hunting caliber to Grant back at the morgue when they were assessing the weight of the projectile fragments Hamish was removing from Luz Calderon. Maybe Grant had used the phrase with someone else. Perhaps it was coincidence that the classified advertiser used that same phrase.

There was one other classified ad containing **BB** in the Los Angeles Times. It said, **Xin loi, Luz!** Ben guessed this was the Romanized spelling of a phrase in an Asian language he did not know. Perhaps it also meant *I'm sorry*. Three numbers followed this cry of pain; **555**. And this classified was also signed **Nitro Express**.

Making the obvious inference that the three digits in the second ad he found were part of a phone number that ended with the four digits in the first ad, he still had nothing. Were the three digits an area code, or part of the phone number's exchange?

The hotel room was furnished with a relic, a paper telephone directory. It was several years old. In the front of it lay tables detailing local codes and exchanges and the areas they served. The three digit number was not listed as an exchange, but that could have changed in the years since this phonebook was published.

On the off chance, Ben dialed (310) 555-2324 on one of the burners Loki had given him. The call dumped to a generic service provider message explaining the recipient was not available, and that no voicemail box had been set up for the line.

Perplexed, Ben stepped out of the room for fresh air. To be sure he was not followed, he took a winding path to a drugstore for more newspapers. He spent the next several hours back in the room scanning them from front page to last. If someone were reaching out to him, classified ads were a departure from the overall Big Money tone of this entire business to date. The two classifieds were cheap. They were vague. Ben was still unsure they were in any way meant for him.

Ben pushed the newspapers to the floor, set the phone book aside, and returned to the Los Angeles map. He sketched the ridges and hillsides where Grant's killer might have staked out the roof. The assumption that the person who murdered Luz Calderon also killed Grant was starting to wear thin.

Ben began a deep search of his own motives for returning to Los Angeles on the bus. Had he returned for Loki? He should have kept going. He was a real danger to her.

There was nothing he could do for Grant. MacCready was right. Nothing was bringing Grant back to life. Luz Calderon was also beyond help. The Los Angeles Police Department would spare no effort to solve that case. In hoping his participation would help close the case more quickly, Ben felt he was being arrogant. *The police might miss something, right?* It was too early to think that, though every passing minute with no breaks or leads made official failure more likely. A shooter was still in town, still at large, and he wanted to draw Ben out with the doctored bullet. Suddenly, Ben felt claustrophobic again.

With the map and the range sketches he had made from the penthouse vantage at the Renaissance, Ben took the exterior stair to the Orchid Suites rooftop lounge. He gazed out to the west, comparing his map to the ridges and valleys before him.

Behind Ben, a man muttered quietly, almost to himself. "My God, I wondered if you would ever come up for air."

Ben turned. A black man in an ivory linen suit sat comfortably at a corner table underneath a broad-brimmed straw Borsalino Panama. Ben knew him. "Knocker" Ellis Hogan.

Ellis had crewed for Ben aboard *Miss Dotsy*, the Blackshaws' deadrise workboat in the Chesapeake Bay, for years. He had done the same for Ben's father before that. Recent trouble on Smith Island had prompted them to abandon making a living on the water to begin very separate callings.

Ben was glad to see his old friend. "I've had a lot on my mind. You're pretty far from home."

Ellis pushed out a chair with his foot. "What's home? I'm home wherever you find me. And unless these old eyes deceive me, all that you've had on your mind for the last five, going on six, hours, is a very worthy young woman."

"Saw her, did you?" Ben blushed.

"Even tipped my bespoke two-thousand-dollar hat to her on the stair. Would have been a crime not to."

Ben sat. "Been in town long?"

"Couple hours. I was in Milan when I got word you were out ripping and running again. Took a minute to wrap up some business, or I would have come by sooner."

Ben was quiet. A few months before, these two men could not have scraped together a thousand dollars between them. Now, because of the trouble with the gold, Ellis was enjoying his retirement in extreme comfort.

"Do you miss the water?" Ben asked.

"It would be sentimental to say yes, but a lie all the same. I wasn't born to it like you, and my last few times on a boat were too damn eventful. How're *you* holding up?"

"More questions than answers. I was shown a file about the dead singer."

"La Luz," said Ellis.

"The same. A friend from the service wanted my help in the matter. Now he's dead, too. And can I just say that the flight over here left a lot to be desired?"

"Tell me about it," griped Ellis. "On my flight, the champagne was too sweet. Americans like Brut on the label, but syrup in the bottle. And my hot towel before landing was lukewarm."

"You poor thing." He wondered what Ellis already knew of the drone flight and its abrupt end. Ben still weighed how much to trust Ellis. "That does sound distressing. I think the killer is calling himself Nitro Express."

"Catchy. You're a hunter too, Ben. So hunt! Or are you having your usual qualm before the storm, you sensitive, peace-loving, non-violent hippy artiste."

"A little late for that. My flight was hijacked. I'll fill you in. But it isn't that simple here, just going out and catching this guy. The C.I.A. or some O.G.A. is all over this. And if you'll recall, I'm supposed to be dead and buried and gone to my reward. This is no time for a resurrection. Bad for business."

"I take your meaning," Ellis said. "So you're headed back east."

Ben's anger surged. "I don't know who the enemy is, and I'm no cop. This isn't my fight. Not like before."

Ellis studied Ben. "A friend is dead."

Ben could see Ellis sizing him up on the question of how he would behave if Ellis were the dearly departed and needed a touch of vengeance. "Yes, a friend is dead, and the shooter is looking for me."

"That's the best news I've had all day. Let's get to work."

CHAPTER 38

LILY MORGAN GRABBED at the phone. It was a private, encrypted line in her Washington, D.C. office. As the recently appointed
Secretary of the Department of Homeland Security, she still took pleasure
in all the perquisites of her new job. She had been the senator (R) from the
great state of Wisconsin until a few months before. A horrendous national
tragedy, the first nuclear attack on American soil, which came in the form
of a terrorist's dirty bomb detonating on a small island in the Chesapeake
Bay, had not hurt her career. There were a few whispers that she had
known of the plot beforehand, and failed to stop it in time, but those were
easily smothered.

Her evolving symptoms of new variant Creutzfeldt-Jakob disease,
which she had likely contracted from contaminated cattle bone meal with
which she fertilized her beloved roses, had not halted her rise in power.
Slurred speech, memory impairment, her twitching left hand, and her increasingly awkward gait were never mentioned by staffers. Such traits were
regarded as normal accompaniments of power inside the Washington
Beltway; at least they were viewed as tolerable quirks. In times of disaster,
be it nuclear terror, or an incurable disease eating holes in her brain,
Secretary Morgan somehow managed to hold fast to her home state's simple motto, *Forward*.

"What!" Secretary Morgan barked at the phone.

She heard the unctuous voice of one of her chief operatives,
MacCready. She had inherited MacCready from the former DHS head, and

though at one point she had intended to clean house, sack him, and staff-up fresh, she had forgotten to do it. The Swiss cheese in her head was letting her down. And so MacCready happily endured in his old position, but with new opportunities.

MacCready said, "Good morning, Lily. And how are we feeling today?"

Morgan exploded, "*We?* Do you have a fucking tapeworm? What's going on?"

MacCready was growing used to his boss's drive-by mood swings. Early in Lily Morgan's tenure, he had ruled out feral bitchiness as the cause of her attitude. He had done some spade work, and found the doctor who had diagnosed Lily's noggin issues.

Far from crumbling at the prospect of working with a difficult employer, MacCready had taken a leaf from Lily's operating manual and become proactive. He helped the diagnosing doctor to permanently disappear on a hunting trip, along with the pertinent medical records. Then he made sure that any new physician she went to was properly terrified into being utterly discreet. Secretary Morgan, never an angel, was now MacCready's personal gorgon to quarterback as he saw fit, at least until she succumbed to her illness or became totally unmanageable.

"My apologies, Madame Secretary. Just a figure of speech. Do you have a minute?"

"Of course I have a minute. I own time and space. I just let you run them for me."

"And I do thank you for that. Lots of fun. I wanted to speak with you about the unfortunate singer in Los Angeles."

Secretary Morgan's tone softened. "Go on."

"We're data-mining all the media, the papers, social-media, and we think her death gave us exactly the push we need. She's front-page stuff. Above the fold. Special bio sections added. There are TV and radio news segments galore, and two competing network long-form documentaries, and a biopic already in the works."

"Who's playing Luz?"

"They're talking about Salma Hayek."

"I love her, but for Luz? Too old. Seriously. She could direct the shit out of it though. You do realize that in capping that girl, you have probably put me out of fucking business?"

MacCready was incredulous. "What are you talking about?"

"Yes. Luz was one of mine. Why do you think she got on your screen? I fucking made her huge! I was going to employ her in something so big you can't even imagine, MacCready. But you killed her."

He started tap-dancing. "Luz was Grant's last sanction. And you had the other little problem that seemed more urgent."

MacCready tried to wrangle Secretary Morgan's attention back to his point. "In any case, we're tracking more than seventeen hundred hashtags related to Luz's death. More importantly, we're also tracking approximately twenty-four thousand *possible* hashtags in relation to your—um, your *primary concern.*"

Lily tensed. "And?"

"And I am happy to say, things are very quiet. Luz's tragic yet highly visible end has, in total accordance with our algorithm, preemptively displaced the primary concern into media oblivion. It'll never see the light of day."

"It cost me enough, but that's what I like to hear," Lily Morgan purred.

"The only reference to the primary concern, the Papa Charlie as we're calling it in the back office, was in *The Kenya Times.*"

"What? Are you kidding me? What page?"

MacCready was one of her operatives with an unspoken Deadly Force writ appended to his job description. If she were ever truly unhappy with his work, his pink slip might arrive from the barrel of a gun, the edge of a knife, the pressure of a garrote on his throat, or poison. The only positive aspect to a summary and terminal dismissal by Lily was that his death would take place so soon after his firing that he would not have to clean out an office, or even file for his benefits.

MacCready preferred to live, so he calmed Lily with concerted élan. "It appeared on page four. Bottom of the page. Two column inches. The article referred only to a missing set of files from a shipping-office burglary in Nairobi. The word *yellowcake* appeared only once in the article. The BBC might pick it up, but not likely."

Secretary Morgan was not to be pacified. "You idiot! The BBC is so broke that their reporters infest that whole continent. Cheap to send them to Africa. Cheap to maintain bureaus. I never heard so much boring, inconsequential bullshit come out of the Beeb as when they crank up their Africa wonks. It's how you know it's a slow news cycle for the Brits. Africa-Africa-Africa! Election violence, famine, diseases, insurgents. Their reporters will bite on your page-four mention like it's the moon landing. And that's not good. I have lots of business interests there."

"But Madame Secretary, that was in yesterday's paper, and today, there's nothing. Absolutely nothing whatsoever. The Papa Charlie is buried."

"All the same," said Lily, "you think maybe we need another little pincheroosky to keep things on the down-low? What about a school shooting?"

"We are having some luck introducing the strep virus to bring on acute PANDAS reactions in kids. It works best in prepubescent children actually. That will make for amazing headlines. The tots get severe, acute onset OCD symptoms, and they turn into Children of the Corn. That's in the experimental phase right now.

"That said, we do have a few unstable elements closer to tipping into rampage shooters if we really need to. Emotionally disturbed adolescent outcasts with access to guns. We're lacing their mac 'n' cheese and hand pizzas with supposedly helpful, legal psychotropic drugs that actually boost suicidal ideations in younger people. We don't even have to cook the drugs ourselves, which saves us a bundle. The pharmacy shelves are full of them, and the child therapists on our payroll are prescribing pills like candy; they're monitoring some very volatile cases right now. But the shrinks can't overdo it, or the kids shoot themselves first, and that never makes even a regional headline these days. The other problem is that we catch absolute hell from the gun lobby whenever we exercise that option."

Lily all but guffawed. "Even though gun sales go through the roof when folks think this or that peashooter is about to be banned?"

"Right. But everyone has a public position to take in the aftermath of events like that. The North American Pistol and Rifle Association is no different. They got so rich as the mouthpiece of the gun lobby, they slacked off their homework, and the old chestnut of *now is the time to grieve, not write new legislation*, well it's wearing thin. They need new material. So, the mass shooting option is problematic, and might actually be overused for now. It's why we went with the PF-PD vignette for the yellowcake problem this time around."

"The *what* vignette?" Lily sensed she was falling behind.

"Sorry. Public Figure-Public Death. I'll be the first to admit, sometimes a grievous wounding in front of news cameras offers a longer-term media meme displacement than a grisly fatality, because there are plenty of follow-up reports on the victim's condition. They have real human-interest staying power. Several news cycles or more. Funerals of non-celebs don't get much more than local coverage unless Al Sharpton shows up, or the Westboro crazies.

"Anyway," MacCready went on, "right now, we maintain a roster of potential events, and celebrity candidates, including a rating of their effectiveness to shift a news meme either through death, adulterous scandal, suicide, or down-low trysting with tranny hookers, and we update their rating four times every day. It's like the IMDb, but for complete lowlife shitheads. Also our meme displacement estimates can predict a story's exact page relocation in a subsequent news cycle at an accuracy rate of 94 percent. We project the column inches, and even the page *position* at only 47 percent and 56 percent accuracy, respectively, but that's still good. On social media, we can quiet any embarrassing chatter, and curtail problem hashtags by 70 percent in twelve hours, and by 96 percent in twenty-four hours."

Lily beamed. She was almost giddy with the possibilities. Her schemes were so audacious, some were bound to go wrong, and this MacCready and his algorithm offered cover-up options that would have made Nixon's head spin. She could distract Congress, the press, even the president from ever knowing what she was doing even if something went south. She was bulletproof. But just to be sure, she asked, "Is there anything on a *back* page of that rag in Kenya that you can shove to the *front* page?"

MacCready did not mind Lily's heritage media metaphors despite the prevalence of so many digital news outlets. The *page* had become a standard unit of measure for the Meme Displacement Algorithm.

He said, "It's an idea we're working on, but at the moment, the program only functions one way, in the direction of displacing troublesome front page memes toward less conspicuous positions, and mostly by redirecting and overwhelming the reporting resources with bigger news. It still feels like we're doing brain surgery with a lead pipe, but even though there are more news outlets today, we also have more interpretive resources. Our work has become so much more predictable since the Kennedy and Dr. King vignettes of yore."

"Well get on that, will you? What about using some *good* news? How does that play in Peoria?"

"Short of the Second Coming of Christ, good news doesn't have much relevance in current Meme Displacement Theory. But we're making great strides. For now, we'll watch the Kenyan paper like hawks. Working preemptively as we are to suppress the primary concern on the yellowcake, the only thing the world is hearing about right now is La Luz, or crickets."

Secretary Lily Morgan was appeased for the moment. The death of Lucilla Calderon might not be a bad thing, after all.

CHAPTER 39

ELLIS HOGAN CHANGED out of his linen suit into cotton desert camo BDU pants, and a black polo, and hung the suit in the closet in Ben's room. "That there's my urban ghillie suit," he said. "I never get a second look wearing that thing. Like I'm invisible."

"I get the same effect in coveralls for a lot less money. Now let's get up that hill."

Ellis and Ben mounted up in a rented Toyota Land Cruiser left just outside the Orchid's underground parking lot. They stopped to buy a small pair of Nikon binoculars at a sporting goods store, then used the map and the SUV's GPS to navigate to the higher elevations of the Santa Monica Mountains. On a crest, they pulled over on the switchback road outside a fenced microwave and cellular phone facility. The cell towers rose in the northwest above the iconic Hollywood sign which itself loomed over the downtown area.

Ben said, "That sign is protected pretty much like the U.S. borders with Mexico and Canada. Infrared cameras, microphones, motion detectors, patrols, and such."

Ellis looked at the city sprawling below through the binoculars. "You really want to go down there? I hear there're rattlesnakes, and mountain lions, and actresses."

"Not to mention this shooter likes to watch his last position, and say it with bullets if anybody shows up to poke around."

"Very professional on the one hand," said Ellis.

"Keeps him stuck in the general neighborhood, on the other."

Ellis shrugged. "Take my chances with the snakes and the ingénues."

Ben and Ellis scuffed and shuffled down the steep hill to the catwalk behind a chain link fence protecting the big white letters farther below.

Ellis asked, "You going to hop over?"

Ben thought about it. "Do you think the shooter did? This is close enough. I just wanted to see what the he was looking at when he took Grant down. Can I have those binoculars?"

Ben focused on the rooftop over a mile away where Grant died. The sheet-metal gun hide had been disassembled already. "I'll be damned!"

"What you got?" Ellis peered into the distance with his naked eye.

"There's somebody on that roof."

"You said MacCready locked it down tight. Can you see who it is?"

"No. Need stronger binos, or my scope. I tell you one thing. He's waving right at us. Wearing a hoodie. Waving."

"Shut the front door!" The usually laconic Ellis was impressed. "You think it's Nitro Express?"

"Who else?"

"I declare, the *balls* on this cat."

Ben lowered the binoculars, tried to make sense of the apparent connections, the shooter's strange, unpredictable moves. He felt they were maneuvering around the circumference of a large circle, but they remained always fixed diametrically opposite each other, never drawing closer.

Ellis reconsidered. "Could be anybody down there, Ben. Sure you got the right roof."

After glaring at Ellis, Ben looked at the Hollywood sign's security cameras on their pylons. One camera was aimed from below the sign uphill toward their position. Ben pointed it out to Ellis. "See that camera?"

"You said he might have used video feeds to direct fire on La Luz. You think he's tapping them wherever he wants?" Ellis asked.

Aiming the binoculars at the tiny figure on the distant roof with his right hand, Ben absently raised the middle finger of his left hand.

The person on the rooftop glanced down at something in his hand, perhaps a smart phone, and then looked up toward Ben and Ellis. Then slowly, he raised his left hand. Though the binoculars' resolution did not allow Ben to discern individual fingers, the body language was clear.

"He's hacked the video feeds up here," Ben confirmed.

"Some very fancy business."

"I'm telling you, Ellis, this mess is sob wet with cash."

"Don't forget the main thing," said Ellis. "Nobody else is up here. That bastard reckoned you, and *only you*, could back-figure the dope on that shot and arrive here. But this time, he's not shooting. And look there."

Ellis indicated the ground fifteen feet to their right. Four bright new .416 Rigby shells, all fired, stood like a quartet of headless knights on their primers in the dirt next to the fence. "That does it, Ben. You know this shooter. And he knows you."

Ben raised the binoculars, and looked back at the faraway rooftop. The small figure had vanished.

CHAPTER 40

BEN AND ELLIS ate takeout chicken in the hotel room, sipping cola from plastic cups.

Ben said, "Might could be I made a mistake telling MacCready to go to hell."

"You never go wrong being a little rude to power. It keeps them crazy baldheads humble. And you bought yourself some time here without MacCready watching you."

Ben was not so sure. "He has resources. And this shooter, my God, he has serious bank for equipment, for intel that goes broad and deep. It's impressive."

"Feeling out-gunned, Ben?"

"Feeling out*spent*. In a flash town like this, it's like I'm the low-budget, low-tech insurgent trying to take down the Great Satan. Thinking I should pay MacCready a call. Tell him I reconsidered. Eat some crow, for Grant's sake."

Ellis and Ben had agreed to leave the four spent cartridges on the hill in case the police managed to discover the shooter's position for Grant's murder. Ben did not want to have any kind of physical evidence in his possession lest he fall afoul of MacCready, or any other amped-up authority struggling to tie a bow on the killings. That left Ben with what little intel he had gathered so far. The rest was supposition. Grant had not lived long enough to enlighten Ben about the ill-fated drone flight, and the ambush at Pyramid Lake. What struck Ben now was how quickly Grant had arrived on the stony shore to exfiltrate him. He knew there were some elite quick-response teams out there, but they were forward operators, in war theatres. Grant's appearance on American soil, with full tactical and medical units aboard, was astonishingly fast.

Perhaps Grant and the Osprey had been trailing the drone from the beginning of its flight in New Jersey. The Osprey could have kept pace if the drone had flown lazy S-turns while the tilt-rotor flew a great circle course. Roughly three or four in-flight refueling intercepts would have kept the Osprey aloft the whole way across the country. In that case, why did Grant not simply offer Ben a lift from McGuire? And why the expanded headcount, the operatives and the medics. What had Grant expected Ben to encounter on a clandestine cross-country flight?

Ben recalled clearly now that Grant's fast rope unit and the medical team on the Osprey all looked fresh, and rested. They did not look or smell like they'd been flying all night without a change of clothes. The redhead who dressed Ben's cuts smelled of lavender soap, which should have been a no-no on such a crack team in case of patient allergies. It was a helpful mistake for Ben's reckoning. Only Grant looked fatigued, and that was because he was dying on his feet from cancer. The picture forming in Ben's mind was that the Osprey was close when the drone spat him into the lake. The proximity, the timing, it all felt like a rendezvous, but Ben could not figure out its underlying purpose.

Ellis looked straight into Ben's eyes. "Listen to me. Don't go to MacCready. Not yet. What do you really have to offer him at this point? Good will? It sounds like he was happy to see your back. You could give him that engraved bullet, and show him the classified ads, which are pretty weak if you ask me. You could lead him to the Rigby brass up on the hill by that sign, if they're still there. But if MacCready's in a bad mood, he could nail you for tampering with evidence, or for withholding evidence. Who knows what playbook he uses, if any? I bet, from what you told me, he could have your ass renditioned straight to hell, and you'll never see daylight again. Do your homework first, then dime the killer to MacCready. Then let MacCready decide what to do with him. Stay out of it. Stay away. If Grant was a friend, he didn't tell MacCready anything about you. After this is done, you could get yourself dead again. You could still have a life."

This was a different sound from Ellis. Usually, he advocated action of the most clear-cut, decisive, and aggressive kind, even on U.S. soil. Ben wondered if coming into money had made him careful.

Ben cleansed a chicken thigh bone. Grant had drawn Ben away from New York with the message on the wall of his building. Once Ben read the murder jacket on La Luz, he believed he had been tapped because there was a counter-sniper mission on which he was to find and put down the killer. The engraving on the bullet that snuffed Grant meant that the shooter was part of the small coterie who knew the cipher; just five men left alive from Ben's days in the service. Six men, if Ben counted Ellis, to whom he had explained the simple sequence. Seven men, counting the messenger who braced Omega in New York City. So, seven men, and a woman all told, for Ben had taken a great risk and confided in Loki. The number of people who knew the cadre's encrypted call sign ballooned without limit if Grant had written it down, or divulged it to MacCready as part of their casework.

Ben would have to scour his memory to see whether anything having to do with this business jibed with any of his buddies from the service. So far, only Grant seemed involved.

MacCready was another matter requiring thought. He did not seem at all unhappy that Grant had died. From MacCready's smug manner, it was clear he had no objection to receiving bloodstripes, his field promotion due to the death of a superior. He had stepped onto that rooftop in plain sight, filled with confidence that he would not be killed. Ben did not sense that MacCready was brave under fire. It seemed he was wily, and somehow guessed or knew the firing was done.

One of the cellular phones Loki had provided began to blare. The number that came up was (310) 555-2324. Ben recognized it as the same number, minus the area code, that was split between the two Nitro Express classified ads.

Ellis eyed Ben. "You expecting that lovely woman to call?"

Ben opened the line with the speaker. He did not say anything.

An electronically disguised voice said, "Thanks for coming to town, Ben. We're going to have some fun together."

Ben and Ellis stayed quiet. The robotic voice continued, "The man with you. Do him a favor. Tell him to go. Soon. He's not invited to this party. Sometimes I miss my shots, and hit people I don't mean to."

The line went dead.

CHAPTER 41

THE STRANGER'S RELIEF was palpable, but temporary. Following the telephone call to Ben Blackshaw, a restorative sleep flooded in, resulting in three hours of sweet oblivion. No recurrence of the nightmare. No dreams at all. The killer made two more telephone calls on waking, and managed to find what was required on the second one. Instructions were given. Payment was offered. A downpayment was wired. The hired gun had never outsourced a mission before, but time to plan was paramount. Now that Blackshaw was emotionally engaged, it was imperative to keep him moving while other decisions could be made, and preparations ironed out.

The deadly visitor knew that the reprieve from the nightmare would be brief. This was borne out in the next period of collapse, which some called sleep, when once again the familiar metropolis of the vision was ransacked by invaders.

The dreamer woke on the floor next to the bed once again, bathed in sweat. Vomit puddled in the sheets, and the hotel room reeked of bile. In the core of the killer's being, only one lasting solution to this torment was becoming clear. Ben Blackshaw would have his part to play, but only if he was willing to help an old friend; an old friend he had never met.

CHAPTER 42

MACCREADY PACED ON the top level of the Santa Monica Civic Center's parking garage among the solar panels that made up the roof. By day, the sun would have warmed his scalp through his thin, wispy hair. At night, when business took him to Los Angeles, he enjoyed the lights of the amusement park rides at the Santa Monica Pier, without actually visiting there. He even admired the parking deck's LEED-sustainable whimsy, the vertical multicolored lights that covered the outer walls of the structure like a fair ride that took you nowhere, but festively housed your car when not in use. Janie had MacCready's car parked up the street.

MacCready wondered about his attractive young driver. He had flirted with Janie shamelessly, but was always met only with professional politeness. She never seemed tempted to improve her professional stature by accepting his invitations to dinner, for drinks, or for sex. He could wear her down eventually. He was MacCready after all.

Superiority infected MacCready's mood. All the world was at play. He believed the grazing public was so soul-sick that they were desperate to crawl out of their own heads, and flee their own lives. Grownup children wanted, no, they *demanded* that distractions and amusements lie close and ready in every prospect.

Having that singer popped had been his stroke of genius. Grant had taken the suggestion, and acted upon it. In ordering the death, MacCready felt he had disturbed the ambient sounds of pleasure that thrummed through the world zeitgeist so profoundly that nobody had their heads on straight anymore. Even the Luz Calderon haters were completely taken up with the passion of their disdain in the face of her eulogies. They were unaware that the breaths and heartbeats they squandered bleating that La Luz was nothing special could never be recovered, carelessly tossed as they were on the altar of venal pleasure, and burned as a smoke offering to the God of Lives Unlived. At least the primary concern was safe for now. The embarrassing stolen yellowcake story in Niger was stone cold in the press.

Hell, MacCready wondered, *who he was kidding?* His mood darkened abruptly. He knew he had to call the Secretary of the Department of Homeland Security with disappointing news. And she was a crazy as a shithouse rat. For MacCready, this was going to be a night almost completely devoid of levity or diversions. Almost, but not quite. He patted the lower cargo pockets of his new field jacket which bulged and sagged with the weight of their contents. *Soon,* he thought, soothing himself. But the call had to be made first.

He had smoked his Lucky Strike to the filter. Now he ground it out under his heel into the face of a solar panel. Then he dialed his encrypted phone. Secretary Lily Morgan answered on the third ring. "It's MacCready."

Lily got straight to business. "Are we good?"

"For the most part."

Lily stage-whispered, "Good, because I think there's a unicorn in my office."

"Oh dear." MacCready groaned inwardly. For such a keen mind, the Secretary's hallucinations were banal. "Lily, may we talk about business for a moment? Would the unicorn mind?"

Lily paused. "He says okay. Putting you on speaker so he can hear."

"Please don't do that." MacCready pinched the bridge of his nose. "This is private."

"Of course it is. Why did you call?" Lily sounded offended.

"You remember the singer who died?"

"Yes. Stop talking to me like I'm a damn child!"

MacCready suspected that would be difficult. "There is a slight issue with the operative who handled that matter."

"What issue?"

"Okay, are you familiar with Project Ark-Light?"

"I'm guessing you don't mean the B-52 bomber push in Vietnam in 1965."

"No, ma'am."

"Then we're talking about storing data in DNA. I loved that project. I made sure it was financed when I was in the Senate." Now Lily was sharp. She was plugged in. But MacCready always had to remind himself she was insane.

MacCready said, "Well, it seems we got pretty good at it. I mean, all fifty-three trillion gigabytes of digital human knowledge now fit into a space the size of a slice of pound cake."

"So far, you're making me hungry. And angry. Bad combo."

MacCready proceeded with caution. "So, now we can cache data in living DNA, not the artificial stuff. Actual human DNA. We can crank it into the genome, or the epigenome, which sits on top of the genome, so to speak. That turned out to be easier. So that's what was done."

Lily Morgan, Secretary of the Department of Homeland Security asked, "Am I supposed to know this?"

"I really think so. The idea was to cache critical information, NATO plans, wargame results, things like that. Crucial top secret data." MacCready was not enjoying this.

Lily stopped him. "Okay. What about hardened data storage? Is brick-and-mortar totally out of vogue?"

MacCready said, "That's just it. Past a certain point, about eight months ago, a decision was made to stop storing critical intel and crucial data in hardened silos. They're vulnerable. The NSA is buried in the massive amount of data it's collecting. So instead, the idea was to cache it in DNA which isn't hooked into the internet at all. DARPA got good at this stuff. Anyway, there was this plan that got cached, one in particular."

Secretary Morgan became wary. "What plan was that, MacCready?"

"It was your soup-to-nuts detailed strategy, as worked out with the Joint Chiefs, and their chairman, to invade a certain OAS ally. You remember?"

"Sure. I think the Organization of American States is as useless as tits on a boar. I still think we could stick it to them."

MacCready hated dropping bad news. "No doubt you're correct. And your invasion concept resonated with some important folks a few blocks away from where you are now. The point is, that idea got stored. Through Project Ark-Light. In the DNA of two different human subjects."

Lily said, "Holy shit! Did we run out of lab gerbils? But it's in their genome, right? It's not as if they're aware of it. Do we have a line on who they are, and where?"

"No, they had no idea what they're carrying. The data infusion was performed during routine physicals. The important thing is that plan, *your* plan, is in their *epi*genome. But what the boffins at DARPA are telling me now is that dicking with the *epigenome* changes things."

"Is that right?" Lily's voice had no inflection. This was a bad sign.

"Yes. It changes outcomes. Alters personalities, sometimes significantly. Especially if there's a data bleed."

"A data bleed? What the hell is that?"

MacCready was not happy revealing this part. "Apparently, that's where the information actually begins to leak out of the DNA. I suppose that's the best way to describe it. So it leaks out of the DNA, out of the epigenome, and into the carrier's subconscious, and then into consciousness. The cached individual gains awareness of the data through an unforeseen mind-body conduit, roughly speaking, from nature to nurture."

Lily asked the next logical question. "MacCready, where the hell are those human flash drives?"

MacCready tried to lighten his tone. "Good news, and bad. One of them is dead. Suicide. The bleed became too intense, and there were acute personality deficits that the bleed seems to have complicated. Apparently, this man's ancestors were from the country specified as the plan's target for the invasion. He told a therapist that he had some kind of apocalyptic vision having to do with this home country, and that it was so intense, he ultimately could not tolerate it. He has been cremated, so there is no DNA for a foreign power to harvest."

"That leaves one. Kill him." Secretary Morgan was never fazed by issuing a kill sanction.

"Good idea, Madame Secretary. But that's a problem."

"What is?"

"On the other matter, I mean. One subject is dead. And that leaves one. But the folks upstairs say we *must* keep him alive. That's from the very top."

Lily Morgan raised her voice. "You're saying we need to have some-body walking around with a damaging, incriminating strategic plan of inva-sion of an ally floating around in his bloodstream, a plan with my name on it? Really? I mean, the Joint Chiefs and I were riffing this out on cocktail napkins at a bar. We were drinking tequila!"

The farcical circumstances were not lost on MacCready. "I understand. And yes, it is in his bloodstream. But this concept is actually affixed to every single solitary cell in the man's body."

Lily was angry, a thrill of panic in her voice. "Not encrypted? In plain English?"

"Unfortunately, yes. The caching method was so revolutionary that no one thought a further level of encryption was necessary."

Lily sounded hoarse. "Where is he?"

"We're not really sure."

"This was my plan! I was going to do it when I got into the White House. You have got to be kidding me!"

"I wish I were. That's why I called. The stolen yellowcake problem, the one we killed the singer to displace back a few pages in the media, it's less important now."

"You're telling me!"

MacCready said, "It's less important because the operative who killed the singer is the same person carrying the invasion blueprint."

"Jesus Christ in a chicken basket! They put that plan in a soldier. *Our* soldier!"

MacCready's voice was calm, but his heart hammered. "It's happened before. All our agencies are drawing on the same finite pool of qualified candidates. Test pilots become astronauts, who become senators. Video gamers fly real drones. Actors become presidents. But we're not consulted. They just uploaded him. He was a fine soldier at one point, and maintained in the reserves, but DARPA figured he wasn't catching any frontline action these days, and yet he could defend himself if called upon. Boy, were they wrong. He seemed to them like a good candidate, for the same reasons he fit our profile like a glove. Trust me, I was pretty harsh with the DARPoids when they started asking *me* what he was doing, and where they could get in touch."

Secretary Morgan was spitting with rage, "The plan is in a corrupt soldier who's chirpy as hell to work for the likes of *you*, who is highly, extremely skilled in killing anything that comes near him, and who is out of his ever-loving gourd? You gave that responsibility, and that kind of power, to a pie-eyed stark raving homicidal lunatic!"

MacCready yearned to point out Secretary Lily Morgan's own neurological circumstances, but let it go. Instead, he said, "The decision was made by bureaucratic scientists, ma'am. Like I said, the idea as it was explained to me, was to cache the plan inside someone who could and would defend himself, and in doing that, they could also unwittingly defend the data cached in his DNA."

"Why not stuff that plan into some fat, boring housewife, or a secretary with zero ambition who likes knitting and watching television, and then lock her up in a hotel room or a prison cell for the rest of her life where she would be happy and safe? The timing on this is awful. Premature."

MacCready said, "You're pushing on an open door here, ma'am. The problem is, we need to bring the operator in. From my last few chats with him, he's sounding symptomatic."

Lily bawled, "So, shoot the bastard! Is that so hard?"

"We don't really handle him face to face. It's a work-from-home situation. A telecommute. Even the voice is encrypted. He sounds like Darth Vader on helium when we talk. Very weird. And the important thing is this: we cannot kill him, because your plan, in all its enhanced detail, is going hot on Pennsylvania Avenue."

"Oh my God!"

"The target nation is so embroiled in the South American debt crisis that POTUS and the Joint Chiefs feel that forcibly locking that country into a kind of American-run receivership is the best way to ensure that the financial cancer doesn't metastasize and go the way of Europe and the Middle East."

"I don't believe this," Lily Morgan hissed. "The Joint Chiefs and I were shooting tequila and bumping skag. What the hell are they snorting in the West Wing to make this idea actually sound feasible now? If something goes wrong, where am I?"

MacCready ignored the question. "Eliminating this subject would be for the best all around. I would hate to think what would happen if the invasion fails, or takes more than a few days."

"My name is really all over it?" Lily asked.

MacCready said, "From what I was told, the invasion is called the *Morgan Guaranty Thrust* in your honor. Every byte of data has *Lily Morgan* as the watermark. They want this operator brought in and scanned to recover the blueprints. Which brings me to our next issue. We need to groom a replacement to continue the DHS's Meme Displacement work, especially in the run-up to this proposed invasion. Having a reliable operator working for your office will be crucial to manage the meme flow during and after the invasion. My former boss, Grant, had a line on someone who might be right."

Madame Secretary Morgan growled, "Why are you bothering me with operational bullshit? Ramp up the new guy as fast as you can. We'll decide if we want to ice Mr. Flashdrive in due course. And one more thing, MacCready."

MacCready was ready for this call to end. "Yes, Madame Secretary?"

"What the hell do leprechauns eat? This one only speaks Gaelic."

He trod carefully. "I thought you had a unicorn in the office."

"MacCready, you're just a complete banjo retard, aren't you. Unicorns don't exist." She terminated the call.

MacCready took several deep breaths. His boss did not want the invasion plan revealed with her name on it now. Yet she wanted to put the plan into action in some delusional administration in which she was actually the President of the United States. *God help us*, thought MacCready.

He lit a Lucky Strike and drew on it deeply. He peered over the side of the parking deck rooftop and was cheered to see a family of five exiting the garage and starting down the sidewalk toward the amusements on the Santa Monica Pier. Mother and father, and three children under age ten. He followed them, strolling along the roof unseen above.

MacCready left the cigarette in his mouth, and quickly reached into his jacket cargo pockets, removing two heavy M67 fragmentation grenades. He hefted one in each hand. They felt like cool plums to him. Killer plums. It was like cupping his own balls, as he imagined their lethal power.

The deaths of Grant and Strahan had been covered up well enough. MacCready and his cadre had seen to that. Grant had died of cancer, so the media was told. Strahan, it was given out, had expired from an apparent heart attack. Detective Dario, the lady cop on the roof, had died of food poisoning, as her obituary would report. Of course, the local medical examiner had been bypassed on these deaths in favor of a MacCready's own doc', and discouraged from squawking with clear and present threats to his family. MacCready had simply hired Lieutenant Borskein. The murder of La Luz would keep the unfortunate, though natural, deaths of the other three well off the front pages, but MacCready felt that he needed to carry some additional insurance just to be safe. Something unusual. Something freaky and weird to keep the journalists busy.

He took another look over the edge of the roof, and saw that the family below him was making progress down the sidewalk toward their evening of fun. He hooked the thumb of each hand into the pin of the grenade in the opposite hand. MacCready held the little bomb in his left hand upside down to make access to its pin easier. He took a deep cleansing breath, then spread his arms wide. The pins he had straightened earlier slid free of the fuse mechanisms without effort, and dangled from his thumbs. The levers, or *spoons* as they were called, flipped free of the grenades, igniting primers which lighted the time-delay fuses.

Feeling like a god once more, MacCready grinned for the instant he let the fuses *cook* the three second delay in his hands.

He whispered, "Frag out", and dropped the grenades. They clanked onto the sidewalk, one falling behind, and the other landing in front of the happy family.

With the agility of a Little League shortstop, the youngest boy dashed forward, scooped up grenade and held it high for his parents to see. MacCready's high position prevented his viewing facial expressions, which he thought a real pity, but the father did reach toward his boy. He, at least, had the germ of an idea something was wrong. MacCready ducked back to avoid the whizzing fragments to come. An instant later, the grenades cracked in quick succession.

MacCready looked over the roof's edge one last time. The shortstop was reduced to small fleshy chunks of humanity. The other, older boy lay still, also brutally sundered. The last child, a girl with pigtails, wailed, writhed, and sent several arcs of bright arterial blood across the sidewalk and the garage's wall. The father was down, not moving. The mother, despite the loss of her left leg below the knee, crawled screaming toward the tot perishing amidst the ruin of her family. Grinning, MacCready flicked his cigarette over the roof's edge.

Not fully satisfied, but feeling much better than before his talk with Lily Morgan, he calmly made his way to the stairwell. Shortly, the garage surveillance cameras he had ordered shut down an hour ago would reboot, having missed his entire performance.

He reached ground level enjoying the din of howling Samaritans who needed to believe that the volume of their bleats would somehow change the carnage before them. Musing contentedly upon the mother crawling toward her dying child, MacCready made a mental note: *three grenades next time.*

CHAPTER 43

BEN AND ELLIS finished the last of the chicken in silence and considered the strange call with the distorted electronic voice.

"How did he know the number for that phone?" Ellis asked. "It's prepaid. A burner. Did Loki tell him by mistake, or under duress?"

"I don't think she tipped anything. She's careful. This fellow's got amazing intel resources. Likes to keep his distance. He's a shooter, yes, but thinks more like a hunter than a soldier. Anyway, that call's from the same number I found split up between two classified ads in the newspapers. I had tried the number myself from that phone."

Ellis said, "And he knows about me."

"Probably saw you up at the sign. Wants me all to himself. Maybe you should go while you can."

"Miss all the fun? Like hell. Did you recognize anything in what he said? Cadence? Phrasing? Word choice? Anything ring a bell?"

"I should have spoken up. Maybe talking to me would kick something loose from him. Something I can pinpoint. But no, nothing he said reminded me of any one of my friends in particular. He kept it all very neutral. No jargon. Let's go."

Ellis looked sideways at Ben. "Where to?"

"He's controlling the situation with threats to bystanders, and that pisses me off. I have to take the innocents out of the equation."

"Head for the open. Okay. Joshua Tree maybe? That's four hours away."

Ben shook his head. "We're going to need plane tickets."

Ellis grimaced. "You don't want to fly commercial. Again, too many bystanders. And that's way too broad a digital trail if you want to lead him someplace. Going to have to be more subtle, or he'll smell the trap."

"True. I want to make it look like I'm running. We don't have time to drive, and God only knows if trains go where I'm thinking."

Ellis reached for his suitcase. "Get packed, and let's go."

Ben stood up. "There. I'm packed."

Ellis smiled. He took the cellular phone that had just been used, removed the battery, and stomped the phone to smithereens, and dropped the fragments in the swimming pool as they left the room.

Ben said, "I still have two phones. They're blown too, like as not."

Ben and Ellis each took two taxi rides over the next thirty minutes, dropping the remaining cell phones in the cabs' back seats. Anyone tracking the phones would not have a clear picture of their destinations as the cabbies continued trolling the city during their shifts.

Ben reunited with Ellis near the La Brea tar pits. They walked to a car rental office in the neighborhood where Ellis obtained a small Fiat. Ben waited outside.

Ellis drove Ben south, instead of east toward LAX.

Ben said, "We need to catch a flight. So, where the heck are you going?"

"We're flying out of Torrance. Lower profile. It will look like you're avoiding the beaten path, and running like hell."

They drove onto the five hundred acre aviation preserve once known as Zamperini Field. Ben expected Ellis to pull into the terminal parking lot, but he drove to an unmarked gate in the chain link security fence, flashing the lights in a seemingly random sequence. A man emerged out of the darkness, and opened the gate. Ellis drove onto an isolated ramp.

From a distance, no lights showed inside the Embraer Legacy 650, but the cabin door was open. Ben and Ellis ditched the Fiat on the ramp, left the keys in the ignition, and approached the plane. The man who opened the gate got in the Fiat and drove it away.

When Ben and Ellis reached the plane, the air stairs deployed to the tarmac. They boarded into an opulent cabin with minimal red lighting that would preserve night vision if need be.

Ben sat in a rear-facing club chaise. "Ellis, you are full of surprises. You bought this?"

"I've rented it on an indefinite basis. It's actually a repo. The repo company president and I are friendly since the service."

Ben had agreed to share the gold proceeds from their last crisis on a fifty-fifty basis with Ellis, who was his partner throughout the attack on Smith Island. Ben had divided his half among all the other Smith Island residents, as he believed his father would have wished. Ellis, therefore retained the largest aggregation of monies of any individual involved in the affair. Though other Smith Islanders held Ellis in a certain unfavorable light, Ben stood by his friend, and by his original agreement on the split. The advantages to keeping his promise were beginning to have very positive returns.

In fifteen minutes the Embraer was airborne. Ellis said, "We took off filing for Spokane. Care to redirect us?"

"Refile for Mexico City."

"Not the last time we're going to do that on this flight, is it?" Ellis relayed the new destination to the pilot on the intercom handset. "The cell phones in the cabs will buy us an hour, maybe two," he told Ben. "The rental car will be tougher to trace, but once they find the right rental company, it's got a GPS chip. The guy who took the car is instructed to ditch it near the field. Again, we show okay tradecraft, but not great. So, I figure your shooter's support team will be at Torrance within thirty minutes after that. Five minutes to scope departing flights. They'll see the original filing, and then they'll see the new one."

"We'll be refiling at least twice more," Ben said. "Keep them on their toes."

"Resources will be alerted, and deployed along the route we fly. Fool them often enough, they might stand down so they can focus better when we actually land."

Ben said, "Confusion to our enemies."

The flight continued without incident. They served themselves simple yet delicious box lunches from the aircraft's galley. MREs for the well-heeled. Ellis used the intercom to convey two further flight plan changes pointing the aircraft ever farther south. Ben never saw the pilots.

Hours later, over Peruvian airspace, Ben gave Ellis one final filing. "Put us down at El Loa, at Calama, Chile."

Ellis relayed the message to the cockpit, then unstowed a heavy case from an aft luggage bin. "Got a little something-something for you."

Ben leaned forward when Ellis snapped the case's four latches open. "Is that what I think it is?"

Ellis grinned wide. "A man on the go needs options."

He lifted the lid on the case like a magician. Ben eyed the flocked blue velvet lining. The inside of the case looked more luxuriously upholstered than the jet cabin. On the case's top shelf lay a heavy, engraved, dis-assembled rifle stock and bolt action as well as a long telescopic sight. "You're not serious."

"As a Hambrusch heart attack," Ellis said.

Ben lifted the top shelf out, revealing nestled below not one, but three individual barrels with engraved wood fore-stocks. Each barrel was bored to a different diameter. There was matched ammunition for all three calibers. Any of these three barrels would fit the single stock perfectly.

Ellis touched each barrel in turn. "Here's your .338 Lapua Magnum like the shooter used on Grant. This next one here's a straight .416 Rigby, but not necked down at all. A .416 cartridge, and a .416 bullet. And last but not least, .600 Nitro Express. Like what the shooter used in that cannon on Luz Calderon, but not as big, and for certain, not as fancy."

"I can't take all three barrels where I'm going," Ben said. "Too much weight."

"You have the options, based on your plan. I was going to give it to you for Christmas, but I figured you could use it now."

Ben thought of the encounter he was planning. "Customs will be fun with this thing."

"Customs is for folks who go through Customs. We are not custom-ary. But on that note—if you're sure Calama's where we're putting down ..." Ellis stepped to the back of the cabin and made several calls over the course of the next thirty minutes.

The Embraer landed at El Loa, and taxied, true to form, to an unlit, isolated area of the field. Two vehicles intercepted the aircraft. The Mercedes sedan was a rich man's cast-off, definitely better suited to the smooth pavement of the airport environs. The other vehicle was also Mercedes by birth, a Unimog 1300L. This heavy-duty all terrain truck with high ground clearance was, by the look of its equipment, lately discharged from service in the Chilean army.

The Unimog's driver, a crisply uniformed Customs officer, hopped down from the truck and met Ellis at the door of the aircraft. The agent produced a stamp from a small belt wallet, and plied it over Ellis's genuine passport, and Ben's counterfeit documentation, which Ellis produced like a magician, having seemed to plan for every eventuality. Though not magic, it impressed the agent deeply when Ellis handed over more than the $320 U.S. for two Tourist cards. The agent saluted Ellis, and climbed into the sedan next to the driver. The sedan pulled away and disappeared down the ramp. Time from the opening of the aircraft door until the documentation was examined and found in good order, two minutes.

Back inside the jet, Ellis found Ben checking the contents of a light rucksack Ellis had brought out from the aft cabin. Ellis looked at Ben, smiling sheepishly, "We're here."

"Much obliged, Ellis. I'll repay—."

Ellis held up a hand. "No, you won't pay me back. First, you *can't*. You don't make that kind of scratch after your ridiculously magnanimous gesture back on Smith Island. Your father might be proud, or he might think you're a fool, sharing out your half to everybody else like you did, but the result is you're not as rich as I am, and never will be. Second, I consider this trip a business investment. You need to kill this bastard and get back to your walk-down in New York, and get back to your work. Have your fun now. Breathe your fresh air. But before the blood dries, you're going to be wheels up and halfway back to the big city again if I have a say in it. So don't thank me. I'm just looking out for my own interests."

Ben said, "Thanks anyway."

Ellis changed the subject. "Did you choose your weapon?"

"Go big—"

"—Or go home? I wish you could Ben. Truly. You sure you need a .600 for this? I mean, you must be more afraid of the shooter than what this gun will do to *you*. Kills on one end, maims on the other."

"I'm sure."

Ellis persisted. "It's not much good past two hundred yards. Doesn't seem like your best bet to take down a man. Not like a .338. Kind of unsniperly."

"I understand what you're saying. Thanks for worrying."

"You need a spotter."

"I need my lines of retreat protected."

Ellis regarded Ben, apprehension drawing at his features. "To hell with you, then. Drop me at the Sonesta."

The Unimog was solid on the rough roads from the airport into Avenida Balmaceda where the Sonesta Hotel rose into the starry sky. Ben said, "You think he's going to find me?"

Ellis was encouraging. "That's the idea, isn't it? It looks like you exfil'ed Los Angeles like a scalded owl, with a few flaps at amateur trade-craft to cover your line. Once he traces you down here, he'll get cocky, fig-ure you for a coward trying to drop off the face of the earth. When he knows where you really are, there will be fear, then worry. A rancid sweat will break. And all that happening in the next several hours. Good luck, you badass picaroon."

He strolled into the hotel lobby with his suitcase in tow.

Ben drove east out of Calama into the desert night.

CHAPTER 44

BEN'S UNIMOG CRAWLED over the lunar terrain to the edge of El Tatio. It was still dark, but the geyser field, the third largest in the world, was easily discerned by its hissing and roaring eruptions. He had trained here long ago on a joint exercise with members of Chile's elite 13th Commandos Company *Escorpión*.

Surrounded by volcanoes, many of them active, the field's water was heated by magma below the surface until it surged into the air in columns of wet steam. Ben shut the big truck down, collected his pack and weapon, and walked straight into the field. The sun would come up soon. Ben had to be ready.

He stepped with great care. There were places where the crust underfoot was thin, and might crumble and give way, dropping him into boiling mud or the scalding water below.

Ben had another reason to tread gently. He had been living at sea level for several years, in Maryland, and lately in New York City. He was now picking his way by starlight through a natural minefield at an elevation of nearly 14,000 feet. His head pounded from altitude sickness, and he felt nauseated, as if he were coming down with the flu. His heart rate was elevated well past the stress level of the task before him, and his breathing was rapid, even when he stood still to get his bearings. Dizziness threatened his every leaden step, but he kept picking his boots up and putting them down like an automaton.

In the dark, Ben was more certain of his path when he was near active fumaroles belching their low clouds of vapor, or jetting towers of white steam into the night. When the geysers lay quiet between eruptions, Ben had to slow down to hear the mud and water percolating just below him to avoid tumbling into the rocky ducts. The night air was below freezing, and after an instant of warmth, the steam that billowed up from the ground near his path left him damp and chilled.

As Ben walked, he worked hard to push down fear. He was armed and in a foreign country, as he had been many times before, but now his government offered him no support. If caught, he would be disavowed by any friendly diplomatic or consular authority, and abandoned to live out his life in a Chilean prison. If his prospects could be any worse, it was likely that an American operative was tracking him down for the kill. Ben was sick of getting backed into corners where he had to defend himself with violence. He was furious that he was forced to run to draw fire away from those he loved. He had left the service with every intention of living in harmony with others. Ben was beginning to think he carried this trace of death with him wherever he went.

He felt a moment of pride at his dead reckoning skills when one hour of careful trudging finally brought his objective into view. An abandoned geothermal power collection unit had been built on top of one of the hotter, more potent geysers in El Tatio field ten years before. The cost of moving energy from such a remote, hostile environment to where people lived and needed the power soon proved an unworkable investment. The tall gantries of vents, pipes, chimneys, and tanks were rusted to ruin in the geyser moisture. Corrosion was otherwise an oddity in the Atacama Desert, one of the most arid places on the planet.

Ben went straight for the derelict plant, hung his jacket among the pipes and braces, and left the Hambrusch's .338 barrel projecting forward in sight, but without the gun's stock attached. He knew that any sniper would try to find him among the power plant's shadowed mechanisms. Even if the structure had been ruled out as a hide, it would remain a distraction to the onlooker's subconscious. Like a Vegas magician, Ben understood that misdirection worked on many levels. For a moment, he considered swapping the .338 barrel for the .600 as Ellis had suggested. In the end, he kept to his original plan, and took the bigger barrel with him.

After setting up the decoy, Ben walked east from the power plant, finally bearing north, and taking a less obvious position at a lime-encrusted rock formation fifty yards closer to his entry point to the west. He lay down in a ground depression behind low scrub in front of the big rock. The air was cold, but the earth was warm from the geothermal energy surging just below the crust. If anyone studied the rock searching for Ben, they would be naturally be studying the rock's silhouette, for the head and shoulders of a man, a scope, and the barrel of his gun poking out from behind. Due west, in front of this formation, Ben would lie fully in the shadow cast by the rising sun.

Ben stashed his pack between himself and the rock. He placed a fresh egg taken from the Embraer's galley into a steaming rill running within arm's reach from a hot spring. Twenty minutes later, he had a hard-boiled breakfast.

He wondered if the shooter would take a run at him this morning after all. The trail from Los Angeles was obvious enough to a killer with such an enviable array of intelligence resources. Was he impatient to clash with Ben? Or would he wait until nightfall when the light advantage would reverse to favor someone looking east with the sun at his back.

There was also the question of tourists. Knocker Ellis Hogan's wealth would not buy Ben immunity if a hapless hiker visiting the geyser field was gunned down. Dawn was favored by tour guides because the sun shone through the steamy mist in an otherworldly way that improved the guides' tips, and helped tourists feel they had slipped the surly bonds of strip malls and gone somewhere fresh and interesting. As ever, Ben would need to make a positive, ironclad identification of his target before squeezing the trigger.

The sun rose, burying Ben's position in a growing shadow in front of the rock. The light crept down the slopes of the western volcanoes surrounding the geyser field, drawing his eye away from any approaching trouble on the ground. So much incredible, compelling natural beauty was proving to be a powerful distraction. Killing was easier in places Ben found ugly. For him, a setting devoid of scenery jibed better with the grim nature of the work. Yet again, he wondered how he had entangled himself in this maelstrom of lies, second guesses, and murder.

Ben noticed movement amidst the steaming fumaroles, sinters, and rock formations, about one hundred yards away. He led the shadow in his scope, and took up the trigger's slack. Four more shadows materialized in the steam. A light breeze, the first of the morning, pulled the veil of vapor back to reveal a small herd of llamas foraging among the scrub bushes. Ben let out his breath. His head still pounded with altitude sickness.

After a half an hour, the sun was beating through the geysers when they erupted, refracting and scattering the light as if emissaries of a star had landed to shine here for the morning.

Ben thought he saw a man slowly walking among the spouts. The range this time, two hundred yards, the extreme end of the .600's accuracy. Confirming the intruder's presence, the llamas spooked and trotted south away from the stalker. As often as not, the figure was obscured by the jets of steam in this fantasy realm, as well as by his circuitous passage among the distant rock formations. Ben put his scope on the man. The intruder carried a rifle. Ben watched the shooter take a kneeling position braced against a luminous calcareous sinter that looked molten, as if it would burn the man on contact. Ben figured there were few hikers up here with rifles, and little game of interest, excluding himself.

The kneeling man fired. The gun's single report cracked out again and again among the mountains. In the chorus of reverbs, Ben heard a bullet clang into the ruined geothermal equipment and spin away with a hornet's bombilations.

The shooter was probing a likely shadow the quick and dirty way, testing the decoy Ben had set up there, trying to draw him out. Another shot split the thin air, but this one came from Ben's right. The rifleman by the rock turned quickly and snapped off a shot. Another gunshot cracked out from Ben's right. Rock fragments must have broken from the sinter; the kneeling shooter dropped his gun and staggered away from cover, clutching the side of his head. Injured and disoriented, the shooter wandered a few steps onto a hillock of lava crust.

He could have held directly on his target with the .338, so flat was its trajectory at this range. At this distance, with this higher caliber weapon and its heavy load, Ben had to elevate the gun barrel to the point that it blocked out the intruder. Ben was shooting blind, more like a mortarman, than a sniper. He corrected for the range, and the slight breeze on instinct, and squeezed the trigger. The chubby, blunt .600 Nitro Express round streaked from the Hambrusch's barrel, treating Ben's shoulder to an angry mule's kick in parting. The slug described a lead rainbow through the air, then struck the ground one foot in front of the stalker. The thin lava dome fractured beneath him, and his own weight did the rest, shattering the rock like an eggshell. The man dropped into the earth. Ben heard his screams fly out among the mountains for several horrendous moments as the stalker scalded to death. The echoes made it sound like more than one man succumbing to agony and terror. Ben had heard this before, when three Iraqi insurgents had burned alive in a Mosul house fire rather than flee into the open where they knew Ben watched, his rifle trained in waiting. As in Iraq then, the shrieks sickened him now, even though they meant he had done his job.

The stalker was down, but Ben stayed in position. He was unsure of the second shooter to the right. Several minutes passed. Then Ben saw Ellis limp in from the south toward the shooter's last known position, carrying what looked to be the twin of Ben's Hambrusch rifle. Ben stood, slung the pack onto his shoulders, and tracked toward Ellis.

Ellis had bled heavily from a wound on the outside of his right thigh. Since getting hit, he had torn the pants leg open, and now held a QuikClot hemostatic dressing over the wound. A Hambrusch rifle, this one with the .338 Lapua Magnum barrel affixed to the bolt action and stock, was slung over his shoulder.

Ben said, "Nice gun."

"Never give a gift I wouldn't like to have myself. But I should hang it up. I didn't hit him. I thought he made you back in those works. I rushed the shot."

"You flushed him out."

"You flushed him to death. Look down there."

Ben peered carefully over the edge of the fractured lava dome. The body of a man lay with head, shoulders and chest pulled up onto a small ledge. The dead man's raw hands still gripped a small projection of lava, his fingertips scraped to the bone in the last moments of life as he tried to climb out of the superheated mud bubbling around him.

"Harsh, Ben. For God's sake, you could have just shot him."

"Sure, but then he'd look all shot," Ben said. "Now he looks unlucky. It's why I needed the big gun. Wasn't shooting a man."

Ellis gave a short, mordant chuckle. "You were shooting a whole damn planet."

"Here's the bad news. All our talk about how much lead time we had before they got onto us was pure bull. That's our pilot. He flew us here."

Ellis looked more closely at the body. The muddy white shirt was indeed decked with the captain's shoulder boards that many commercial pilots wore. "Damn! It's a pilot, but might not be ours."

Ben was disgusted with himself at having been deceived. "When did he take command?"

Ellis shrugged. "Hell if I know. The jet's original owner ordered the crew lavatory en suite to the flight deck so he wouldn't have to rub elbows with the help. Guess that backfired on me."

"Damn it Ellis, how did we miss that?"

"It's sloppy, I know. But we're still standing here, and he's down there."

"Hold on. Dope it out. Whoever's on to me has been on to *you* since Milan, or else this guy came aboard while you were on the ground in Los Angeles."

Ben picked up the dead man's rifle, a scoped Winchester 30-6, and dropped it into the fumarole next to the body. After collecting the elements of his decoy from the geothermic generation plant, he gave Ellis a shoulder to lean on. They slowly headed west out of the geyser field.

"This place reminds me of hell," Ellis said.

Ben walked in silence. Then he said, "We have a problem."

"Other than me getting nicked pretty good, I'd say we're okay. Ready to get back to the big city?"

"Hate to break it to you, Ellis, but that fellow back in the hole didn't kill Luz Calderon, or Grant."

It was Ellis's turn to fall silent. They trudged on.

Ben continued, "His stalk was bush league. His first shot at the old machinery revealed his position, which was obvious anyway. He was bored. He wasn't shooting at anything, least of all me."

"He got me," said Ellis.

"No, he got lucky with a snap shot. Maybe he hunts birds, the way he's quick like that, but he's no soldier. The proof is you're still alive. Kneeling a couple hundred yards like he was from you, the person who shot Grant would've drilled out your coconut. This guy couldn't qualify at a county fair shooting gallery. I murdered a rank amateur."

Ellis stopped walking. "Hold it. If I read you right, you'd feel fine if this guy had been a better shot? A better opponent? That is so fucked up, I don't know where to begin."

"This isn't war, Ellis. It's all dirty. There's no honor. It's not how we're supposed to do things. I'm going to say it, it's not *American*. I'm turning into a goddamn freelance terrorist."

"I've seen you get like this—"

"You want to make something of it?" Ben's voice had a serrated edge.

"I was going to say if you didn't feel this way, I'd be afraid of you. Afraid *for* you. I'm glad you're my friend."

They made slow progress, picking their way more carefully now that the weight of two men was concentrated over fragile lava tubes where only one man would wisely walk.

They returned to the road and found the Unimog, and a blue Jeep CJ7. Ben said, "Please don't tell me the Jeep is yours, and the shooter hitched a ride with you?"

Ellis was in pain, and not given to quips. "I got a lift from the night bookkeeper at the hotel. That Jeep must be the pilot's ride."

Ben examined the Unimog, the undercarriage, the engine compartment, fuel tank, and the seating. No triggers. No explosives. The brake and fuel lines were intact.

Ellis said, "Cocky. Thought he would get you, zip-zap-zoop, and be done. Maybe get himself a new truck in the bargain."

Ben fired up the Unimog, then helped Ellis into the passenger seat. He broke Ellis's Hambrusch rifle down and stowed it. He wrapped his own rifle in his coat, and handed it to Ellis.

As they drove to the airport, Ellis said, "There was a copilot."

"Let's hope there still is."

CHAPTER 45

THE SAME CUSTOMS officer who had welcomed Ben and Ellis six hours before hopped on the Unimog's running board at the airport to ease their way through two barricades to the Embraer's remote parking area. With paperwork swiftly attended to, and a pocket bulging with fresh cash, the officer drove away.

Ben boarded the aircraft and turned left through a bulkhead door toward the flight deck and crew rest area. The crew lavatory door was unlocked. Ben opened it. A blond man in his late twenties lay unconscious, bound with several obese passenger seatbelt extensions, and gagged with a cloth rag and oxygen tubing from the overhead mask. He snored loudly on the toilet. His white shirt bore the epaulet bars of a first officer. Ben freed him, and with a few shouts, slaps, and shoulder shakes, the copilot slowly regained consciousness.

Ben helped Ellis board the jet and found the first officer struggling to make a pot of coffee in the galley. He was still mocus, slurred his speech like a drunk. Likely he had been drugged by the man they had killed in El Tatio.

Once he was sure the copilot could manage his coffee mug with both hands, Ben descended to the tarmac and circled to the plane's external cargo hold. He opened it and found the captain. Ben checked for a pulse, and after observing the mottled skin, judged the man had been drugged during his preflight walk-around in Los Angeles, and had not survived their long trip at Flight Level 36, or 36,000 feet, in the super-chilled, unpressurized hold. He looked around the airport for a suitable place for the captain's remains, and finding none, simply left the dead man where he found him, and closed the cargo compartment door. There was no denying the simple fact that the flight home couldn't hurt him any worse.

CHAPTER 46

A CAFFEINE INFUSION slowly stirred the recently promoted captain back to life. He did not make a heroic recovery, but revived sufficiently to oversee the Embraer's refueling. Then he filed a flight plan back to Los Angeles.

Ellis's wound stopped bleeding within half an hour of takeoff. After making sure his friend was comfortable for the trip, Ben sat in the cockpit's right seat. He asked the new captain, whose name was Dale Engstrom, what had happened to him and his former boss. He had already asked Dale for the story twice before. With each recitation of the facts, Ben hoped to find Dale's involuntary sedation clearing. He needed to learn additional details Engstrom might have forgotten in the haze, and wanted to verify he was lucid enough to fly. Ben also wanted to gauge whether Dale was clean, or part of the pall of filth that seemed to follow him wherever he went.

"What did your replacement captain call himself?" Ben asked.

"Bill. Said he was Bill Wilson. Back in L.A., Bill shows up on the flight deck and tells me that Evan, I mean Captain Voskamp, the pilot I flew in with from Milan, said he'd been called away suddenly on a family emergency, and Bill would be pilot-in-command, wherever the client wanted to go. I told him that didn't sound right, mostly because I've been flying with Evan for two years, and he doesn't have any family. And if he was called away, why'd he leave his flight bag and carry-on in the cockpit?" Dale pointed to the bags in an open locker. "Then Bill gets this look in his eye, and then he acts like he sees something weird over my shoulder. I turn to see what it was. Oldest trick in the book. I feel a sting in my neck. Next thing I know, I've got a migraine, we're in Chile, and you're slapping me around like it's a first date."

"How long after he introduced himself did he drug you?"

"What's it matter? Less than a minute. And no, not long enough to figure out *Bill Wilson* wasn't his real name, if that's what you're asking. So where's old Bill now?"

"Family emergency."

Dale took that in. "And Captain Voskamp? He's where? In Los Angeles?"

"No. Sorry. He's not anywhere."

Dale shot Ben a quizzical look. "I don't follow."

"Okay Dale, you need to sack-up for some hard news. Your friend's currently in the external cargo hold. In L.A., Bill Wilson overpowered him first, probably doped him, and then stuffed him in there. Cold and altitude did the rest. He probably didn't feel a thing, if it's any consolation."

Dale's face blanched with anger. "I'll ask you again. Where's the guy who did that to the captain?"

Ben spoke evenly, "In a very warm place. Never coming back. Let it go."

Impotent rage and resignation vied for command of Dale's emotions. "Who are you people? I mean, Mr. Hogan's hurt pretty bad."

Ben ducked the question. "Can you fly this thing back to the States?"

"If you keep the coffee and aspirin coming, I'll be good. But I'm not flying you anywhere."

"You're staying here? You have family in Chile?"

"You left a friend of mine dead in a cargo hold."

Ben grew impatient. "Dale, I appreciate your loyalty. Your esprit de corps, and all that. Commendable, sure enough. But we need to get Stateside. All of us. If you start hollering here, and turn up with a body on your plane under suspicious circumstances, you'll spend the next year in a jail fielding questions you don't have answers to. So fly the plane. It's what you do. Mr. Hogan back there is rich. You will be paid like crazy. Get your buddy back home to an American grave."

Dale thought about it. "Los Angeles, and no further."

Ben said, "Okay. But just so's you know, Dale, if we have a problem with you, if I find out you're a friend of Bill, I'll choke you out cold, and then some."

"Then who lands the plane?"

"Same as always, Dale: *gravity*." Ben did not elaborate on the thought. Dale's expression said he did not need to.

CHAPTER 47

DURING THE TAKEOFF, the coffee did its job, and the pilot did his.

Ben joined Ellis in the main cabin. His friend was ashen with pain. Though a few Percocets were meandering their way through his bloodstream, they had not yet hit in earnest.

Ben got to the point. "How did we get out of that geyser field alive?"

Ellis squinted at Ben. "Trick question?"

"Put it like this: how come when that guy, whose go-by was *Bill Wilson,* how come when Bill was dead in that hole, we just figured the shooting was over? You gimped right into the open easy as pie."

Ellis's expression darkened. "Either you think I'm in on it—"

The question had crossed Ben's mind. Ellis had arrived very quickly in Los Angeles from half a world away. Ben had placed only one call to Smith Island before leaving New York City, to make sure the studio lair was cleaned out of gold and other precious or incriminating items in his absence. How had Ellis learned of this mission? Had Ben's Smith Island contact alerted Ellis to help him once again? That was the only possibility Ben cared to entertain, but there were other more nefarious ways for Ellis to get wind of his trouble.

"I'm sure you're not in on it," Ben said.

"It's that, or you and I have both started dancing to a strange rhythm."

"That's more like what I'm thinking. When Grant was killed on that roof, MacCready strutted out into plain sight, right in the kill zone. But no more shooting. Not a hair on his head grazed. And today, when that airdale, Bill, went down the mud hole, you walked out into the open, and then I walked out. And nothing. Quiet."

"We were damn stupid when you think about it."

"Extremely. We both know better. Who's to say there weren't five more men supporting the first one? If he was a genuine sniper, there would have been a spotter at least."

Ellis shifted his weight in the chaise, easing pain in his leg. "Something about mud-man's amateur ways put us at ease?"

"We're assuming the shooter in L.A. acted alone. We're both assuming that any *other* tactical operator we meet on this detail is likewise acting alone, when all our training says *pairs*, at a minimum."

"Prolly took a team to build that shed and haul that gun to the roof, even if it was done in small pieces in off-hours. Yes, the exfil' from out them geysers could have been bad for our health."

"But it wasn't. We got the guy. The *only* guy." Conning this puzzle began to banish Ben's fatigue. "Mud-man had no tactical support. And he didn't get onto the Atacama because he followed after us thanks to some highfalutin strategic digital tracking we know of, but because he was sitting right up front on this plane, flying the damn thing himself the whole way."

Ellis's voice was softening as the Percocets began to work. "Low-tech. They were onto me sooner than I thought."

"That supergun on the roof in L.A. was state-of-the-art." Ben thought out loud, hoping something would gel in his own mind though Ellis drifted off. "The Dallas tableau in the building by the Dolby Theatre, that's highly organized stuff. Overkill."

"Evolutions," mumbled Ellis.

"Come again?"

"Like basic training," Ellis slurred. "Do an exercise, finish it, and it ends. Rest a minute, then comes the next training element."

"But the geyser guy was a punk."

"He was your rest interval. Put it like this. He was the *entr'acte* between headliners. And that L.A. shooter? He's waiting for the main event."

CHAPTER 48

MACCREADY'S HOTEL ROOM at the Beverly Hilton reeked of opulence, and good marijuana. An unusually corrosive level of contact with Department of Homeland Security Secretary Lily Morgan was wearing him down, and a few luxuries went a long way toward compensating for the unpleasantness.

He had enjoyed a bath and an in-room massage. A split of champagne chilled in an ice bucket while he rolled and lit another joint. Reveling in the delicious plush terry of the hotel bathrobe, he felt restored enough to dial the number that by now was etched on the inside of his skull.

"The new guy's not coming along," he said.

"It's the old guy everybody's interested in," Lily snapped. "Myself included. Got a line on that fucktard yet?"

"Not exactly. I've tried to reach out, but he's not responding."

Secretary Morgan tried to be helpful. "Did you offer money? A nice juicy new gig? Lure him in that way."

"Tried it. Seems he's not falling for it. He's been with us for so long, I think he knows all the angles."

MacCready looked over toward his suite's bedroom doors, and gave a start. Ben Blackshaw loomed there. A muscular, older black man with a cane stood at his side. Ben held a pistol loosely in his bear paw of a hand.

"Madame Lil', a couple of leprechauns just dropped in," MacCready said.

"Damn, those little bastards are everywhere. Call me back!"

MacCready broke the line, remained seated, and leaned back in his chair. "Howdy boys."

"Ellis, meet MacCready," Ben said.

Ellis said, "Hi, MacCready. What's your first name?"

"Just MacCready."

"Like Cher," Ben added.

"But bigger tits," Ellis said.

MacCready bridled, stood, "How much of that did you hear?"

"Enough," Ben acknowledged. "The *new guy*? Who's that? Reckon you interest me, MacCready."

The stout handler crossed to the balcony. "How was Chile?"

"Aw, I sent you a postcard," said Ben. "Didn't you get it?"

MacCready glanced over his shoulder. "The gun. Put it away. I work for you. Haven't you figured that out yet?"

"Fire him, Ben," said Ellis. "He makes the world a hostile work environment."

"In due course. Where's the operator who killed the singer, and Grant?"

MacCready said, "You first. Where's the agent who went south with you?"

"His name is mud," Ellis said. "You know him?"

"He was *not* one of ours. A sub-contractor. I didn't approve him." MacCready looked at Ben and held out his hands palm-up, then jabbed a thumb toward Ellis. "Who's Uncle Tom?"

It looked as though Ben flicked the pistol an instant before it fired. The plush furnishings and treatments ate up the report as they were designed to do. MacCready howled and leaped into the air. He fell hard to the floor gripping his left foot with both hands, blood flowing from the empty place where his big toe had been abruptly detached.

"God dammit! What the fuck! Jesus! Ow, shit!"

Ellis flinched. "Damn, Ben!" He picked up the burning joint from where MacCready dropped it, and tossed it in the wetbar sink.

Ben said, "Sorry. Just went off. Accident."

MacCready roared, "Jesus! What the hell! Where is it? Where's my goddamn toe?"

"I saw something fly under the bed," said Ellis as he limped into the bathroom. He returned as quickly as his own injury allowed with a thick white towel which he tossed to MacCready.

Ben sat down in the chair MacCready formerly occupied. "What did Grant tell you about that business at Pyramid Lake?"

"Fuck you!"

Clearing his throat, Ben languidly let the barrel of his pistol point at MacCready's other foot. MacCready was frantic and distracted, but he got the message.

"Yemeni al-Qaeda sleeper cell," MacCready grunted. "In place in Reno for six years. We were planning to bust them all, but Grant wanted to impress the boss. So he tipped them some intel. Your flight path. The freqs and encryption for the drone's controls. And then he let you handle the whole problem. Saved everyone a lot of court costs—and dicey press."

After a moment taking this in, Ben said, "Let me ask you again. How do you get in touch with the shooter?" He had already tried the phone number from the newspaper for the second time. Again there was no answer, and still no voicemail set up on that line.

MacCready rolled on the floor, the rictus of pain twisting his face. "Oh my God!" He tried to hold the towel in place with one hand while rooting under the bed for his missing digit with the other.

Ellis extracted a bottle of mineral water from the suite's refrigerator, and twisted off the plastic top. MacCready held out his hand for the bottle. But Ellis took a swig and sat down on the edge of the bed. "Getting shot makes you thirsty, doesn't it? I took one in the leg along about sunrise this very day, and I could drink a hundred gallons. Oh and it smarts like fuck-all, too."

MacCready howled in frustration, and plunged his arm back under the bed.

"Flesh wound," said Ben.

"My flesh, wasn't it?" Ellis protested. "Don't you mock a man's pain."

"MacCready, you need to talk faster, and get some medical treatment before you bleed out," warned Ben. "You look pale, doncha know."

The bath towel MacCready wrapped around his foot was saturating red. "You are in fuck-tons of trouble right now!" he sneered.

"Would that be metric, or imperial fuck-tons?" Ellis asked.

Ben said, "How exactly do you reach this guy?"

Spit flecked on MacCready's mouth. "Do you have any idea who I work for?"

Ben looked at Ellis. "Didn't he just say he worked for me?" Ellis shrugged.

MacCready pleaded, "So thirsty—Got it!" MacCready held up the toe with a pain-crazed look of victory in his eye. He spilled the melted water out of the ice bucket and dropped the toe in. "Sew it back—" Again, he tried to wrap his foot with the towel. The blood was running scarlet.

Ellis took another swig from the bottle and held it out to MacCready. MacCready reached for the bottle with blood-drenched fingers. Ellis drew it back. "Quit rolling around on the floor, man! Tell us how to contact the shooter, and you can have water and beer, hookers and doctors, and pain-killers, too. Take care of that foot problem."

"Are you nuts? You can't kill that guy. He's—he's a national security asset."

"So we're agreed you know who he is," Ben said. "He reports to you. You knew he was going to hit the singer and Grant."

"No! Grant must have been a mistake. The shooter was just supposed to engage you on that roof. We were really setting *him* up."

"You're light-headed," said Ben. "You're not making sense."

MacCready reached a gory hand toward Ellis's bottle. "Water goddammit!"

Ellis warned, "Language," and did not budge.

"He was supposed to *engage* me?" Ben pressed.

MacCready rolled onto his side still holding the towel to his foot. "Grant said you'd be more likely to stay if—if the operator took a couple shots at you. You'd stay, and you'd get the guy for us. But everything's changed. You can't kill him now. Now we need him alive."

Ben sorted the paradox out loud. "You gave the shooter instructions to throw down on that roof, to set it up for *me* to go after this same shooter, which is what Grant wanted me to do anyway, but without setting me up."

"No," said Ellis. "It sounds like Grant set you up for the lake."

"Exactly!" shouted MacCready.

"This whole thing is nuts," marveled Ellis.

"The shooter's going to be retired from active duty," MacCready went on. "He's got very serious mental health issues. You *were* going to—to take him down, and—" He stopped talking.

Ellis shook the few sips of water remaining in the bottle to tantalize MacCready, "And what?"

"And then Grant was going to hire *you* to fill the vacancy." MacCready pointed hard at Ben, flicking blood off his fingertip.

Ben and Ellis exchanged incredulous glances. "And what's the job description exactly?" Ben asked.

"Make headlines!"

CHAPTER 49

BEN HANDED ELLIS a warm paper-wrapped bundle from the bag of takeout food. They were holed up at the Renaissance Hotel, in the penthouse. Ben figured that MacCready would not expect him to retrace his steps to the first place Grant had billeted him. In retrospect, Ben had no idea how much Grant had briefed MacCready of the details of his arrival in Los Angeles an eternity ago. At least, Ben believed, MacCready would not suss out where they were for several hours, provided the pain killers afforded the nine-toed bureaucrat with anything like clear thinking.

Song, the desk clerk who had checked Ben in the last time he visited the Renaissance, made no sign of recognition. Nor did she balk at the large, heavy, wheeled steamer trunk vented with air-holes that Ben and Ellis brought with them. Because Dale's sedated body made the trunk heavy, Ben availed himself of a bellman's cart, but once again, no bellman.

In the room, they both stared like wolves at the sandwich wrappers, and carefully unclothed the burgers within. Ben sniffed his, and got a wistful look on his face. "I would kill for a helping of roast goose right about now."

Ellis took a bite of the hamburger and set it aside. "LuAnna made a fine oyster fritter, didn't she? Before everything happened."

Ben could say nothing. Any talk of his wife, and particularly of her exploits in the kitchen, was too painful to contemplate. Ben was a long way from home and felt it all the more acutely with every mouthful of fast food.

Ellis put the newspapers they had taken from MacCready's hotel room at the Hilton onto the penthouse's large conference table. He started with the *Los Angeles Times*.

Ellis said, "A man my age, I like to start with the obit's. Make sure I'm not there." A moment later, he angled the newspaper toward Ben, and said, "Damn. MacCready's got some juice."

Ben scanned the false reports of the deaths of Grant, Strahan, and Dario. Disgusted, he spat his mouthful of burger into a trashcan.

Ellis turned to the classifieds.

Ben threw the rest of the burger away. "I'm still ticked we wrecked the one phone that the shooter had a fix on."

"I know," said Ellis. "He foxed us, sending in the relief pitcher. You had the right idea, trying to draw him off. Should have worked." He kept up his scan of the small ads while he talked. Then Ellis read aloud, **"BB2AM Caca dau! Nitro Express"**

"That's definitely him!" Ben said. "What's *caca dau?*"

"I haven't the faintest notion."

Ben knew from hard-won lessons when Ellis was telling the truth, and when he was hedging. "It's Vietnamese, isn't it? The way you said it, I can tell you've said it before, with the right accent and all. What does it mean?"

Ellis relented, "It means, 'I'll kill you.' Nothing we didn't know before. What do you think he's doing?"

"MacCready said the shooter has mental problems."

"We could have asked him more about the situation if he hadn't passed out."

Ben was irritated by Ellis's dig. "He wouldn't have told us anything at all if I hadn't got his attention."

"Just surprised me, is all," Ellis said. "Not like you to—"

"To *what?* I had to move things along. I know you like to play the heavy. Didn't mean to step on your toes."

"No pun intended, I'm sure." Ellis turned to the next classified page and ran a gnarled finger down the first column. "Oh boy. Okay Ben, what does *Kasumigaseki* mean to you?"

"Not a blessed thing."

Ellis penned a circle around the classified ad, and showed Ben. The salutation was there. **BB2AM**. Then the word **KASUMIGASEKI**. And the signoff, **Nitro Express**. Ben shook his head. *No idea.*

Retrieving a laptop they'd bought that afternoon, Ellis booted it up. He typed the word into a search engine. "It's Japanese. Means the *Gate of Fog*. In Tokyo, it's where the cabinet ministries are mostly located. And it's the name of a Tokyo metro stop."

"You think that's where Nitro Express wants to meet up?"

"The metro station was one of the ones hit in the Sarin attack by that cult in 1995," said Ellis. "Five days before that, the same cult tried to spread a botulin attack there. This Nitro Express dude likes drama."

"And retro crime scenes. What's wrong with this guy? He's got too many frequent flyer miles or something. Can your plane get us there?"

Ellis walked over to a closet, and pulled open the door. Dale Engstrom, the pilot, lay groggy on the closet floor next to the vented steamer trunk, bound at the wrists and ankles with zip ties. Though gagged with duct tape, his eyes spoke of burgeoning fury.

Ellis said, "Good morning, Dale. You hungry?"

Dale hesitated, then nodded.

"How you feel about sushi?"

CHAPTER 50

THE EMBRAER FLEW for an hour before Ellis returned from checking gear in the aft onboard luggage space and noticed that Ben was sitting upright with eyes closed. His friend was not asleep. Ben's body was not lax in the way of repose. His muscles were still quickened with life, but his vitality was focused inward. Ellis said nothing to disturb the contemplation. The dead captain's remains had been removed from the cargo hold the day before by two local men who valued Ellis's cash flow, especially when a significant part of it streamed in their direction.

"This is bullshit," Ben said, opening his eyes.

Ellis creased an indulgent, inquisitive look onto his face, and waited.

Ben was angry. "We're on a jet. Again. Before, we were trying to lead this Nitro Express shooter someplace away from populated areas."

"Which we managed to do," Ellis threw in. "But the dude in Chile wasn't the shooter we are looking for. He was a proxy. A place holder who kept us busy, presented a real-enough threat, made us feel productive, but not much more. We're pretty sure we have no hostiles aboard this time?"

"Cap'n Dale's pissed as hell about his treatment, but you saw him. He was *not* understanding the urgency. We'll settle up with him in a way that helps him forgive and forget. Meantime, we're heading to a very populated area where this Nitro Express guy wants to square off. What if we change course now?"

"MacCready will let him know we are not headed to Tokyo. MacCready doesn't like you very much." Ellis's eyes lit with new understanding. "And that's why you shot his toe off. So he would continue to help Nitro Express, not you."

"You got it. So the shooter can follow us. He'll take MacCready's help, but I'm not a hundred percent sure this guy is marching to MacCready's drum anymore."

"MacCready said this fellow had mental problems. That doesn't always make somebody a pushover."

"That's the first thing any bureaucrat says when somebody disagrees with him, or disobeys," said Ben. "This one's crazy, or that one's not well. It's as much a cliché as resigning to spend more time with family. This feels like a mop-up operation for something. I wonder if Nitro Express got ahold of some intel he shouldn't have. You don't put a good gun-hand down for no reason."

Ellis chuckled. "You think he's going to chat with you? Have a feast of reason and a flow of soul over some warm sake?"

"Ask Dale if he wouldn't mind refiling for Wakeham Bay, up in Quebec, most direct route," Ben said. "I think we'll need a couple fuel stops along the way. The moon's just about full, which will help me. If Nitro Express doesn't tag along, we'll try something else."

Ellis tapped the keys of his laptop. "Ben, that's on the Hudson Strait. Above the Arctic Circle! What the hell is way up there, *eh?*" Ellis's philosophy and fatigue, interwoven with painkillers, had made him as close to silly as he would ever be.

"A quiet place to kill. Or be killed."

CHAPTER 51

WAKEHAM BAY AIRPORT had a single gravel runway, laid out along the magnetic azimuth 15/33 of the compass. On touchdown, the jet yawed a few degrees on either side of the runway centerline until the thrust reversers slowed it enough to make mechanical braking safer. On rollout, the noise of pebbles blasting up from the landing gear onto the Embraer's belly was terrifying.

Dale checked the damage after landing, and refused to fly the aircraft again. No tires blew, but the nose wheel sidewalls were scored deeply enough to be dangerous. He went on about Foreign Object Debris ingested by the engines. Here above the Arctic Circle, the local fixed base operator was not equipped to handle repairs of aircraft heavier than Cessnas, and deHavilland Otters, Beavers, and Aviat Huskies.

Hopping-mad airport management threatened to call various authorities because of the Embraer's deep rutting of the strip. Ellis's thinning bankroll bought them a respite with Customs, but very little goodwill. Dale was paid off handsomely, and stayed at the field to find a seat on the next plane out. This was not a graceful entry into town.

An elderly Inuit woman drove Ben and Ellis, their gear, and what little food and drink was left in the aircraft's galley, into the village of seven hundred souls. The place was quiet, with broad and dusty streets leading to the bay itself. Rounded highlands surrounded the hamlet to the north and south, and sloped to the stony shore. The houses were all built for warmth.

Many were maintained with scavenged materials. There was a whiff of the shantytown in the atmosphere.

The two men put up at the Wakeham Bay Hotel, a seven-room outfit with twin beds, and common showers and lavatories. They bunkered in the room for the night, avoiding a visit to the town's cooperative for chow. Ellis's leg was aflame from getting grazed the previous morning. True to form, the wound was more excruciating, not less, on the second day, despite an infusion of pain meds better suited to a rhinoceros with an abscessed tooth.

They noted two aircraft arrivals at the field. One was a small, single-engine plane by the sound of it. The other was a twin turbo, on the lighter side, maybe a Beechcraft King Air.

"He's here," Ben said.

Ellis scratched at his stubble. "Last time we decamped Los Angeles, he sent a substitute along."

"That was a test. This whole business is a damn test. MacCready calling this shooter a national asset? Why? And why should we keep him alive all of a sudden? Why change gears like that? Reckon everybody upstream of the problem is flat out confused. Everybody downstream, meaning you, me, and this shooter too, we just want to wrap up this detail and get home."

"Amen," said Ellis.

They dropped off to sleep for a few hours. Ben rose long before the sun, snacked on food that was getting to be past its prime, and shrugged into his jacket. Ellis stirred and sat up on his elbow.

"I'm going for a walk. Progging by the water."

"Hold on." Ellis swung his legs stiffly off the bed and put his feet on the floor. He took a breath and tried to stand. "Whoah. Damn, that ain't working."

"You sit tight. Back in an hour or two." Ben shut the door.

He walked to a repair garage he had noticed on the way into town from the airfield. The mechanic, a grizzled white man in his sixties, was already on duty under the hood of an old pick-up truck. A greasy shirt, striped like old mattress ticking, bore a patch with the name *Alan* stitched on it.

Ben's introduction earned him no more than a glance from the mechanic. "I need a car for a few hours."

Alan cocked his head to the side. "Drive half an hour in any direction, and you'll come to the end of whatever road you're on."

"Still, a few hours at most. See the sights. The tide going out is a wonder, so I'm told."

"I'm working on my truck here, but it's not ready. Drive stick?"

"That I do."

Alan appraised his customer. "Five hundred dollars."

"Pretty steep."

Alan swept his eyes over Ben and went back to work under the truck's hood.

"I have a hundred," said Ben.

"You have a goddamn jet. A broke-down jet, but it's a jet airplane all the same."

Ben took a sheaf of bills from his pocket. There would be no disputing this kind of logic, and time was wasting.

Alan pocketed the money, led Ben around the side of the garage to a detached shed, and pulled open the door. Ben peered into the darkness. Something was looking back at him from the depths of the garage bay. Alan switched on an overhead light.

A time machine roared forward toward Ben from another age of motoring. Two large headlights bracketed a chrome V-twin engine like silver eyes. The sleek, gleaming red body was slung between the two open fender-and-spoke front wheels, and drew Ben's eye past a small windscreen, and a two-seat leather cockpit, arriving at a gentle boat-tail apex that seemed too narrow to cowl a pair of drive wheels.

"Where's the rest of her?" Ben asked.

Alan squinted at the uncouth Philistine standing before him. "She's a Morgan 3 Wheeler."

"For Christ's sake! Does she run?"

"I took delivery of her brand new just last year. Retirement present to myself, except I forgot to retire. And yes, she goes like hell. But that'll be three hundred bucks more. Not sure a fool like you should be allowed to have this kind of fun."

After taking another hard look at this fascinating whip, Ben shut his mouth and forked over the surcharge.

The five-speed gearbox offered simple, smooth shifting as Ben maneuvered the 3 Wheeler through town toward the water. When he reached the frozen shore, he turned south on the narrow coast road, and pressed the accelerator down. The V-Twin S&S X-Wedge engine growled, hurling Ben forward. As the freezing wind cut through every stitch of his coat and clothing, he felt the fatigue of the last three days peel away. The road blurred as it rushed past, and Ben found a strange moment of peace in the speed, snarl, and chill.

Too soon, Ben ran out of road. He braked the Morgan to a stop in a cul-de-sac. To his left, ice encrusted Wakeham Bay as far as he could see. With a heart full of regret, he pressed the dashboard button. The engine fell silent, like a lioness that had spied worthy prey. The quiet was not empty. To Ben, it was the harbinger of the hunt; the caesura before the slaughter.

CHAPTER 52

THE TIDE EBBED into the Hudson Strait with incredible speed. Ben discovered he was not the only one picking his way along the shore. Several Inuit families also studied the pack ice as it fractured into plates and dropped away from the full flood heights of an hour before.

The Inuits were waiting for the tide to ebb completely. Even in late winter, with the moon full, Ben knew the tide waters of the bay could plummet nearly forty feet. With the sea rushing out from underneath, the ice would ruck and rear into vaulted passages giving the courageous residents direct access to the sea floor where mussels lay just below the newly exposed bottom. The tasty eating was worth the risk, but the harvest had to be fast. Access to the bounty lasted only a half hour at best before the waters returned, flooding the new chambers, shifting the stranded floes as they regained buoyancy, and sometimes crushing or drowning hungry men who lingered too long to collect a few more delicious bivalves.

Perhaps sensing Ben's darker purpose, the Inuits gave him a wide berth. Ben glanced over his shoulder twice, and saw no one who seemed out of place in the vast waste.

Another thirty minutes of walking put more distance between himself and the Inuits. One more glance back stretched into a study. Now someone was there, one hundred yards down the shore; standing still on the ice in the shadow of an arching rock. Ben could not get a clear look at the figure. All around him, the huge frozen slabs groaned and popped like gunshots as they fractured and settled lower. One plate of ice split near Ben's feet. He stepped aside to avoid tumbling under the newly formed block. A moment later, Ben wondered if he had blinked and missed something, or whether he had imagined seeing the lone watcher in the first place. Now the ice was empty.

Ben glanced to his right, and saw a crevasse yawn open in the ice revealing cracked crystalline teeth. From his coat pocket, he took an emergency flashlight pilfered from the Embraer. He knelt, and drew the Bersa. Now was the time. This was the place. Ben stayed low, took four quick steps farther out onto the flow, and slid down the new ice face into a dark cold maw.

CHAPTER 53

THE ICY LABYRINTH glimmered in those thinner reaches above Ben where sunlight struck the peaks of upthrust slabs and refracted the light down to the bay's floor where he crept. The alluvial reek bloomed heavily from the freshly exposed sea bottom. He took a few further steps, then stopped to listen. Only the ice groaned and growled around him.

He pressed forward, now ducking below frozen arches, now scrambling over slanted, shattered floes as large as half a basketball court that had slid under neighboring tablets waiting for a giant god's inscription with new laws to be erased and forgotten in the melt.

Ben stopped again to listen. The ice tectonics had gone silent. Now he heard nothing but a slight trickle of water. The tide was at full ebb. His heartbeat quickened. He had about thirty minutes to complete the mission, and find a way back on top of the ice before he was pulverized or drowned. Ahead, he saw a light flicker. He scented greasy smoke. He pushed carefully around a block of ice. There, he found an Inuit man kneeling on the bottom next to a kerosene lantern, filling a pail with mussels he scraped from the chilly mud.

"Nice day for it," Ben muttered.

The Inuit stared at Ben who stepped past him through the narrow frozen corridor. The expression on the native's face was comment enough on Ben's sanity.

Ben himself wondered if he were chasing a phantom, risking his life for no other reason than to avenge a dead man who was past all caring, or simply to wreck some undertaking of MacCready's for nothing more than the principle of the thing.

He saw a shadow behind an ice wall to his right and fired the Bersa before he could even think of the consequences. The bullet smashed the ice, fractured it. A spider web of fissures radiated from the impact point, and the wall began to settle under the weight of the ice table overhead. Ben dived through an opening into another chamber, lost the pistol, but kept moving, hoping the more vertical ice sheets would save him from a cave-in. The void in which he had shot the gun collapsed behind him with the thunder of cannon fire.

He pressed ahead, and scrambled straight into a solid barrier of ice with no opening. The chamber was deep enough below the surface that no sunlight reached it. Ben played the flashlight over the frozen, mud-daubed wall. The beam of light faltered. Ben rapped the flashlight against the ice four times to knock corrosion off the battery contacts and revive the light.

Ben heard four distant raps on the ice in front of him, as if in answer. He said, "Is that you?"

No one answered. Ben thought the taps must have been a freak echo. Then, a soft voice, muffled through an unknown thickness of ice, replied, "Hello Bravo-Bravo-2-Alpha-Mike. I don't know. Is it me? I can't be sure these days."

In the arctic netherworld, Ben found that sound was nearly impossible to triangulate, but something made him turn to his left and look down. Lost in the shadows at the bottom of the ice wall was a narrow depression in the mud.

Ben crept quietly toward the depression. "Kinda existential for a killer, doncha reckon?"

"The absurdity of my existence is becoming more difficult to bear."

"I can help you with that. You murdered an old friend of mine, and a cop."

Ben switched off the flashlight. He was unsure if its feeble beam would betray his position through the ice wall, nor if that mattered. He felt for the depression, peeled off his coat, and crawled into the cold, wet flume, pushing mussels from his path as best he could. Old empty shells sliced into his fingers and palms.

He was head and shoulders into the tunnel when he heard the voice from just ahead, "I can hear you scuttling across the floors of silent seas like a pair of ragged claws. Grant was my friend, too. We worked together for years, but he was suffering terribly. The cancer."

"You shot him out of mercy?"

"Compassion. We're part of the same family, Ben. I would do the same for you."

"I don't intend to give you the chance."

Ben burrowed, squirming deeper into the tunnel. There was absolutely no light. The mud and clay greased his way below. The ice slab was so cold it felt as though it burned his back as he passed beneath it. Ben hated tight spaces. Tight, cold, dark spaces were a trifecta of horrors for him. His SEAL training helped push him along, and he despised this murderer far more than he was afraid. He inch-wormed forward using his toes to push, and his hands and elbows to pull himself deeper in.

"Okay," said the voice. "But you don't have much time. The tide's coming back in for both of us."

The killer was right. There was now an inch of water at the bottom of the tunnel through which he was sandhogging. The second proof of the tide's return was not the growing sensation of cold water, but an event. The enormous slab of ice above Ben lifted away from him. It did not rise a great deal. Two inches, no more. Nor did it rise for very long. After a moment of enjoying the little bit of extra space, in which Ben took two deeper breaths than he had managed before now, the ice slab settled again. It dropped down hard, and much lower than before, pressing Ben into the mud, pinning him. He panted, snorting and sputtering, and could barely lift his mouth and nose out of the wet ooze for air.

Water flowed into the cramped, frigid half-pipe. The voice was muffled, drifting farther away in the narrowing, sodden acoustics of the tunnel. Ben could not be sure what he heard, but it sounded like, "The dreams, Ben Blackshaw. The dreams might kill me before you do."

Ben felt a hand rooting and scrabbling in the mud ahead of him. It grabbed his right hand, and nearly yanked his shoulder out of its socket. Like a neonate in an icy primordial birth, Ben was hauled forward into a new chamber, with a wet flatulent sucking noise. A gray light seeped in from above. Ben choked, coughed, spitting mud and grit from his mouth, snorting it out of his nostrils, digging it quickly from his eyes. He groped for his flashlight, but it was lost under the ice behind him, along with his knife. Unable to see well, he suppressed all the convulsive urges to cough and shiver, held as still as possible, and listened.

Now the plates of ice in the bay were beginning to shift, grind, and groan again as the tide flooded back. In the next several hours, the rifts between the slabs would be remodeled and refrozen, cementing the fragmented field into a solid sheet again. Ben heard the massive movements all around him, but sensed he was alone in this new chamber.

He followed the only apparent escape route through a narrow gap that, if he still had his sense of direction, led straight out toward deep water away from the safety of shore. He pushed through the gap into another chamber with ice slabs shifting above and below; in the next moment, the lead through which he had just passed crunched closed with the sound of a demolished building rumbling down to earth.

Ben dodged around cold shifting surfaces, scrambling forward, and nearly died a dozen times slipping into deeper chasms. The side walls slid past each other with a roar; great cold molars tried to chew him to pulp. While he searched for a way back to the surface and the air, he also kept a sharp eye out for the killer. The passages seemed ever-changing. He wondered if he truly followed his opponent, or if the wrenching underscape of ice was steering him to new alleyways.

Now water surged and rushed in below him. In one instant, the ice was dry as he scrambled for a new lead low in the wall ahead which promised brighter sunlight through the riven crystalline roof. A moment later the chamber through which he struggled was flooded neck deep in frigid water. He jackknifed for the passage he had seen. One shift, one pinch or squeeze from these giant boulders of ice, and he would be crushed.

Ben swam through the opening, and found himself in a long crevasse. He clawed and kicked forward and up, his face pushing into an air pocket that barely allowed his nose to clear the surface. It was like trying to breathe at the very apex of an A-framed igloo.

With a fresh lungful of air, Ben pushed down against the ice slabs that were constricting him and moved on through the narrow channel. More light showed ahead. He surfaced fully afloat in a larger chamber, with a manhole of open sky directly above him, and three feet beyond the reach of his upstretched hand. He submerged, got a foothold on a ledge, and pushed up, breaching like a dolphin. He missed grabbing the edge of the opening by inches. This must have been the freezing edition of what the scalded pilot felt like in that El Tatio fumarole; safety just out of reach, and death all around. As Ben fell back into the water, the edges of the skylight shattered, and crushed closed.

Ben dived again. Again he swam hard toward a light that glowed ahead. The path was suddenly blocked by a wall of ice that had no bubbles in it, no air at all; it was as clear as a pane of glass. The ice around Ben gave another explosive shift, and the invisible wall burst in front of him. He swam over a knife-edged sill into another narthex that was nearly pitch dark, gulping air as the tide rushed in to kill him.

Ben's eardrums were battered by the thunderclap of breaking plate ice. A solid sheet surged from below, forced him upward toward the chamber's roof. He rose fast, a rodeo cowboy bucked toward another granite-hard stratum up above.

With another discharge of big cannon, the ice roof above him split into open air. Before he realized what had happened, Ben was lying on the surface ice, with water sheeting off it into the bay, and threatening to wash him into a lead with it. He hacked his fingertips into the hoary ice, caught hold of a sharp outcropping, splayed his feet, and rode out the plate's gyrations.

The broad sheet on which Ben lay pitched steeply, then settled into a regular rhythm with the bay's two-foot waves. He was a quarter mile from shore, with a deadly barrier of shifting ice and open seawater blockading his path to land.

"Need a lift?" The man's voice was accented, but the words were plain enough.

Ben looked over his shoulder and saw a handcrafted umiak with a family of five Inuits aboard. The mother and the two young girls, and the teenage boy, stared at Ben as if he were a weird arctic specter risen from the depths to haunt them. The father grinned at Ben, and beckoned to him to slide over to the edge of the ice slab.

In less than a minute, Ben was shivering in a hide blanket on the bottom of the umiak in a macabre embrace with the deliciously warm, bloody corpse of a seal.

CHAPTER 54

THE HAMMERING CEASED when Ellis opened the door to the motel room to see a ghoul swaying on the stoop. Ben's eyes blazed red. His skin was blue. The blanket he clutched was a sodden membrane, and bloody like his mud-caked clothing.

"You going to stand there and die, or come in and die?" asked Ellis. "I don't care, but you're letting out all the heat."

CHAPTER 55

THE EXFILTRATION FROM Quebec Province required a full day. Though quicker than Benedict Arnold's retreat from the city of the same name two hundred years before, it was just as ignominious, and nearly as fatal. Ellis's leg wound showed signs of festering before antibiotics could start their work. Ben was exhausted, recovering from hypothermia. His increasingly labored work of breathing suggested the onset of walking pneumonia.

Several hops in discreetly hired light planes brought them to Lincoln Park Airport in northern New Jersey. After a slow midweek shift at the airfield's eatery, the Sunset Pub and Grill, a waitress was willing to pick up extra cash driving the men into New York. It was difficult for Ben to gauge exactly where to ask the woman to drop them off. Too far from Ben's bolthole, and the walk might kill them. Too close, and she might remember too much if questioned. There were so many innocent victims strewn about this business already.

The door to the basement den was still secured with a chain and padlock. Ben patted his pockets. He said, "I must have lost the key."

Ellis stepped forward and lifted a metal chain from around his neck. There was a single key dangling on it. "Forgot you gave me one of these?" He unlocked the door.

Though Ben had been away from the New York lair only a few days, it felt like an absence of years. But so much had gone wrong, so many decisions had proved destructive, that the oppressive walk-down was now a sanctuary.

The gold bars Ben had left under the tarp were gone. So was the swan sculpture that was the current work in progress. The call he had made before departing earlier in the week had been to friends on Smith Island. They had sprinted north to retrieve the treasure, lest it fall into unfriendly hands. Not a scrap, not a filing, not a single spattered drop of precious metal remained.

Only the furnace and the worthless rough furnishings were left behind. The basement was cold. Ben flipped the switch to turn the furnace on. The subsonic electric pulse filled the air. The single dangling light bulb dimmed for a moment, losing out to the furnace's heavy amperage draw.

They had talked very little in the last twenty-four hours other than to address the logistics of their travel.

Now Ben spoke as if in the middle of a conversation he was having with himself. "He's dead."

"Likely."

Ben shuddered. "All that ice. The water coming in. It was like a ship that kept sinking over and over again in the same bad dream."

"You sound a little messed up about that." Ellis broke a fevered sweat. An infection was coursing through him.

"Yes, but I'll get by for now. You agree he's dead, whoever he was." Ben knew he was seeking confirmation on something about which neither of them could be sure.

Ellis sighed. "Might never find the body. Water doesn't always give them back."

Ben recalled a dive the previous fall that had ended badly. "I heard that. His hands were small but strong. But he yanked me out from under that slab of ice down there. I crawled under it to get my mitts on him, but he saved my life." Ben studied the cuts on his palms. "Said shooting Grant was a mercy killing. A friend helping out a friend."

"Please don't do me any favors like that. Don't forget, MacCready said this fellow was nuts. Sounds plenty confused to me."

"That was the last thing the guy said down there before he hauled me out," Ben said. "Talked about Dreams. Nightmares. Said they might get him dead before I did. Mind you, I might have missheard. I was busy drowning at the time."

"He doesn't sound like a national asset to me. What was MacCready talking about with that?"

"We can't stay. They already found me here once."

"That's why they won't look here again too quick. We covered our tracks better coming in than you did going out. Reckon we've got nine, maybe twelve hours."

Ben grinned, coughed. "Because we're so good at guesstimating trouble."

"Touché."

"Sit tight," said Ben. "I'm going topside."

"Does it look like I'm going anyplace?"

Ben climbed the fire escape carefully, slowly. Winded by the time he reached the parapet, he had puffed past Omega's window. At this late hour, she was most likely out plying her art on the walls of the city. Regardless of the time, dropping in on her again was out of the question. It was not as if they parted friends.

This would have been the moment for a contemplative cigarette or three, up there in the shadowy loom of the city street lights radiating from below. The cold would drive Ben back downstairs before long, but there were decisions to make. He had answered Grant's call, but had not completed the mission. Grant had been doomed by disease, but what few heartbeats remained to him were cut short by this assassin who claimed to be Grant's friend. How many nursing home staffers killed with justifications of euthanasia? And now, the case was most likely closed, the killer, gone. Put to a grisly end beneath a field of grinding ice.

MacCready remained a problem. He would be furious at Ben, for the casual removal of that digit, as well as the failure to bring the target in alive. Ben had made it eminently plain he never fully supported that mission, nor felt allegiance to MacCready's rank as Grant's successor. That creep could still make trouble though, Ben knew.

CHAPTER 56

DEPARTMENT OF HOMELAND Security Secretary Lily Morgan stood on her desk and looked down at MacCready. Her office door was closed. The regiments of red scorpions birthed from her current hallucination ranged across the floor around her underling's feet. She heard their carapaces tick, clack and scrape over one another as they hunted for unknown prey.

MacCready's injured foot was swathed in trauma dressings and a garbage bag. Rain made the outer wrap necessary. He wanted desperately to sit, but his boss was still standing.

Lily Morgan breathed deeply to maintain her equipoise. MacCready was adamant that there were no other living things beside themselves in the room. Madame Secretary suspected that her mind was going, but wished to keep it to herself as best she could. The racking dissonance within her cranium did not improve her mood.

"So it's been twenty-four hours since you heard from your operator?"

"Last word was that Ben and this black guy were on their way to a little town way the hell up in Quebec," MacCready said. "My assets were tracking them closely."

"I hope that's a good sign," Morgan said. "Twenty-four hours isn't very long. How was your nuthatch operative doing?" She twirled her right index finger next to her temple.

"The recurrent dream was becoming more intense with every episode. The data bleed was progressing to the point that sleep was no longer desirable. He had a suicidal sound to his voice when we talked last."

Secretary Morgan wanted to mention the scorpion, big as a Maine lobster, picking at MacCready's bandage with its pincers, but she refrained. "Works for me if that guy offs himself. The DARPA people don't have someone looking for him do they?"

MacCready was insistent they did not, but waited until Lily tired of repeating *DARPA-people-DARPA-people-DARPA-people* to herself before he spoke. "I told them I'll see to bringing him in alive."

"Whoopsie."

"So the compromising data he was carrying probably went with him. No one would know to scan any DNA he left behind."

Lily considered. "This Ben guy might have done us a big favor."

The sledgehammer throb in MacCready's foot made agreement difficult, but he managed to give a politic nod.

"Did Ben show any aptitude for our Meme Displacement Unit?" Lily asked.

"Aptitude, yes. Attitude, no. Not a real patriot."

"So that's it, then. No invasion blueprint means no invasion for now. My name is cleared. You on the other hand, might be in a jam with the administration."

MacCready shrugged. "If the Joint Chiefs and POTUS want to attack an American ally to save the world, it will happen. There are enough idiots on the Hill to cosign anything if the case is cleverly made, and it will be profitable. It just won't happen with your stamp of approval all over it. And DNA data caching, or at least the protocols for choosing the right recipients, will have to be reassessed. It was too Dick Tracy. Do you want a hand getting down from there?"

"Fuck no! Are you out of your mind? Those *things* are all over the place."

MacCready ignored Lily as he answered his ringing phone.

CHAPTER 57

A FEW MINUTES on the roof, and Ben was feeling the cold. His tolerance for brisk weather was all but eradicated after his near-drowning in the Hudson Strait. It was time to step back down the fire escape, huddle by the furnace to get warm again, and talk with Ellis about what came next. This safe house, and perhaps the plan to convert the gold bullion into works of art, and thence into cash, might be ruined now as well. Sunsetting the entire operation for a time seemed a wise course.

He stood up slowly from the beach chair someone had brought to the roof for sun in warmer seasons, and heard a splintering thud, followed by a sudden splash of liquid, a big steady stream of it that reminded him of a city fountain. Ben searched around him in the weird light. Glancing up, he saw it.

His building's iconic redwood water tank, which stood girded by steel bands over the roof on a lattice of thick beams, had sprung a leak. A big leak as thick as Ben's thumb. Water flowed in an arc to splash noisily on the rooftop. An instant after Ben noticed the first stream, another leak broke out just one foot to the left of the first. This tank was not failing from rot. Ben realized someone was shooting at him, making holes in the tank from a great distance, and using enough of a noise suppressor that the gunshots were inaudible over the dull roar of traffic and the peel of sirens.

Ben ducked low, astounded. This was MacCready's work. He had found them. Or perhaps the shooter had survived the ice. He thought he saw the flash of a muzzle from two buildings over. He looked back up at the water tank. A total of seven holes gushed. They had been shot with deft, but whimsical precision. Together, the perforations formed the eyes, nose, and mouth of a dot-matrix visage. Ben marveled. A damn smiley face! His opponent still lived.

PART 4
EARGESPLITTEN
LOUDENBOOMER

CHAPTER 58

MACCREADY WAS TIRED, furious, and experiencing a new and devastating level of pain from his gimped foot. Numerous instant release Roxys were not helping, though he was beaned out from bumping crushed pills for the last two hours. Forgetting any sense of dignity, he lay sprawled, moaning in the back seat of his car.

Janie, his pretty driver, maneuvered down into southern Maryland from Washington D.C. with MacCready's injured foot dangling by her face as her only front-seat companion. His foot was beginning to stink. He wondered if it were normal, run-of-the-mill foot funk, or something more gangrenous in nature fouling the car's atmosphere.

There was an Asis Rigid Hull Inflatable Boat, or RHIB, waiting for MacCready, moored to a pier at Point Lookout State Park. It was a Department of Homeland Security boat, but unmarked as such. Per MacCready's orders, the boat had been prepped with a very large plastic chest, actually a sealable shipping container for human remains. It fulfilled all international requirements for transporting bodies via traditional air carriers, as well as those civilian carriers with military contracts. As far as MacCready knew, the bottom of this casket was already covered in a four-inch bed of crushed ice, as he had requested. A number of additional bags of ice were stowed aboard the boat in various lockers.

The four-man team following in the black Taurus would help with the recovery operation. MacCready would dismiss the boat's captain. The captain would no doubt complain that MacCready and his men were not qualified to handle the RHIB. MacCready would let the captain know Janie would be running his damn boat. MacCready knew Janie fairly well, and when he vomited during the boat ride, as he always did, at least he knew she would not blab about it. The handpicked quartet of operatives would also keep mum. They would not breathe a word of MacCready's failings, or they would simply disappear. That kind of discretion was important. He did not mind it being known that he had been shot. That was cool. He did not want it rumored he was a seasick landlubber who was *not*, in fact, MacCready: *Ready* for anything.

The phone call MacCready took in Lily Morgan's office had required his best ingenuity. He remembered the strange, distorted voice. He remembered his acute disappointment that the problem was not yet handled. MacCready's mind had filled with lists of tasks yet to be completed. First thing to do, take this crazy maniac down a peg.

The shooter said, "I'm following him still." *Him.* Must mean Ben the Overrated. Why had Grant placed so much stock in that guy? What kind of fixer would Ben ever make if he could not, or would not, wax the current talent?

MacCready had excused himself from the Secretary's office, leaving her pacing on top of her desk. "What the hell happened in Canada?" he asked.

The shooter sounded woozy. "Got close. Got very close."

"That's for hand grenades and horseshoes, my friend."

"You said you could help with the nightmares. I really don't think it's PTSD after all."

MacCready felt like he were talking to an idiot. "Finish what you started, and we'll get you into a great hospital."

Secretary Morgan needed this shooter wrangled in from the cold, but MacCready felt that Ben's death was a worthwhile postponement to regaining custody of the killer's incriminating DNA. MacCready admitted to himself that he would be ecstatic no matter who in the pair killed the other first. The taking of his toe had been a humiliation.

The voice had said, "Mr. MacCready, I don't believe you anymore. I don't think I'm a veteran with mental troubles. It seems much, much more serious."

MacCready was angrier now. Angry enough, and frustrated enough, to resort to the last tool left in his meager kit, the truth. "You're not ordinary. Is that what you want to hear? In fact, during your last physical, you got loaded up with some data. Not quite experimental, but not quite state of the art, either. And it didn't go in like an implant, or a suppository. So, you're not some low-life drug mule. The vast amount of data you hold in your possession is actually in your cells. In your very DNA. Exciting to be part of that, isn't it? But the information, it seems, is making your head funny. We need you to come in once you take care of our buddy Ben."

There was a pause that made MacCready believe that the line was dead, the call had dropped, or worst of all, that someone had actually hung up on him.

But the voice came back, more quietly. "You can remove this data? Because I think I know it front to back. Apparently the plan in me was war-gamed extensively. All the outcomes were included in the data bolus. All those people dead."

MacCready was incensed. "You are now cleared Top Secret, soldier. Ultra Mega Top Hella Secret! You were never meant to know what was entrusted to your care. You are a courier. You were never intended to look inside the pouch."

The voice on the phone persisted. "You can remove it?"

"Yes, of course! You don't think you'd be cached with information vital to national security if we couldn't retrieve it, do you? Easy as taking a letter out of an envelope."

The shooter was still not satisfied. "Will doing that help me forget what I've seen?"

MacCready softened his tone. "What you're experiencing is commonly called a *bleed*. Your brain is assembling the data in your cells into the aggregate concept. Who knew brains could do that? When the data source of the bleed goes away, the shadow of the data, what you're experiencing in your sleep, goes with it." MacCready was chewing up the scenery, and almost believed that load of crap himself.

"That's reassuring to know. But who is George Calvert?"

MacCready stayed as calm as he could. "No idea. There's a nuclear plant in southern Maryland with *Calvert* in the name, and some cliffs. It was the name of Lord Baltimore. Is *he* in your dream?"

"No. The name's somehow linked to a place I feel drawn to visit. Irresistibly pulled."

MacCready was sick of the delays. "Can it wait until we untangle your noodle?"

"I wish I could ignore it. I'm going there next, I think. MacCready, this plan that I'm going to completely forget, will it ever be put into action?"

MacCready knew he had to play this one just right. "The thing is, the blueprint you carry is the only copy in existence. Amazing isn't it? The trust that's been placed in you, and you alone, is colossal. Presidents don't get the kind of access you've got. But here's the thing I need you to understand. You don't get to make the call on whether the blueprint is ever used. The bleed has afforded you a privilege of insight, but not any rights. You hear me, soldier? And after you come in, when the data is gone, and you've forgotten the few details you possess now, and the dreams stop keeping you up at night—when all that happens, and the plan is put into play by decision-makers well above our paygrade, then you will be just as surprised as anyone. Isn't that cool? You might be deployed in the very operation you're protecting now, without even realizing it."

"It's like you said, MacCready. *Cool.*"

MacCready sensed his troubled operative might be coming around, but was not certain. "We understand each other. So, forget George Calvert, okay? When your current sanction is finished, you just come in, and we'll tidy up that cranium of yours, ship-shape and Bristol fashion."

The voice was wistful. "I want that more than anything. The dreams are intolerable."

"Soon, my friend. Soon you'll be just fine."

George Calvert, it turned out, was not such a mystery after all. His team of operatives found the site in question, and it was confirmed by the troubled shooter.

Janie kept the car rolling south toward the boat. MacCready wondered why she was leaning toward the window she had opened an inch, like a chain-smoker driving in winter.

CHAPTER 59

NITRO EXPRESS APPRECIATED Ben Blackshaw's sense of propriety. They had unfinished business, yes, but it would not be right to wrap things up in an alley like rabid dogs. MacCready had obliged by providing GPS data for the phone currently in use by Ben's friend. Once again, Ben and his buddy had not scoured their possessions of all the telltale electronic raft. It seemed as if they intentionally left a trail of breadcrumbs. All well and good. Though there was a shared sense of mission between Ben and the killer, they would not exactly be carpooling to their appointment with destiny.

When the nemesis assassin had stalked in via rooftops, fire escapes, and alleys to where Ben was lying low in New York, the name *George Calvert* was freshly scrawled on the wall by the door. Of course, by then Ben and his friend had left the city. Taking incoming fire is a great motivator to relocate. They were traveling south now. It took a little while to decipher the meaning of *George Calvert*. And when the killer finally made the connection, it became urgent to make MacCready aware of it, too. The more, the merrier. But MacCready was not very quick.

The lopsided smiling face the shooter had blasted into the water tank was perhaps overly silly, but *acting out*, as high school counselors called it, was a reasonable counterfoil to the horror of the dreams that both plagued sleep and shattered the killer's waking life as well. The face was just a brief flicker of mirth in the morbid darkness.

To hell with these nightmares! The dreamer had limits. The killer had standards. The assassin was a political operative working with a fine brush on a worldwide canvas, but not a genocidal animal. Not a monster. The spectral mass destruction of innocent noncombatants was horrible compared to the creative biffing of individual targets of various unwholesome stripes. No matter how often the liquidator repeated the fact that the Visigothic ransacking that played out in the nocturnal visions was nothing more than a dogged hoax of the mind, it provided no comfort. So much blood. So much misery! Such ruination of a vast and rich culture. And now, thanks to MacCready, the hired killer's suspicion was confirmed; the vision was a harbinger of reality; the stranger, no longer a mere factotum operative, was the living key to Pandora's Box.

CHAPTER 60

HAPPINESS RARELY FILLED Ben's heart during the last few months as it did the moment he stepped aboard his old deadrise workboat, formerly known as *Miss Dotsy*. Even though there was a new name on her transom, Ben knew her to be rightfully his. Sensed it in his DNA.

Ellis and many of Ben's neighbors had salvaged the boat from the swamping she had suffered late the previous fall. Over the past few months, *Miss Dotsy* had been restored to even better condition than when she came down her boatyard slipway to touch water the first time decades before.

With a warning call from Ellis, local friends had readied and fueled the deadrise, and left her moored in the Small Boat Harbor in Crisfield, Maryland. There, Ben and Ellis abandoned the rental car they had driven from Newark Liberty Airport.

Ellis watched Ben take in all that was familiar about *Miss Dotsy*, and note that much of her was new. By the sound of her, the original Atomic Four still banged away in the engine box. She was still steered by a fore-and-aft tiller on the starboard side, amidships. Now there was a thirty-six-mile Garmin GMR 18 HD radome mounted over the cuddy cabin. Ben thought that was a little too yachty for his humble standards, but he was grateful for the thought that went into the choosing, buying, and installing of it. All that care, and a sweet Awlgrip paint job, made this a happy reunion. Ben wished he were in such fine shape himself, but springtime was proving rough on a body.

The real surprise was the toilet installed forward in the cuddy cabin. That had probably been added with his wife's comfort in mind. Had LuAnna been aboard, Ben imagined it likely she would have looked askance at the item, and whispered to him as soon as she could that it would have to be removed. As one old friend had said of her, she was no Miss Fairy Pants. But LuAnna was not aboard today.

Next to the commode lay a ragged black heap of Lycra-covered neoprene. His old diving wetsuit. How Ben hated it now. A shiver ran through him from the harrowing days he spent zipped into it during the previous fall. When he was the service, it was an insulating second skin. Now it lay on the deck like something he had sloughed, as if he had outgrown it. Ben stripped and pulled the wetsuit on. At least for now, it was dry.

Without a word spoken between them, Ben could tell Ellis was suffering a low-grade fever as they set out through the complex channels and shallows that guard Crisfield. His hands shook. He had donned and doffed his coat several times in the last ten minutes. Ben simply could not ask him to act as a spotter on this last mission. Ellis was too ill.

They passed Old Island, which was marked by the single chimney of a ruined menhaden rendering plant. Time and Tangier Sound had swept all other traces of the factory into oblivion. Ben wondered if Smith Island would look like that one day.

They bore to the northwest, north of the Martin Wildlife Refuge, but kept south of Jones, Pry, and Holland Islands, and thence setting out into the Chesapeake Bay. Ben dared not cruise in close to Smith Island. He feared he might not be able to wrench himself away from home to carry on and finish the business ahead.

A cold spring rain beat down on them, which was just as well, as it would keep visibility to a minimum for anyone who did not know their way in these waters. The bay was running two to four feet. Not life threatening, but sporty enough for ailing, wounded, exhausted men.

After a little over an hour, the hulk came into sight as a darker shadow on the night horizon. Whitecaps rolled past her nearly four hundred fifty foot waterline. The old liberty ship did not rise and fall with the waves. She was aground, and had been since the Johnson administration. The name on her stern was different today, but when she was launched, she was the *SS George Calvert.*

PART 5
BLOWING OUT
AND
NECKING DOWN

CHAPTER 61

THOUGH NEVER A fan of vampire lore, the assassin known as
Nitro Express felt metaphysically lethal pushing up the lid of the casket
aboard MacCready's boat, and carefully climbing out. Things had been quiet
for several minutes. The sound of MacCready retching during the boat ride
had provided some amusement on the way. Then, MacCready had sworn a
great deal while transferring from the RHIB to the derelict liberty ship. His
assistant, Janie, and the four squad operatives that Nitro Express had totted
up from their desultory conversation during the crossing had all tried to
help MacCready. Unfortunately, he was the type to get himself into inextri-
cable trouble before he thought to ask for help.

The stranger hoisted the .950 JDJ rifle, by SSK Industries, out of the
casket where it had also lain on the trip across the bay. The single-shot bolt-
action rifle weighed more than one hundred pounds. It was inconvenient.
The ammunition was enormous; the lathe-turned slugs were a half pound,
comparable to rounds from an M61 Vulcan Gatling, and cost fifty dollars a
pop. But with rusted ship materials to defeat, this was the weapon for the
job.

Once again, as the shooter gazed up at the old vessel, there was an
abiding sense of approval of Ben's choice of venue for the proverbial
deathmatch. Like the mysterious killer, and like Ben as well, this ship had a
history of service in nearly every branch of the military. Beginning with the
Coast Guard, as a training ship, she then had been listed with the Army, as
part of the appropriately named DAMP service, or Downrange Anti-Missile

242

RobertRobert Blake Whitehill

Program, for tracking rocket tests. Then came her brief service in the Air Force. Finally, she was a Navy ship.

In her last incarnation, in the mid-1960s, she had been scuttled on a shoal, and used as a live-fire target ship for pilots sortied out of Naval Air Station Patuxent River. Pax River had stopped pocking her with holes of varying calibers in the early 1970s. Today, the name *American Mariner* was peeling off her stern. She had been passed around, well-used, terribly abused, and left for dead. The stranger could relate. So could Ben. For two people detailed to kill one another, they were eerily alike.

CHAPTER 62

MACCREADY'S EGO FOUGHT against the pain in his foot and briefly won out. He climbed slowly up the rusting companionways of the old ship to a place that felt natural to him as the leader of this operation: the bridge. It had been rough going. The missing toe made every other step agony. Finally he arrived. Though stripped of all navigation equipment, the bridge offered a commanding view of the foredeck. The action would take place there, MacCready imagined. He gazed to port and starboard, pretending to maintain a vigilant scan of ever-changing conditions.

He noticed that Janie was not with him. After a foggy effort, he remembered she had stayed on one of the many lower decks to keep watch, and to radio him when the other players tied up to the ship. He had told her to remain behind, hadn't he? He believed he had made his wishes known out loud but he could not be sure. Perhaps she knew him so well that she had intuited the need to picket below. A polluting level of painkillers made the rock-steady *American Mariner's* deck feel as though the Chesapeake was running high, though not nearly as high as MacCready himself.

MacCready mused with confidence on his unit operators. Odie Rance was a Blackwater washout who had become zealous in Kandahar in 2009. He had suffered his own mental troop surge, slaughtered a few too many civilians on an unauthorized solo patrol, splattering hearts and minds instead of winning them in a Rudyard-Kipling-on-Angel-Dust affair that could never be swept under the oriental carpet.

Rance was packed off stateside before the locals could skin him after a hastily assembled shura. Odie Rance liked to shoot first, second, and third. Asking questions simply did not enter into the equation, ever. MacCready had recruited Rance personally, and brought him into Jerry Grant's team. Grant had not been pleased with the choice. That was no longer an issue, of course.

Chalmers Coffin was practically mute. He spoke on patrol only through hand signals. At all other times, he was quiet to the point of insubordination. He did not inspire camaraderie in the usual way, through friendly banter. He inspired awe with his close-action marksmanship. He was a phenomenon, perhaps the very model for any character that the director John Woo ever created, minus the pithy patter and catchphrases. He spoke with his guns. Deemed far too creepy by buddies and commanding officers alike, he was promoted to a desk, and from there, summarily managed out of the Army, at which point MacCready recruited him for the team.

Maximo Serano was masterful with a knife. He talked nonstop until a patrol began, wearing down the good will of his fellow soldiers with quips that were never as funny as he wished them to be. Perhaps his greatest sin was his own gale of laughter that punctuated his attempts at humor. When a patrol went hot, Serano seemed to evaporate. Within moments, enemy fire in one area would begin to fall silent, though his buddies were lighting up other sectors with every gun and mortar they carried.

Serano would reappear when the fight was done, drenched in blood, and sporting a bootlace strung with body parts slashed free from their original owners. No disciplinary action ever cured him of taking the macabre souvenirs. With the final infraction, a military police officer tried to confiscate Serano's most recent pecker necklace. The MP went to the infirmary for two hundred forty-nine stitches, and three units of blood. Serano went to the brig unhurt, and received an honorable discharge in exchange for a stint with MacCready's unit where his bloodthirsty traits were appreciated rather than reviled.

Declan Flaherty was a steady enough hand most of the time. He spoke normally, was not loquacious. He was horrifically sensitive to ridicule, which put him at odds with his fellow squaddies in a coiled business where tension-relieving trash talk was the *lingua franca*. A green replacement had tried to get chummy with Flaherty with some good-natured ribbing. The FNG had died from a traumatic brain injury following the bare-knuckle obliteration of his maxillofacial bones, including Le Fort I, II, and III fractures, with his orbits reduced to small change, and a piledriver's pulping of the softer tissues. MacCready had scored Flaherty for his unit easily enough, because no one wanted Flaherty around. All told, they were an effective, if motley bunch. With any luck, settling affairs far out on this godforsaken old ship might prevent anyone who mattered from getting hurt.

CHAPTER 63

BEN PENETRATED THE hull of the *American Mariner* through a rusty waterline wound in her forward holds. The tide was high. He swam through the jagged gash and stopped there, just inside the welded outer plating, standing on the for'd peak saltwater ballast tank with his head just out of water. He watched carefully to be sure that Ellis was in fact departing the area of the old hulk aboard *Miss Dotsy*, and not lingering to try something stupid, heroic, or both, in aid of Ben's mission.

Miss Dotsy was hull down in dawn's dark waves within a few minutes, and completely gone from sight a few minutes after that. At least Ellis would soon be safe at his home on Smith Island.

Wave surges broke in through the holes in the hull, and were amplified in height and power as they whipped through open spaces of the big cargo bays into the confines of the companionways. Ben could not move quickly. The waves threatened to drive him onto rusty fangs of old equipment, or the corroded, submerged members of the rotting Liberty ship herself.

As Ben patrolled and searched, he felt the old ship growing on him, and yet changing him. He was adapting his tactics in the moment, but he was also evolving the overall strategy for his life to come. That is, if he survived the next few hours. He knew a gunsmith who adapted ammunition for new loads of powder, new weights of bullet, and new calibers. Expanding the forward end of a tapering cartridge, or blowing it out, accommodated more powder. Reducing the neck of the cartridge where the bullet is seated, necking it down, meant more explosive force driving a

smaller, faster round. This old ship was having that effect on him. Even
though Ben was exhausted, he was gaining a deadly concentration and
focus.

Shouting. Definitely MacCready's bellicose squawk. He was lambasting
someone for nearly shoving him overboard. Ben had expected the Nitro
Express shooter to come alone, had envisioned some kind of Wild West
showdown. Now it seemed there was a larger force to contend with.

Ben half swam, and half crawled, inching carefully along the starboard
wall of the No. 1 Hold, and latched onto an old mount for securing cargo.
He raised his waterproof pouch above the surface, opened it, and extracted
a diving mask rigged with a flip-down night vision monocular. Ben had
saved it from what little remained of Knocker Ellis's flying arsenal, along
with one other item, a very special pistol. He rubbed spit inside the mask,
fitted it over his face, gave the straps around his head a final tug, and
switched the monocular on. The cavernous hold glowed a beautiful green.
Ben visually collapsed the space, quickly scanning it sector by sector. The
hold was unoccupied, save for himself, but it was filled with the din and
echo of the waves. He could not hear anything useful, but at least now he
could see.

A narrow catwalk spanned the aft bulkhead near the overhead, with a
heavy, round-cornered door opening in the bulkhead into the darkness of a
companionway. With a prayer of thanks for Ellis's eclectic taste in guns, he
drew the weapon holstered on his right hip, a Tulsky Oruzheiny Zavod
four-barreled SPP-1M smooth bore pistol. Each barrel was loaded with a
4.5 mm cartridge tipped with a single steel dart almost five inches long. This
was an ugly, pragmatic, utilitarian pepperbox of a weapon. It sported a trigger guard, big and looped, like a Winchester's lever, to accommodate a
frogman's finger fattened by a wetsuit glove. The upside was that, despite
its lack of rifling, this gun would fire in air with reasonable accuracy. The
truly beautiful part was that this pistol would shoot straight and true underwater, and was lethal out to twenty yards, even when triggered as deep as
sixteen feet. Ben knew if it were discharged at a greater depth, the effective
range was drastically shortened. After four shots, it was worthless, not because of a cheap design flaw, but because Ellis had no more of the scarce
four-shot clips.

Ben kept his head low, trying not to let the waves smash him into the wall of the hold nor wash him off his precarious position. He saw Chalmers Coffin, the quiet close-quarters marksman, enter the hold from the catwalk hatch thirty feet above him. Coffin also used a night vision goggle to survey the space. MacCready's team was no doubt patrolling and clearing the ship from bow to stern, hunting him. Gripping the wall with one hand, and holding the pistol in open air with the other, Ben took careful aim.

A growler rolling in through the gashed hull eddied into a whirlpool of water in the confined space. The vortex sluiced Ben off his perch, and washed him into the middle of the hold. His training failed him, and he inhaled water, momentarily sparking a bout of panic; he was about to drown.

Chalmers Coffin fired three quick bursts of armor piercing bullets at Ben with his Heckler & Koch MP7A1. Against every instinct, Ben struggled down and away from the air and into the abyss of the hold.

Coffin's conventional bullets destabilized into harmless slugs in the water. Ben had only one instant to act before the hold's silt clouded his monocular's view. He aimed up at the man on the catwalk and pulled the trigger twice. Two steel darts raced toward the surface, breached the water like sprites, and went home.

Coffin stopped shooting. Ben surfaced to see the operator stagger back against the bulkhead with a dart wound in his chest, and another in his throat. Coffin pawed at his neck, but the dart had punched through a ring of cartilage, pinned his trachea closed, anchoring its point deep in his fourth cervical vertebra. Coffin's chest wound was not doing him any favors either. Suffocating, the stricken operator stumbled forward and pitched through the rusted catwalk stanchions, plummeting into the frothing cauldron of troubled black water below.

Ben surfaced, cleared his lungs, gulped a quarter breath of air and dived again, closing on Coffin's twitching form with strong swift strokes. Ben heard the scrape of his knife blade against the steel dart as he slashed Coffin's throat. Coffin sank slow and limp into the depths trailing smokelike plumes of blood.

Surfacing again near the port wall of the hold, Ben waited for the operator's backup to look for his overdue partner. Once again, MacCready's bunch seemed to favor lone wolf tactics. Teamed pairs had apparently become passé. After a few moments, with no one making an appearance, Ben went hunting. By himself. *When in Rome ...*

In a cold flat crawl, he slowly pulled himself aft through the roiling waters in No. 1 Hold. He had to dive again to locate the bulkhead door and swim into the next hold. Fortunately, the scuttling party had left all the watertight doors open, or removed them altogether for scrap, decades before.

Ben had to make his way by touch through the zero-visibility water. At the hold's bottom, there was no light for the night vision monocular to aggregate and project onto his retina. He knew the boat well enough, though. True, he had not visited the wreck since his teenage years, yet after decades, the darkness bound up inside the confines of the hull felt familiar. Swimming through murk like this still made Ben wonder what lay just beyond his reach. His training gave him the tools to quell the childish claustrophobic freak-out lurking deep in his psyche, hoping to claw its way to the forefront of his thought to obliterate reason.

The bottom of No. 2 Hold was a maze of collapsed iron ribs and trusses. It had been almost clear of detritus when Ben had dived it in his youth. The scuttled ship had begun collapsing in on itself more rapidly since then. Ben maneuvered carefully, vigilant to avoid lacerations and entrapment in the entangling jumble. The submerged junk venturied the cold water into a weird undertow that tugged Ben down hard toward the hold's sole. He as much climbed the sunken girders and braces as swam upward for air. He surfaced behind a piece of the hold's hatch cover. The water was a gentler eddy there.

After three slow breaths to recover, Ben peered out from behind the hatch cover. No one else was in sight. He slowly climbed out of the water on the slick crisscrossed members of a rusted truss. Lying flat on the catwalk, he tried to hear any intruders over the rumble of waves in the open forward hold he had just left. The old ship roared and creaked, but revealed nothing. Ben crept aft.

He had almost reached the aft bulkhead of No. 2 Hold when another operative, Declan Flaherty, put his head through the hatch from the companionway. The operative spotted Ben through his NVGs in the same moment. Ben's SPP-1M and his knife were still holstered from the climb out of the water. He had only two shots remaining in the awkward handgun.

The operative swung his H&K toward Ben, who ducked behind a section of the hold's wall that had subsided well out of true from rust, gravity, and time. In this makeshift shelter, the faint gray of early morning light filtered through old bullet holes in the ship's side.

The operative opened fire, the bullets punching small mounds into Ben's side of the sheet of metal, sending rust flakes flying. The bullets did not penetrate. Ben's hand touched a battered 25 mm round, perhaps fired from an old F4 Phantom's external XM-12 gun pod decades before when the ship was still used for naval air gunnery practice. It took a split-second for him to see by its faintly reddish hue it was a dud tracer. Without thinking, he shut his eyes tight and side-armed the slug around the edge of his shelter. Whatever had caused the round to fail to ignite when it was fired, time had destabilized the magnesium tracer compound in the shell's base, making it very touchy. The shell clanged off the bulkhead, and the darkness of the hold lit up as if from a tumbling spotlight as the round's flare came to life.

The operative staggered back, tearing at his NVGs, his eyes blinded in the sudden searing light. Swearing, he stumbled, fell hard on his ass. With the impact, the old catwalk broke free of its rusted bulkhead fasteners, tilted violently, and dropped the operative into space, his H&K firing quick convulsive bursts. Before the water in the hold could break his fall, he landed on an upthrust broken conduit pipe, and was impaled through his gut, back to front. The screams were terrible, but Ben had heard their like before. A quick glance round the metal plate told Ben the operative had lost his grip on the H&K. A *coup de grâce* for the miserable man was out of the question. Ben had no ammo to spare, and the operator's throat was out of reach. Before the banshee howls attracted company, Ben had to boogie.

His route into the companionway from which the operative had emerged was compromised with the loss of the catwalk. He had a choice. He could climb out on deck, and take his chances in the open air, or descend once more into the treacherous waters of the hold and continue aft the hard way. Ben was sure he had not eliminated MacCready's squad, nor was it likely one of the two men he had killed was Nitro Express. There was an unknown, but significant amount of soldiering left to do.

Ben grabbed the edge of the catwalk and rolled forward, head-first like an acrobat. From there he swung himself until he was hanging below it with both hands. A short sway and a drop to a pipe, and he eased himself back into the water. He moved on the surface from one chunk of debris to another along the port wall of the hold. When he reached the aft bulkhead, he took a breath and sank into the darkness. The bulkhead door opened into the No. 3 Hold. Ben pulled himself in, and slowly rose up into the hold's airspace.

This hold seemed to be clear of MacCready's agents. Ben stayed stock-still against the forward bulkhead for several minutes to be sure. Nothing. The pattern of one operative per hold seemed broken here. Of course, he could be swimming below the operators who, prepped only for work in the dry, might be rampaging through the upper decks. A louder, roaring basso peal told Ben the weather was going to hell. A spring squall might be on the verge of breaking over the *American Mariner*.

Ben released his grasp of a stairway stanchion and skirted the hold's open water. Keeping to the bulkheads and walls, he reached a half-submerged door into the machinery space housing the great-triple expansion reciprocating steam engine. He sank below the surface, and hugged the doorway's sill as a he passed into the new space. He turned toward the starboard wall, and kicked for it without coming up for air. Then he dived down past the boiler, and picked his way in amidst the massive 2500 horse-power engine's piston, eccentric, and connecting rods, gliding over the crankshaft and gently rising up to finally let his face break the surface in a passageway aft and under the stout low-pressure steam cylinder.

Ben climbed the old stairway past the second deck and crept out toward the main deck. From the end of the passage, he observed two operators hunkered on the aft deck in the rain. They were staring forward, watching for him. Evidently they believed they had the advantage of numbers. They appeared clueless that their two squaddies were done for. They had the slack look of men trapped in a tedious bullshit detail. Ben retreated the way he had come. He knew a way to flank the agents who waited for him. The route to achieve this advantage was so dangerous, it might save them the trouble of killing him.

Ben descended the stairs passing through the upper and intermediate levels of the machinery space, and back into the water in the lowest level. Though the *American Mariner's* three-story engine had been left in place to serve as ballast after scuttling, the drive shaft had been salvaged. The trunk that housed the shaft reached fifty feet aft from the machinery space over the keel. Watertight while the ship was in service, the trunk was now completely flooded. Surmounting its farthest end was a vertical escape trunk that gave onto the aft deck behind the intruders' position.

Ben wondered for a moment when the *American Mariner* had begun to feel as though it was *his*, but then let it go. He avoided hyperventilating. Breathing normally saturated his blood with 98 to 99 percent of his capacity for oxygen. Woofing more air improved on that very little, while it would definitely spike his risk of passing out from hypocapnia, or low blood-carbon dioxide levels, which would disconnect his natural urge to breathe. Without that sensation, he might metabolize all his oxygen in his free dive and simply gray out, or black out with little warning.

Ben sank into the dark, feeling his way down to the bulkhead where the fifteen-inch propeller shaft had been removed. Fortunately, a larger stuffing box had also been displaced from the bulkhead to facilitate the shaft's salvage. Ben felt his way into the thrust recess, and passed over the first bearing platform that buffered the engine from the torque and the fore-and-aft forces of the propeller. There were nine such bearing supports, like loggers' X-framed sawbucks made of iron. The last one lay a few feet beyond the opening of the vertical escape trunk.

Ben pulled himself deeper into the shaft tunnel. It was inky black. He swam as carefully as he dared without wasting time and with it, oxygen. If the No. 3 Hold was any indication, the clear spaces of his youthful incursions might be cluttered now with wreckage. He felt his way past the second bearing mount.

Ben sensed the beginnings of the telltale burn in his chest. He was free diving thirty feet below the surface of the Chesapeake. He was aware that ever more oxygen was consumed for a given activity the deeper one went. Ben was already fatigued from negotiating the ship's three holds and the engine space. Now he was deep in the core of a ship, and if he changed his mind, or ran into trouble, swimming straight up was not an option. If he died here, his body would never be found.

He pulled his way past the third, fourth, and fifth shaft bearing mounts in the tunnel. By now he had a simple side kick-and-stroke rhythm established, and was letting his mind soften and relax to keep anxiety at bay. Nothing like panic to help the depth burn out his oxygen.

Ben knew the MDR, or Mammalian Diving Reflex, was helping him on this swim in far more important ways than hyperventilation ever could. This evolutionary vestige of man's ancient, marine existence was causing his heart rate to slow. Though he was moving by virtue of his arms and legs, the blood vessels in his limbs were constricting to shunt blood back to his brain, heart, and lungs. The MDR was also contracting his spleen, dumping oxygen-rich red blood cells into his circulatory system. A phenomenon called blood shifting was sending plasma to the vessels in his lungs to keep them from folding in on themselves from the increased pressure. Hyperventilation looked dramatic, and butch, but the MDR worked automatically for free-divers without the macho *blow-your-house-down* pantomime.

He swam on past the sixth and seventh shaft bearing mounts, keeping to the top of the tunnel to prevent stirring up silt on its floor. This was a gesture borne more of training than practicality. The tunnel might have been completely full of muddy water, but the total lack of light would have kept him from noticing. Eyes open, or eyes closed, it made no difference.

The least likely hazard, but the one that might be most alarming, was encountering another living thing in the tunnel. For Ben, the odd sensation of getting kicked on the heel of his boot came out of the blackest realm of improbability. The kick was not a martial blow at all. It felt casual, like an unintended happenstance. It did not hurt, but it served as a limbic alarm; someone was down in that tunnel with him. Someone had swum undetected directly beneath Ben, and passed him unwittingly, headed in the opposite direction toward the midships machinery space.

Ben stopped, tucked his knees to his chin, drew his knife, and shoved off the port side of the tunnel to hug its starboard wall. He did not want to be rediscovered where he first made contact with the other swimmer.

Ben was trying to sort out how best to subdue an opponent he could not see, when the intruder switched on a small LED flashlight. The tunnel was all but silted out with the passage of two divers and their evasive maneuvers. No beam reached out from the flashlight to expose Ben. It simply illuminated an area of water a few inches from the lens, and no farther. Ben knew where his man was. The silver flash of the intruder's blade flickered quickly into the flashlight's wan, murky loom, and disappeared. Now, it was an easy decision. Ben, it seemed, had brought a water pistol to a knife fight.

Ben drew the SPP-1M, and judging by the half-moon the knife had described through the disc of light, figured the blade was gripped in his opponent's left hand. The light was in his opponent's right hand. Ben aimed at the darkness between, and pulled the trigger once. The brief flash from the gun caught the surprised expression on the intruder's face as the steel dart punched through his right goggle lens, penetrating his eye, and driving into his brain. The flashlight spiraled to the bottom of the tunnel. Ben did not bother to retrieve it.

He swam onward, his lungs starting to sear for breath, the tinnitus-like ringing growing to a din in his ears, with a bass surge of blood roaring through the lower registers. Ben realized he had lost count of how many bearing supports had he passed. Though his only path lay along a straight line, he was lost. He swam on.

Finally, in a forward thrust of his hands, he rapped his knuckles on a dead end. Had the tunnel collapsed? He explored the face of the obstruction with his fingertips. It was vertical as best he could judge, intentionally placed and secured, and not haphazard, like debris. Groping farther down the barrier, Ben's hand passed into an opening; this was the shaft entry through the large peak ballast tank. Beyond that was the hull's stern, and then the Chesapeake. No way could Ben squeeze through the two fifteen-inch apertures between him and the freedom of open water. He knew he had wasted breath swimming too far. The shaft tunnel escape trunk was now somewhere in the blackness above, but behind him.

His lungs burning, Ben could feel muscles in his neck and face fighting to open for a gulp of sweet air. He swam, pawed, and groped. The shaft tunnel roof expanded over him, making a wide vertical passage. Without exploration, Ben threw his body upward into the void. He was rising inside the dark tube, perhaps too quickly. As he surged upward, pulling on the slimy rungs of the trunk's ladder, a small spot of gray formed out of the murk; the escape route's opening to the drizzling dawn sky on the main deck.

But he was not home free. Now he needed to watch for a deep-water blackout, when latent hypoxia could suddenly cause an irresistible urge to inhale, killing him within feet of the surface. It had struck Ben once before on a salvage dive from *Miss Dotsy*, but Ellis was not there today to reel him in to safety.

After too long underwater, Ben's face broke the surface. He peeled off and dropped the mask and monocular, trying hard not to hiss and huff and blow like a walrus as his aching lungs involuntarily filled and emptied like a blacksmith's bellows. No syncope this time. No drowning alone. Yet there were still other ways to pack it in. If the second operative on the stern was waiting for his buddy to climb out of the escape trunk, Ben had won the fight in the tunnel, but lost the element of surprise.

Ben could, he reasoned, catch his breath, then drop back down the escape trunk, and retrace his path through the shaft tunnel, past the dead intruder, and surface back into the machinery space. Then he would have the entire ship as his hunting ground. None of the remaining operatives, neither the Nitro Express shooter, nor MacCready, would have a clear line on his whereabouts. But daylight would soon invade the portholes and shell holes in the ship, and the light was not Ben's friend. He assessed the risks of his only two choices, chucked out the results, and started to climb the thirty-foot ladder in the trunk tube.

When Ben judged he was halfway between the surface of the water in the escape trunk and the upper end of the tunnel on the main deck, someone put his head into the circle of gray light.

"Serano! You see him?" Odie Rance called out.

Ben stopped climbing. Was this guy certain his friend was coming up, or was he just checking on the off chance? Ben figured the topside sentry would not have said anything if he had not heard Ben's step on the ladder. The tunnel transmitted sound upward like the final brassy length of a giant sousaphone.

Ben hurried up the ladder. He had to climb and talk, and keep this guy from shooting at him. He coughed as if he were choking, and muffled his voice to disguise it. "Almost drowned."

Maybe the weird acoustics of the escape tunnel would make the operative pause a split second longer. Ben picked up the pace of his ascent.

Rance said, "Serano?"

"Quiet!" Ben knew the masquerade was about to fail. He wondered if the operative could see him in the dark of the tunnel. Likely not. He had to act as if he could anyway. Ben drew the pistol. It had one shot left. He kept climbing.

When he heard Rance say the catch-all, "Shit!", he knew the ruse was blown. Ben was still fifteen feet from the top of the shaft when Rance started bringing his H&K to bear down the metal flue. Ben knew he would not have to aim. The bullets would ricochet off the tunnel's walls into Ben's head and body even if his sights were off the mark.

Now or never. Ben hugged the ladder, aimed the pistol and fired. Maybe the bang and flash would get the man to duck his head, even if Ben missed. Ben had no idea if he hit the guy. There was a thunderous report, not a pistol or rifle, but more like a Howitzer. The sound resonated through the tunnel, and perhaps through the entire ship, to the point that Ben felt the detonation shudder as much as he heard it crash down the metal chute to which he clung like a monkey.

What surprised Ben next was that instead of a swarm of bullets, he was pelted by a shower warm sticky fluid. He looked at his hand in the dimness. It was spattered with blood, and a patch of scalp with short-cropped hair. Had he been hit? Was his soul now departing his body and viewing his own remains? He pulled a gobbet of grey matter out of his collar. He looked up. The way out of the tunnel was clear. Nobody up there now, except maybe another armed killer he could not see.

Again, Ben triaged the options. Stay put? No way. Retreat down the escape trunk, and apnea-swim back into the machinery space. Safe, predictable action if he were not already exhausted. So that was not happening. Continue up the escape trunk into view. This was his most dangerous, least predictable course. Someone might be watching the trunk, waiting to cut him down as he prairie-dogged into a kill zone. If it were Nitro Express's finger on the trigger, there might be a split second of hesitation. Ben sensed this eccentric shooter had a need to connect with him before obeying the order to kill.

Ben was still having difficulty tracking the loyalties. Did Nitro Express work for MacCready or not? The four operatives did, without question, work for MacCready. Supposedly, Ben had received an offer to join the payroll, but this was likely withdrawn when the toe came off. Then who killed the fourth operative who was now decorating Ben's wetsuit with gore?

Ben decided. He bulled his way upward as fast as he could. With all the blood and tissue shellacking the tube and the ladder, it felt like he was scaling upstream inside the floor drain of a giant slaughterhouse.

Ben just kept charging at the lip of the escape tunnel, rolling out onto the fantail on the side of the tunnel's mouth opposite where the operative had been standing when he was hit. The overspray of human remains made the deck slicker than the rain by itself. It took Ben two grabs to pick up Odie Rance's H&K, it was so gunked. Ben was reminded of the physical destruction of La Luz. Whoever obliterated this agent was packing a like magnitude of ordnance.

Ben scanned forward. No one in plain sight. No one announced himself by shooting at him. Ben darted forward, threading his way among stowage lockers and winch mounts. The walls of the cargo handling station between the No. 5 and No. 4 Holds were so rusted they would not stop a horsefly, let alone a bullet. He pressed on until he reached the passage into the galley. Still, no shooting. That could not last.

With better concealment below decks, if not actual protective cover, Ben slowed his pace and took more care in his progress. No sense rushing past a doorway to get plinked like a gopher. He cleared each compartment as he moved forward. Arriving at the down stairway from the boat deck, Ben climbed, careful of his footing so he would not crash through a rust-ravaged tread.

Ben knew a one-man search of an entire Liberty ship would seem like madness. But the prey was also hunting him. Even if his enemy was still looking for him in the holds, eventually, he would come on deck. Like a startled blue crab in a trap, Ben knew that to climb up through the decks was the best way to narrow the area of focus, reduce the size of the imme-diate sector under surveillance, and cut the number of stairways from which he could be flanked. Gaining an advantage in elevation, without skylining his silhouette, would also help Ben control the exterior deck areas better. Without a spotter, without support, all Ben could do was reduce risk and improve odds. Guaranteeing his survival through numbers and complete control of the ship was impossible.

At the top of the stair, Ben smelled smoke. Taking it one compartment at a time, he found that the officers' accommodations on the boat deck were vacant, until he came to the last.

CHAPTER 64

BEN PUSHED INTO the forward most port compartment and found a woman sitting cross-legged, full-lotus style, dead center on the cabin sole. A freshly lighted cigarette was screwed into the corner of her lovely mouth. She squinted, watching Ben through the smoke. Her eyes, her black hair, spoke of Asian ancestry. Her skin tone was tanned Caucasian. Something indefinable about her looked familiar to Ben. A Glock lay within reach next to her right knee, but the slide was open, the chamber empty, and the magazine lay on the deck next to the gun. Ben covered her with the H&K anyway.

She smiled. "Cigarette?" She held out a pack of Larks. The same brand Jerry Grant had smoked.

Ben's eyes darted around the compartment. No one else was present. No one was there to back the woman up. Where did her easy calm come from? "Those things'll kill you."

"Not if *you* don't do it first, eh Ben? There were four agents with MacCready. Did you see them in your travels?"

"We met. It ended badly."

The truth about this woman struck Ben without thought, without deduction; a full-blown fact appearing complete and undeniable in his consciousness.

"You killed Grant. You're the shooter. Nitro Express."

The woman's smile contracted. "Three for three, and that's only a small part of today's top story. We don't have much time."

"Reckon that's so." Ben moved his finger from outside the trigger guard to inside, and slowly started to take up the trigger's slack.

The woman dragged deeply on the cigarette. "Could you point that away from me? I am going to tell you something, and it'd be best if you don't jitter. You need to hear it." When Ben did not move, she added, "I've had you in my sights six times since I came aboard. Please?"

Ben breathed in slow and deep, and shifted the machine gun's muzzle a few degrees to one side of the woman's head.

"I'm Annie Vo," the woman said. "MacCready wants me dead. I am the problem MacCready wants you to fix."

"Happy to oblige."

"*MacCready* wants that. Grant, on the other hand, had something else in mind when he called you in. I told him to. It was my idea. What I wanted from him in exchange for helping him die with honor."

"I don't believe you. How did you know anything about me?"

Annie Vo ducked Ben's question. "Look, I understand you're pissed. But Grant didn't believe in the unit's mission anymore. Covering up crises with bigger crises, and outside the rule of law, and eventually on American soil. I was good at it, if I do say so myself, but things were getting out of hand. At first, the target selections were, let's say, deserving of a splashy end. But there was an air of desperation with the last hit."

"You did it anyway. La Luz was just a singer."

"Not quite," said Annie Vo. "She was letting her brand, shall we say, be compromised by laundering money for four different government agencies. Enormous money that a fragmented, desperate music industry was too ready to take credit for generating."

Ben's hand ached to squeeze the trigger. He let Annie Vo continue, in case she said something useful.

"But La Luz wasn't one-tenth as popular as everybody was led to believe. Not at first. She made a deal with the NSA devil eight years ago, and that's when she took off, and eventually grew into the legend she had been groomed for. The problem is, eliminating her was our unit's plan, crafted in-house. We did not know about Luz's work with the NSA. Her cover was too good. The Secretary of Homeland Security, Lily Morgan, was facing some hot water with a theft and clandestine sale of yellowcake, and I don't mean Betty Crocker. Uranium from Niger. She was selling it to *Iran*, who was in a bidding war against North Korea for the stuff."

"No way."

Annie Vo said, "I shit you not."

Ben flinched inside. That was a favorite expression of his roving father, Richard Blackshaw.

"When the unit detailed me to take down Luz Calderon, unfortunately, most of the cash her brand was laundering, and we're talking trillions of dollars, it belonged to Lily Morgan's agencies."

"She's the former senator—"

"Exactly."

Ben was stunned. For the second time in less than half a year, Lily Morgan was party to inverting his world.

Annie lit another cigarette from the first, and expertly flicked the butt out a porthole. "Essentially, in detailing me to target La Luz, Commander Grant knocked down three walls in Lily Morgan's house trying to save the fourth. He didn't know. And she is very, very upset. Yes, the yellowcake story stopped breaking before it ever started, but the Luz Calderon Wash-and-Fold was out of business. The roof is coming down around Lily's ears. Am I going too fast?"

"The politics don't interest me."

"That's where you're wrong, brother. They interest you very much. MacCready kept you on after Grant died for two reasons. One, to kill me. Out with the old. In with the new. He knew I was loyal to Grant, and that I agreed the new mission stank."

"Funny way of showing that, shooting Grant dead like you did."

Annie Vo ignored the interruption. "The second reason was to have you carry on with my mission, which if you hadn't guessed, is distracting a docile public tax base from learning about the grotesquely profitable derelictions of the state."

"Old news. I've been uncooperative."

"That's putting it mildly. You shot off the man's toe! I admire your flair, doncha know. Here's the problem, Ben. Lily Morgan is losing her mind. She has real neurological damage that's impairing her judgment. In a moment of drug-addled madness, she actually conceived a plan to invade

262   Robert Blake Whitehill

one of our OAS allies to the south. Bolivia to be precise. The Joint Chiefs bought in, and so did the Chairman. They liked knowing supply lines for the invasion, for fuel in particular, were already in place in Mexico and Venezuela, even if those two countries did not cooperate at first. The brass liked knowing they could fly home in four hours for the weekend, and then get back to the war just as fast Monday morning. This was to be an invasion of convenience as much as anything. A commuter war. I'd say Canada needs to look sharp down the road.

"And that's how big this money laundering problem is. Luz Calderon's success, great as it was, was actually too *small* to cover the vast sums Lily had to hide. Arms. Drugs. Cheats on food-for-oil shipments. Human trafficking. Lily actually needed an entire drug-producing *nation*, with all its revenue, and all its cartels, and all its banking connections, to bury the money and dig it up again spic-and-span. It's genius in a way. Who would look at a whole country as a money laundering scam, especially one that's desperate to hide its own cash everywhere else."

The mess was bigger than Ben could have imagined. Like Scheherazade, Annie Vo was casting a lifesaving spell with her story.

She went on. "Lily's money is actually dirtier than the drug revenue, because it's tied up with genocide, which is in turn bound up with these bullshit democratic revolutions going on now, particularly in the Middle East. Arab Spring was a crock. It's a violent swap of the fanatics and dictator puppets out front, while the key families, corporations, and international organized crime syndicates in the background stay the same. But in the churn, there is beaucoup money to be made, and great cover for other illicit activities. The South American cocaine aura makes Lily's funds almost perfumed in some banking circles. Guinea-Bissau alone runs 300 million dollars of South American cocaine a month! Now you can see how Secretary Morgan actually outgrew Luz Calderon, except maybe as an ambassador. Maybe even as a head of state, like in her movie.

"Ease up on that trigger, Ben. It's like a Ginsu Knife commercial. 'But wait, there's more!' Lily is icing her yellowcake. While our national and state legislatures piss and moan about legalizing drugs, and whether to get tax revenues from sales, Lily Morgan is planning a vertical monopoly starting with the means of production south of the border, and going straight down the line to the end user on the street. I hear she calls the profit from drug sales an Addiction Tax she can collect from every country on the planet, not just here in the States. But it's not just a tax, is it? It's a business. A *side* business, but still an astronomical chunk of money. Every nickel on the planet will be tainted with blood and misery inside of a decade. Even virtual cryptocurrencies, like Bitcoin, will stink of filth."

"How do you know all this?"

Annie Vo sounded proud. "I have a few well-placed sources. But I haven't mentioned the worst news of all as far as *you're* concerned. Reckon you could hold off shooting me until I've told you?"

Ben said nothing.

"Have you heard of DNA caching?"

"Pretty compact way to store data, sure."

"Compact, and so it's also very easy to hide. No bunker required. No vault. And just one guard on duty 24/7. No conventional copies of the data need exist. No paper files. No floppies, zips, or memory sticks. The NSA stashed the full specs of that Bolivian invasion plan in somebody they thought could defend it no matter what. Two somebodies, actually. The other had a pretty nasty psychotic break and killed himself."

"You're the second person."

"Oh my blessing, you got it in *one*. Yes. Lucky me. What MacCready doesn't know, is now there's a *third* person exposed to the data cache, and carrying it around."

"Who would that be?"

"Remember up north, Ben? I pulled you from under that slab of ice?"

Ben kept his voice neutral. "I recall that, yes."

A flash of anger crossed Annie Vo's face. "Oh. And you were going to shoot me without saying thanks. Nice. That makes this easier. Back there under the ice, your hand was pretty cut up when I got a grip on it. Your palm. Your fingers. Bleeding. A mess. And after scrabbling down there with those sharp mussel shells, my hands weren't in much better shape."

Ben was mute in disbelief.

"Yep. Sorry. It was that simple. The data cache transmits like a blood-borne virus. You'll start having the worst nightmares of your life in a few weeks, when the data starts creeping into your consciousness. At least now you won't have to wonder if you're losing your mind. You can be damn sure of it."

Ben tightened the welds between his body and the H&K. "I heard you had problems. Thanks for the heads-up. But I have to say, you don't seem too bothered by it now."

Annie Vo chuckled. "You're right. I'm not. If you have a plan for hemispheric domination stuck in your DNA, I figured you just mess up the DNA. I have intentionally tripped on the best LSD I could find seven times in the last month. I'll take the flashbacks and flipper babies later on if it means I don't have those dreams n'mare. So far, no hallucinations or nightmares for twenty hours, and that's saying something."

"You talk like you're from around here," Ben said.

Annie Vo had been glib, but now she paused and seemed to grow more serious. Ben sensed she was not afraid of his anger, or his gun. Her new gravitas and confidence were founded in something else.

"Maybe I shouldn't have mentioned all the acid. And talking about Lily and her insanity runs the risk of making me sound crazy like her. Ben, you must absolutely believe what I'm going to tell you."

Ben snorted. "Because everything you've said so far has the ring of gospel."

"Point taken. The thing is, I am not from around here. But my *pappy* is."

Ben's world shook as insights meshed with revelations and intuitions. "The classified ads," he said. "*Caca dau.* You're part Vietnamese."

Annie Vo nodded. "Half. My mother was from Nha Trang. They called kids like me, the ones with G.I. dads, Children of the Dust. I was lucky my mother didn't dump me at an orphanage. Long story short, that's where my luck pretty much ran out until one day, the CIA learned daddy's little girl can shoot."

"Oh *hell* no." Ben's bead on Annie Vo wavered for a split second. "Are we supposed to be having us a *Star Wars* moment here?"

Annie's voice hardened. "You can boil your life down to a pop cultural cliché if you like, but that's my truth you're pissing on."

Ben wanted to protest, but a part of him was already convinced. "People say the damnedest things to keep from getting shot. So Richard Blackshaw is your father."

"As much as he's your'n. He met my mother before he was discharged, and left her after not too long. Looking back, she said it wasn't a serious thing with Pap. Just something the war brought on. That's until she found out I was on the way. She never tried to find him, or saddle him at all. That was before he ever courted and married your mother here. He didn't know about me until I was seven years old."

Ben was having trouble grappling with the latest addition to his family. He wanted to stall for time, but felt foolish the minute he said, "Prove it."

"How? Am I supposed to show you half of a broken medallion, and you have the other half hanging around your neck? Give me a fucking break. Listen to me, Ben. *Look* at me. That's all the proof you need, and it's all you're going to get."

"Have you seen him recently?"

"We caught up in Mogadishu two months ago. It was Take Your Daughter to Work Day. That was strange, sharing a hide with him, spotting for him, while he was throwing down on insurgents. He's a dead shot to this day. That's when he told me about you for the first time. I got a little envious, the way he went on about you. Admires and respects you. So, I thought you and I should say hello."

Ben felt a perverse sense of envy himself, as if he were a boy who had missed out on a special hunting trip with his father. In fact, Ben had gone hunting with Dick Blackshaw when he was younger, but that was in the marsh, gunning for geese. Not in Somalia, taking down human targets.

He kept Annie Vo covered, and said, "So we just sweep your killing Grant and Strahan under the rug? Bygones?"

Annie Vo's anger was riddled with sadness now. "Grant was my boss for years. He was my friend. Yes, you better believe he put *himself* on my list. And yes, it was an honor to help him die like a soldier. Don't be such a damn prig. You'd have done the same thing if he'd asked. But he didn't ask you, because he wanted your hands clean for what's next."

"Which is—?"

"The nightmares were Homeric, gothic, operatic, what have you. I was going to ask you to kill *me*."

"But something's changed. You said you're feeling better."

"Right, Ben. But there's still some unfinished business."

"I'll bite."

Annie Vo said, "MacCready."

"MacCready's what's next?"

"No," said Annie Vo. "Check your six."

Ben turned. MacCready was standing behind him in the doorway to the compartment. His foot dressing was wet, and trailing a yard long streamer of rust stained gauze. His pistol was trained toward Ben, but his aim wavered under a glassy gaze and a cartoonish leer.

Annie Vo swept her Glock up off the deck, pushed the magazine home, charged a round into the chamber, and covered Ben.

Ben lowered his gun and slowly put it on the deck.

CHAPTER 65

MACCREADY AIMED THE pistol at Ben's foot. "This is going to be poetic. Annie Vo, thanks for keeping him busy, but you can put your gun down on the deck, too. Now."

"You know who I am?"

"Grant's records weren't that hard to decipher. I guessed you were a chick when the file on your last physical mentioned a pelvic exam. Lily Morgan feels strongly that you and Commander Grant went a tad off the reservation capping the singer. Luz Calderon was really important, it turns out. Thank God she went down on Grant's watch, is all I can say. Even though I'm the one who suggested doing her. But you, Annie Vo—Miss Nitro Express—have gotta go. I said, *put the gun down.* Oh, and you're out too, Ben. Sorry."

"This is going to be awkward," said Ben. "Aren't I supposed to replace her?"

"Nope. Once again, you were Grant's pick. So now you're in bad odor."

Ben gambled that MacCready was doped enough to slow his reaction time. He enveloped Annie Vo's Glock hand in his own. With no safety mechanism on this make, it was ready to fire. He pushed the gun downward, and squeezed her entire hand. The gun barked, and the jerk of the gun's slide mechanism broke Ben's grip.

MacCready howled, and staggered backward out of the compartment onto a small outside companionway. A hole in the toe of his good foot's shoe was oozing blood.

"Damnit!" MacCready leveled his pistol at Ben.

For the second time, Ben heard the cannon-like detonation that seemed to shake the entire ship. MacCready's thorax and head disappeared in a bloody fountain of bone and flesh. His shoulders and arms flailed and flapped, and the body dropped to the deck, dead before it struck, but still quivering.

Annie Vo holstered her pistol even while Ben was grabbing the H&K. He covered Annie Vo, but she said, "Relax! Please safe your weapon." Then she yelled, "Clear!"

Janie, MacCready's driver, stepped into the compartment from the outside deck, picking her way carefully through the mess that had been MacCready a few moments before. She had the .950 caliber JDJ rifle on her shoulder.

Janie looked at Annie Vo. "Sweetie, tell me straight. Does this gun make my ass look big?"

Annie Vo rushed over to Janie, and gave her a hard kiss on her open mouth. The kiss endured, not just a friendly peck. Unable to look away, Ben felt a hot blush flood up his neck to his face.

Janie broke the kiss and laid the gun down. "We have some mopping up to do, hon."

Ben heard Knocker Ellis's voice calling up from the main deck below. "Hello the boat!"

A few moments later, Ellis walked into the compartment with several large black rubber bags slung over his shoulder. "Hey Annie Vo."

Again, she was surprised. She studied the black man. "You're Ellis Hogan. Pap said you were KIA. Just before he met my mother."

Ellis grinned. "When worlds collide. Don't believe every damn thing you hear, especially from Dick Blackshaw."

Ellis caught Ben's look of consternation. "If your father never mentioned Annie Vo, then it sure as hell wasn't *my* place."

Ben could not argue. Nor could he help asking, "Body bags, Ellis? Am I that predictable?"

"After that mess with you last fall, I don't like to be without. I got six here. How many do we need?"

"MacCready's going back in the ice chest," Annie Vo said. "He's got to meet with an accident somewhere far away from here, and far away from me. Maybe a pedestrian-versus-train scenario. But we'll definitely need one bag for him between here and our boat. Ben?"

Ben did a quick tally. "Three down, but a couple of them are submerged, and they aren't going anyplace. One bag, I guess. No rush on him. Oh, then there's the one by the escape trunk at the stern. He's in pretty much the same shape as MacCready here." Ben looked at Janie. "Was that your shooting?"

Janie curtsied. "One shot, one kill."

"Much obliged. But how'd you shoot that gun twice without breaking yourself in half?"

Annie Vo gazed at Janie proudly. "She's stronger than she looks."

Janie answered for herself. "Annie told me how your folks would brace huge fowling pieces against their boats before firing them. I butted this mule against the ship. My whole right side still stings, but no broken bones."

Ben said to Annie Vo, "Janie's your inside source at MacCready's office."

"The missus has many talents."

Ellis said, "Let's squeegee this fellow up and get ashore."

"I'm staying," Ben announced.

Everyone stopped moving, and stared at Ben. "Your own house is a few miles from here," Ellis countered. "And a whole lot more than that, Ben."

Ben wanted Ellis to be right, for his homecoming to be that easy and safe, but in the end he said, "No. I'm still supposed to be dead. I still have the work to do. This is the perfect place to do it." He spun his sadness into a thread of logistics, "I'll need a generator, a furnace, and all the rest of the gear that was cleared out of New York. I can work here. It's pretty quiet."

Ellis said, "Can we not discuss our business out in the open like this?"

"Annie Vo already knows about the gold," Ben said. "Pap must have told her about it. She shot the smiley face pattern that's stamped on every bar into that water tank back in New York. Just connect the dots and—"

"That'll teach you to get cute," Janie muttered. Annie Vo looked abashed.

"You don't reckon the whole Kennedy Assassination reference in LA was over the top?" Ben agreed.

Annie Vo sighed, "Did I mention there was some LSD involved? I said that, right? Don't judge. But maybe I drew a comparison between my work and another famous government conspiracy, to show I'd made my bones, too. I agree, not my best thinking, but it made sense, right? You probably figured Kennedy was an early effort of one of Grant's predecessors. Both Kennedys were, and the King and Evers killings, too. Ours is a long and storied unit, if heavy-handed in the early years. But it's time to pack it in. That cop on the roof is really getting to me. I swear I'll make good with his family, if he has any."

Ben helped Ellis shove MacCready's remains into a body bag. "Why did Grant want my hands to stay clean?" he asked Annie Vo. "That train left the station a while ago."

Annie Vo shrugged. "If we really want to shut down the Meme Displacement Unit, and stop the U.S. from forcing the entire Bolivian coke industry into American receivership through a massive cataclysmic invasion, there is one more job left. It's going to take a ghost to get it done, but I'm too beat do it alone. Janie does not have the chops." Annie Vo looked apologetically at Janie. "Sorry babe, but it's true. No offense."

"None taken," Janie assured. "I'm not interested, anyway."

"What's the job?" asked Ben.

Annie Vo's answer made him very unhappy. "Madame Secretary of the Department of Homeland Security, Lily Morgan."

EPILOGUE

AS PROMISED, BEN remained aboard the *American Mariner*. Annie
Vo and Janie waited until dark, and then lugged MacCready's remains away
in the ice chest with Knocker Ellis's assistance. Ellis was still torn up with
fever, but at his weakest he was still a force to reckon with. Declan Flaherty,
the impaled operative, was dead. They lifted him off of the intrusive pipe,
and roped him unceremoniously out of No. 2 Hold. When Ellis finally
pointed *Miss Dotsy* for Smith Island, Flaherty went over the side en route,
along with as much of Odie Rance as could be scraped together, in a single
body bag weighed down with Janie's hundred-pound JDJ rifle and several
rounds of spare ammo.

Ben spent his first hours alone aboard the hulk ranging through the
spaces belowdecks, scouting for interior compartments in which he could
resume work processing the cache of gold far from prying eyes. He also had
to ponder whether he was going to graduate from work as a freelance operative to a treasonous, crusading assassin as Annie Vo had urged. It con-
founded his entire world view to suddenly know he had a half-sister. It was
less surprising to know she was an accomplished killer. That much seemed
to run in the family. Their good-byes had been strained, with no attempt
pretended on either side that they would meet again. Ben sensed Annie Vo
was disappointed they had not parted on warmer terms, but his anger at her
did allow him to care about that. Perhaps Grant actually had asked her to
end his suffering. Ben would never know the truth about that. Whatever
their strange connections and disconcerting similarities, Annie Vo had

murdered Detective Strahan on that Los Angeles rooftop, and that left Ben cold.

Another of Annie Vo's less-than-charming acts had been to infect Ben with a terrible blueprint that might cause him to lose his mind, or become a target if his secret were discovered. He had no idea if he would ever resort to LSD to disrupt the plan's hold on his DNA. Perhaps a data bleed would not develop. In the end, Ben wished this distant relation had remained aloof. He could have made it through life quite nicely without ever knowing her.

The next night, old Smith Island friends heaved to next to the *American Mariner* a powerful fiberglass deadrise workboat, the *Varina Davis*. They made Ellis's excuses, as he was now confined to bed by an intensifying fever from his suppurating leg wound.

They left Ben with food, water, a change of clothing, a small camp stove, a sleeping bag, and a few other essentials. Lest Ben think he was on an exotic camping trip, they also brought the gold swan he had abandoned just a few days before. It still needed his finish work before it could go to market.

On subsequent nights, the men also offloaded a small but powerful generator, quiet as a whisper, and designed for use on location film shoots. There were jerry cans of diesel fuel for it. They also brought a new electric furnace, and Ben's crucibles.

Over the next few days, Ben's heart slowly sank as the novelty of place wore away, and he adapted to the new nest, and the new solitary routine. He had the run of the ship's interior during the day. Only at night did he venture on deck for fresh air when no one might notice him. He still had to take care, even in darkness, in case Naval or commercial vessels passed too close to the *American Mariner*, used her as a navigational way point, or turned their Forward Looking Infra Red cameras upon her out of curiosity. As in the New York City walkdown, Ben would not so much abide on the *American Mariner* as haunt her.

The nights proved particularly difficult because of the unwholesome company Ben was forced to keep. The dead men from Pyramid Lake sat in the compartment and stared at him. There was the mud-scalded Embraer jet pilot, with captain's shoulder boards on his shirt, who also kept watch. And there were the four dead operatives who sulked with MacCready's angry shade in another corner. Two of those operatives were always the last to leave come daylight. Their corpses were still aboard the *American Mariner*, and so their apparitions seemed most vivid of all. One day very soon, Ben would have to dive the hold and the shaft tunnel to clear their bones away, or risk losing his mind. But not yet. Now and then, late at night, he went on deck and looked east toward his home on Smith Island.

Ben took pains to widen the waterline gash in the ship's bow just enough to allow him to pull in a surplus IBS, or Inflatable Boat-Small. The boat, supplied by Ben's Smith Island neighbors, was equipped with an outboard motor. Once drawn inside the hull in No. 1 Hold at high tide, Ben concealed it behind a purpose-built screen of tumbled detritus, now invisibly hinged for ease of the boat's deployment.

Late one night, Ben watched with particular longing as *Miss Dotsy* pulled alongside. He had anticipated this visit more than any other. He watched appreciatively as Loki, or LuAnna as he knew her best, masterfully moored the deadrise and climbed the crude ladder Ben had tack-welded to the inside wall of the hold.

Ben held his bride in his arms. "Been meaning to thank you for all your help out west."

"You have a few hours to show your gratitude. And I wouldn't have missed it for the world. Just sorry I couldn't do more."

"Any reason you wanted an alias?"

"Gosh, you had one. Fair's fair," she said. "Truth is, I met you when you were a boy who became a waterman, then a man who became a soldier, then a rascally picaroon, and then my husband. Top it all off with you being a romantical dead artist who's now a—come to think of it, I don't know *what* you are now."

"You're not going to like the answer to that."

"So don't tell me. At least not tonight. And you knew me as a girl, as a cop, as your accomplice pirate bride, and now—I guess you can see I'm getting partial to the fresh start from time to time."

Ben kissed her. "I know that now."

LuAnna looked around the rough compartment in which Ben had set up shop. "Rat-infested basements in New York. Rusted-out hulks in the Chesapeake Bay. You sure know how to show a girl a good time, Ben Republican."

For Discussion

- How is the theme of misdirection woven throughout *Nitro Express*?
- How do you feel about the level of data collection currently in use for counterterrorism surveillance in the United States of America? Does it materially impinge on your life?
- What are your opinions about personal privacy, and surrendering some of this in the name of making our nation safe? Does it work, in your opinion?

Please respond to these questions, or with any other thoughts on *Nitro Express*, to rbw@robertblakewhitehill.com

ABOUT THE AUTHOR

Robert Blake Whitehill is a Maryland Eastern Shore native, and an award-winning screenwriter at the Hamptons International Film Festival, and the Hudson Valley Film Festival. In addition, he is an Alfred P. Sloan Foundation award winner for his feature script U.X.O. (UNEXPLODED ORDNANCE). He is also a contributing writer to *Chesapeake Bay Magazine*. *DEADRISE* and *NITRO EXPRESS* are the first two novels of the Ben Blackshaw Series.

Find out more about the author, his blog, upcoming releases, and the Chesapeake Bay at:

www.robertblakewhitehill.com

Enjoy the opening maneuvers of the next Ben Blackshaw thriller!

RACK TAP BANG

PART 1
FLOTSAM

CHAPTER 1

BEN BLACKSHAW EXPECTED no company. He rolled stiffly off the cot onto the cold steel deck, wishing he had left the furnace on overnight. So much for the warmth of May. It seemed like April showers were still falling hard in spite of the calendar. He could hear the dull hiss and muted roar of the raindrops sheeting down on the deck overhead. There was the thud again. It was not just a dream after all. The muzzy sensation of being awakened too early cleared, but the muffled gong still echoed from somewhere below him, likely near the No. 2 hold, well aft of the old Liberty Ship's bow.

As Ben carefully descended corroded ladders and stairways toward the hold, he knew the *American Mariner* could not have run aground. She had been intentionally scuttled on a shoal in the Chesapeake Bay during the Johnson Administration, and used for aerial gunnery practice by pilots out of Naval Air Station Patuxent River. The airdales of Pax River had stopped strafing the hulk in the early 1970s. After serving all over the world, with a collection of registries from every branch of the United States Armed Forces, from training to tracking ballistic missile tests, this ship wasn't going anywhere tonight.

Ben's small flashlight was covered with a red lens to preserve his night vision, as well as to keep any stray beams from leaking through an inconvenient shell hole and alerting an observant boater to his presence. His heart beat faster, wondering what the hell was smashing into his lonely lair in the middle of nowhere. In the few months he had been hiding aboard the derelict ship, only once had a massive log floated into the hold through the twin waterline maws where decades of winter ice had partnered with brackish water and rust to gash the hull clean through from starboard to larboard. The wave heights and tide had been perfect to roll the half-sunk tree trunk of several tons straight into the hold. It had been dangerous work extricating the log against wind and wave, where at any moment it might have crushed him against the serrated edge of the hull's gash, and sawn him in two. Leaving the flotsam bashing around the cavernous space was not an option. The booming impacts had been intolerable, threatening his sanity like the roar of a perpetual storm.

Had Ben's own Inflatable Boat-Small broken loose from its hiding place behind a screen of wreckage in the hold? No, Ben knew his business with lashings and mooring lines. He prayed that he was not hearing an inquisitive intruder's boat tied up and rhythmically tugging against its painter line, thumping hull to hull in the storm's rising waves. The rotten weather should have kept honest people on shore. Enemies wishing Ben harm had sprouted like toadstools since the previous fall, and like mushrooms, they would thrive on his carcass. Ben cursed quietly, wishing he had brought his Bersa Thunder 380 pistol below with him, but it was two in the morning, he was tired, and if he assessed himself aright, lately he was getting careless.

Ben reached the bottom of a companionway that was missing its two lowest steps, and continued along the passage leading to the catwalk running all the way around the upper level of the hold. Knowing the rest of the way by feel from nights of patrolling the space, he turned the flashlight off. At times like this, a night vision monocular would have been handy. His friend Knocker Ellis Hogan, who lived on Smith Island on the eastern side of the Chesapeake, had promised to provide him with a replacement for one Ben had lost months before. Ellis, at least thirty years Ben's senior, had nearly died of sepsis after being wounded during their last undertaking together, and was still making a slow recovery. Ben was not one to nag, nor would he insult Ellis by asking someone else who was more able-bodied to fill the order. Such was the life of a polite fugitive who depended on his friends for everything.

Ben moved forward with stealthy care. He had once heard that the visual neurology of a life-long blind person was not utterly dead, but was in part plastic enough to be commandeered to transmit a larger than usual share of auditory information, constructing a soundscape from nearby objects through which the blind could navigate. Ben believed it. First as a hunter on the marshes around Smith Island, then as a Navy SEAL, Ben had found he could listen his way through pitch darkness if he relaxed and allowed his ears to help him *see* by dint of a rude kind of echolocation. Instead of scrutinizing the taps of a long white cane, he allowed breezes and footfalls reflected by his surroundings to help him map the space immediately around him. Intriguing as this enhanced sense was in the abstract, tonight he was a civilian a long way from the peak of his training, and he missed the promised night vision gear.

Shunting this regret aside, he let his ears and fingers go to work. He felt along the companionway wall, counting steps between bulkheads, until he reached his hand silently around the jam of the watertight doorway into the hold. He stopped. The hold's upper catwalk lay beyond the doorway, but Ben knew it let out a sepulchral, wrenching moan whenever the metal lattice took his full weight.

Ben listened. The cavernous boom of the striking object, whatever it was, sounded louder here, but now it melded with the rush of waves breaking athwartship through the double gashes in the hold's great space. Something was down there in the darkness, and Ben needed to see it.

He crouched, and angled the flashlight down through the threshold of the doorway before turning it on for a one-second traverse of the space. He could not believe his eyes. It took all his will to rein in the compulsion to turn the light on again and stare at what lay below.

He thought it possible that shadows cast by the lattice work of the metal catwalk played a trick on him, forcing his mind to incorrectly fill in the blanks of what lay beneath. Ben knew a boat when he saw it. It was definitely not his inflatable swirling in the flooded hold. It was a white fiberglass dingy with several inches of water in the bottom. Like the sodden tree trunk before, it must have been sluiced into the hold through the gaping wound in the ship's westerly, or port side. From Ben's quick glance in the feeble red flashlight beam, the boat appeared to be on the verge of washing through the jagged gap in the starboard, or east wall of the hold, and transiting out into the stormy Chesapeake once again. There, as the waves rose with the weather, it would likely swamp, and soon be gone.

Ordinarily this would not place Ben in the least moral dilemma. He had no need of the boat, so thoughts of salvaging it for his personal use did not enter into his mind. From recent hard-won experience, he knew that the wayward boats of others brought far more trouble than they were worth. He definitely did not want some searcher to case the *American Mariner*, or its immediate environs, looking for the little tender.

The problem lay in the bottom of the boat, where Ben was sure he saw a small, darkly dressed human being, a castaway lying full length, head barely propped out of the water on the crook of an arm, and either unconscious or dead.

If Ben stayed where he was, it would be impossible to know whether the hapless intruder was alive, or past all hope. He risked flashing the red beam of light once more. The dingy was now closer to the great starboard tear in the hold, even closer to sluicing away into the night forever.

Ben's instinct took command, winning out over every natural urge to lie low, do nothing, and let the problem float away. With the flashlight off, he pushed through the doorway and felt his way to the hold's starboard side, rationalizing that if a lost dingy might arouse attention, a missing person would draw even more heat. Authorities around the Chesapeake would go on high alert if a corpse washed up. Ben would no longer be safe. No matter whether his morals were lofty or self-serving, he had to do something.

His left hand reached the second ladder on the wall of the hold. Defying the corroded rungs to part and fail under his weight, he lowered himself down as quickly as he dared. When his feet began to slip on the rungs' clinging tidal growth of algae, he used the flashlight for one instant more. To his horror, the dingy had already washed halfway out of the hold. He kept the light on just long enough to sway out from the ladder and clutch the bow mooring line of the dingy. From his lower position, he could not see over the gunwale to the figure lying there prone.

In the darkness, Ben strained against the wave action to pull the dingy back inside the hold, and made the line fast to the ladder with an anchor hitch. By feel, he carefully stepped into the careening dingy.

Ben lowered himself onto the narrow bow seat. He was about to turn on the flashlight one last time to help him look for a pulse point in the body lying just aft of his position. With no warning, he felt a blow, and saw bright starry flashes in his left eye as something cold and hard was jammed high into his cheek bone. He reckoned it was the frigid barrel of a pistol. This was confirmed when the *snick* of the hammer being cocked cut through the howl of wind and washing waves. Ben remained as still as the tossing dingy allowed. A light hand fluttered along his shoulders and arms, and finally yanked the flashlight out of his grasp.

When the red light snapped on, Ben's good eye noted in the blood-palled loom that he was now the hostage of a child, a small girl of fourteen, if she were even that old. She shivered in the wind. What Ben had taken for dark, wet, clinging clothes was her black skin. The girl was utterly naked, and sheened with water shedding out of her hair. She stared at Ben, but the only thing he could see in her eyes, and in the fierce set of her jaw, was a pure and abject fury. *Aw hell no!* thought Ben. *Not like this—*